"Does everyt

"God, I hope so." Brant crushed his mouth to Nikki's again, sliding his tongue past the barrier of her lips as her body melted against him.

"Now what?" She reached for him again, trying to focus on his face, even though it was blurry. At least it was there, *he* was there in front of her, and he wanted her.

And maybe she was stupid for taking him up on his offer.

But it was Brant.

And she'd regret letting him walk away a second time—without experiencing him like this.

Just a girl.

And a guy.

Having a one-night stand.

What could possibly go wrong?

PRAISE FOR RACHEL VAN DYKEN'S NOVELS

The Playboy Bachelor

"*The Playboy Bachelor* was one hilarious, sexy and emotional read."
—CollectorofBookBoyfriends.com

"Van Dyken succeeds with this well-characterized, tightly plotted tale."
—*Publishers Weekly*

"If you want fun—seriously high in the entertainment value department—with a good mix of sexy and emotion, then this is it!"
—AboutThatStory.com

"This was a strongly written story about feelings, friendship, and family. A slow-burn romance at its finest."
—BooksnBoysbookblog.com

The Bachelor Auction

"The first in Van Dyken's Bachelors of Arizona series charms readers with a decidedly modern retelling of the Cinderella story. [A] lighthearted, eminently readable treat."
—*Publishers Weekly*

"Full of romance and wit, this book will be the perfect choice for your next book escape!"
—RomanceRewindBlog.com

The Wager

"Rachel Van Dyken is quickly becoming one of my favorite authors and I cannot wait to see what she has in store for us in the future. *The Wager* is a must-read for those who love romance and humor. It will leave a lasting impression and a huge smile on your face."

—LiteratiBookReviews.com

The Bet

"I haven't laughed this hard while reading a book in a while. *The Bet* [is] an experience—a heartwarming, sometimes hilarious, experience...I've actually read this book twice."

—RecommendedRomance.com

"If you need a funny, light read...I promise you this is a superb choice!" —MustReadBooksOrDie.com

"Friends-to-lovers stories...Is there anything better? And when told in a fun, light manner, with a potential love triangle with lovable characters; well, how can you not enjoy it?"

—TotallyBookedBlog.com

Elect

"Secrets, sacrifices, blood, angst, loyalties...This book has everything I love!...Rachel Van Dyken is a fabulous author!"

—GirlBookLove.com

"Takes you on a roller coaster of emotion...centers around the most amazing of love stories...Nixon has definitely made it to my best-book-boyfriend list."

—SoManyReads.com

Elite

"This is by far the best book I have read from this talented author."

—Book-Whisperer.blogspot.com

"Four enthusiastic stars! This is just so fresh and different and crazy and fun...I can't wait for the next book, *Elect*... Judging by [*Elite*], this entire series is going to be fantastic."

—NewAdultAddiction.com

Also by Rachel Van Dyken

The Bachelors of Arizona series

The Bachelor Auction
The Playboy Bachelor

The Bet series

The Bet
The Wager

The Eagle Elite series

Elite
Elect

THE *Bachelor* CONTRACT

RACHEL VAN DYKEN

FOREVER

NEW YORK BOSTON

Forever
Hachette Book Group
1290 Avenue of the Americas
New York, NY 10104
forever-romance.com
twitter.com/foreverromance

First Edition: November 2017

Forever is an imprint of Grand Central Publishing.
The Forever name and logo are trademarks of Hachette Book Group, Inc.

ISBN 978-1-4555-4213-0 (mass market edition)
ISBN 978-1-4555-9875-5 (ebook edition)

Printed in the United States of America

OPM

10 9 8 7 6 5 4 3 2 1

To Lauren Layne, "wife." I don't think I could have made it through without all of your feedback and willingness to calm me down. You're the reason I finished this book and this series. Your wisdom has been everything!

THE *Bachelor* CONTRACT

PROLOGUE

Colorless shapes moved in rapid succession as the roar of the crowd grew louder by the minute. Nikki clutched the auction paddle with one sweaty hand while making sure to keep her wineglass secure in the other.

She wasn't sure what was louder:

The people.

Or her heart as it pounded against her chest.

At least she didn't have to *see* him.

Then again, she'd never had to see him to feel his magnetic presence. Brant Wellington was and always would be a larger-than-life figure to her, a person who didn't just live up to the hype, but out-hyped the hype.

He'd been her hero.

And then he'd fallen. And stayed down.

That was the worst part.

When people fell, they got up—it was simple logic. You fall down, and you fight to stand again, you fight with everything you have to make sure you can find solid ground.

Not Brant Wellington.

He fell down. And he'd been on the ground ever since.

"The next item for auction!" the loud voice boomed. It was happening. It was actually happening.

Nadine Titus had given her strict instructions. And because she was out of her mind, she'd agreed to follow them.

"Brant Wellington!" the voice announced as a hush fell over the crowd.

And then the bidding began.

Heart in her throat, Nikki waited for paddles to lift—though she couldn't exactly see them, she supposed the announcer, Charles Wellington, would keep everyone up to date with how much was being bid.

A cough sounded to her right.

And then a second loud cough.

That was her cue.

Hand still shaking, she raised her paddle into the air. "Twenty-five thousand dollars."

"Going once," the voice boomed. "Twice."

Her pulse soared into dangerous territory while her mouth went completely dry.

"Sold! To, sorry, what is your paddle number?"

"Zero, Zero, Five." She'd memorized it the minute Cole, her date for the event, had let her know the number.

She stood and forced a smile she didn't feel. A practiced smile. One that would convey her excitement at winning one of the most notorious bachelors in the country.

But she knew the truth behind that smile.

The hurt that still remained. The rejection that haunted her day and night. And still she couldn't shake the feel of his hands on her body, or his hot kisses, and how they always managed to make her melt into a helpless puddle at his feet.

Maybe it was better that she was legally blind, according to her driver's license. Because when she stood, she didn't have to see the look on his face. The look that would solidify how horrible an idea this had been.

Because she was pretty certain that look was almost identical to the one he'd worn the day he had walked out of her life.

And never come back.

She took Cole's arm and let him lead her away. Because even though she couldn't see Brant, she sure as hell could feel him.

And Brant Wellington was pissed.

CHAPTER ONE

Present Day

Get the hell out!" Brant roared as he threw a vase across the room. It landed with a crash on the tile floor, where it exploded into hundreds of blue glass shards.

Bentley stared at the mess, then stepped over the shattered pieces, and continued to make his way over to Brant. "A vase, man? Did you somehow transition into a chick? Is this our first fight? You might as well have thrown a bra. Oh, also"—he walked around the couch while Brant retreated—"you missed."

"I'm drunk."

Bentley's clear blue eyes flashed. "You're always drunk."

Brant's ass collided with the wall. Trapped. He was completely trapped.

In his own apartment.

With the most annoying man on the planet.

Who just so happened to look exactly like Brant minus a few key muscles and with a very unsavory personality flaw.

"Just go." Brant wiped his hands across his scruffy face. "I'm fine. I just need to sober up."

Bentley snorted. "And if I had a dollar for every time that phrase came out of your mouth."

Pain—raw, familiar, all encompassing—wrapped itself around Brant's throat until he felt like he was going to choke. "Why are you here?"

Bentley slowly turned his head and looked around the apartment. Brant knew what his twin saw. Empty pizza boxes. Beer bottles littered across every flat surface. A few empty fifths of whiskey. Clothes strewn across the couch, and white powder on the coffee table.

"It's not mine," he said quickly as guilt stabbed him in the chest at his brother's disappointed look. "I swear."

"Would it matter anyway?" Bentley asked in a quiet voice before he slowly walked over to the table, grabbed one of the small plastic packets, and then disappeared down thc hall.

A toilet flushed.

When he returned, a tense silence crackled through the air as Brant waited for the yelling, the accusations, more pain.

Because if there was anything he knew without a shadow of a doubt, it was that there would always be more. A human's capacity for pain was limitless.

He would know.

Damn it, he wasn't drunk enough if he could feel the pain, if he could conjure up images of her jet-black hair and red pout.

If the air still smelled like her skin no matter how many times he told himself it was a trick of the imagination.

God, he hated her. But not as much as he hated himself.

Nobody hated Brant Wellington as much as he hated himself. He had that market cornered.

And he wore the title with pride. Most days. At least when he was drunk. And not sobering up enough to sense the shattering truth of his reality.

"I'll clean up." Bentley went over to the large gourmet kitchen, grabbed a trash bag, and began tossing bottle after bottle. The loud clang of glass hitting glass jarred.

And Brant just stood there.

What was the point? He'd have another party tonight, and the apartment would get trashed again. Why clean up? Why do anything?

"I'd shower if I were you," Bentley said, interrupting his thoughts. "Grandfather's on his way over, and I think you'll want to hear what he has to say."

Brant clenched his teeth so hard his jaw ached. "I'm not doing it. I don't care if that woman won me in an auction. I've sent her a check to pay back her donation, and every time she sends it back, I send it again. It's not my fault she doesn't cash it."

"Hah!" Bentley barked out a laugh as the clank of glass hitting glass grew louder. "You're an idiot, you know that, right?"

"Says the man who's living with his childhood best friend—and a dog you adopted together. Now who's the idiot? You had it all!"

Bentley froze, the whiskey bottle brushing the top of

the trash bag as he shook his head. "You've got it backward, man. I used to have nothing. Now I have everything."

Raw pain sliced through Brant's chest—and just like that he was transported back to the hospital.

"I have everything." He kissed Nikki on the forehead. "Everything."

She grinned. "I hope he looks just like you."

"And I hope she looks like you," he countered, just as the doctor walked in, his expression grim.

Brant stood.

The doctor took a deep breath and whispered, "I'm sorry, but, there isn't a heartbeat."

Nikki gasped, then started crying softly into her hands. Brant shook his head. It was impossible. The baby was healthy. They were already halfway through their second trimester.

"No." Brant charged toward the doctor. "Look again! She has a bump, I felt, I felt." His voice wavered. "I felt our baby yesterday, it kicked and—"

"I'm sorry." Dr. Jones placed his hand on Brant's shoulder. "It's rare, but sometimes these things happen."

I have everything.

I have everything.

"And because of how far along you are"—the doctor's face hardened—"you're going to have to deliver."

"My baby?" Nikki choked on her sobs. "I have to deliver my dead baby?"

"He isn't dead!" Brant roared. "It's not true!"

The doctor sighed. "I'm sorry. I'll give you a moment."

Brant turned to Nikki.

I have everything.

I have everything.

I've lost everything.

"Hey." Bentley was suddenly bracing Brant's shoulders. "Did you hear me? You smell like shit. Go shower before Grandfather shows up and decides your future. You'll feel better if you don't smell like old pizza, cocaine, and prostitutes."

"Well, that was an uplifting speech," Brant said in a hollow voice, as the memory of Nikki's face haunted him. Like it always did. Like it always would.

"Go." Bentley shoved him toward the hallway. "It wouldn't kill you to shave!" he called just as Brant slammed the bathroom door behind him, slid to the floor, and let out a hoarse yell as he pounded his fist against the cold tile, once, twice—it was going to bruise.

Maybe it would eventually look like his heart.

Beaten.

Bloody.

Fucking broken.

CHAPTER TWO

Click. Click. Click. Click. The pen slid between Brant's fingers, his thumb resting on top as he repeatedly depressed the little button so that the tip at the other end went out, in, out, in... *Click, click, click.*

Anxiety mixed with a heavy dose of anger hit him full force as he and his grandfather continued their epic stare down.

Wars had been fought in this very room.

Business deals won.

Lives destroyed.

This was one battle he wasn't going to lose. Not a chance in hell.

"Yes." Grandfather.

"No." Brant.

It had been fifteen minutes; it was as if the damn man practiced the art of not blinking under pressure.

Click, click. "All day." Brant leaned forward, pointing

the pen in his grandfather's direction. "I can do this *all day*."

Grandfather's eye twitched. "No, you really couldn't. You'd start getting the shakes, and then you'd start sweating, your knee would bounce in agitation as your parched mouth dried up like the damn Sahara—I'm calling your bluff."

Brant swallowed, and then did it again just to prove to himself that he was fine, his mouth wasn't dry. He wasn't having the shakes, and he sure as hell didn't need alcohol to get through the day—he just wanted it, because it made things easier.

Since when have you wanted the easy way out?

Bitterness lodged in his throat.

Since he'd done the right thing and gotten fucked.

Since being kind, good, and hardworking got him nothing.

Since *her*.

"Yes." Grandfather towered over the mahogany desk, his fingers digging into the wood grain. "You're an ungrateful, depressed little shit, so your answer is yes."

"The hell it is!"

"Am I late?" A familiar female voice interrupted their argument, a door slammed, and with each *click-clack* of her heels, Brant felt his testicles actually shrinking from fear. He wouldn't put it past the woman to grab and twist; she'd done it before. Not to him, thank God, but she wasn't the type of woman one said no to.

"Brant!" Nadine Titus, aka Satan's mistress, placed a well-manicured hand on his shoulder and squeezed. He flinched as her razor-sharp nails dug into his skin. The last thing a man wanted was claw marks from a psychotic eighty-nine-year-old woman who screwed his grandfather on a regular basis. "It's been what? A week?"

"Two days," he corrected. "But who's counting?"

Nadine Titus was an enigma. The type of woman who meddled in everyone's business regardless of race, religion, relation—she manipulated, she controlled—it wouldn't surprise him at all if Vladimir Putin was her bridge partner.

"Sorry I'm late." She released his shoulder. Her floral perfume was so strong, he sucked in a breath and coughed. "I had a few minor details to clear with the resort."

Dread crept along Brant's spine.

"Did he say yes?" Her eyes held a challenging glint.

"No." Brant smirked. "And I'm not going to say yes. Besides, don't you have other employees to torture? Family? Puppies?"

"Of course I do." Her smile widened. "I just prefer working with jackasses."

Grandfather hacked out a cough while Brant tried to keep himself from showing any hint of amusement.

"How are your grandsons?" He changed the subject, sliding the pen into his pocket and leaning back into the smooth leather chair. "And the great-grandchildren? Didn't the youngest just have a recital?" The only way to fight with Nadine was to fight dirty—he made it his business to Facebook-stalk the hell out of her family so that he'd have something—anything—to use against her.

Nadine's smile fell. "Yes, and I wouldn't have had to miss that lovely recital had you gotten your shit together and gone through with the auction weekend."

"Damn, did I miss that?" Brant snapped his fingers.

"And the answer's still no. I won't go through with it. I won't see her." And just because neither of them flinched, he said it again. "That ship's already sailed." He stood. "We done here?"

"He's hired." Nadine's red lips spread into an evil grin. Was it his imagination, or was she growing horns before his eyes?

"I didn't apply for a job," Brant said dumbly.

"He'll do just fine." Grandfather nodded his head and pulled out a portfolio, opening it to the first page. "Just sign here, Brant."

"Why does it feel like I'm getting sold into slavery?"

"Oh, honey." Nadine tapped her red nail against her equally red pout. "You should be so lucky."

"I think my sperm just died," Brant mumbled, rubbing his face with both hands.

"Not like they were being put to good use anyway." Nadine smiled sweetly. "Now, I think you'll be happy to know that I'm giving you a hefty signing bonus, a gorgeous corner office, and naturally, the only person above you—will be me."

"Funny, since women are so often beneath me."

Nadine didn't so much as flinch.

"Brant." Grandfather's stern voice sliced through the room. "Grown men would kill for what Nadine is offering."

"Well, maybe that's the problem." A spark of evil ignited in Brant's brain, and a grin slid over his face as he leaned forward. "You don't treat me like a grown-ass man, so what reason do I have to grow up?"

After all, the one and only time Brant had stepped up to the plate, he'd been struck by a fastball and taken out of the game. Sometimes life is better spent sitting on the bench.

Grandfather's expression of disgust was a clear indicator that Brant's comment had hit its mark.

"Read," Nadine barked, shoving the paperwork in his face.

Brant swallowed and reached for the portfolio, struggling to keep his eyes from widening as he read over the details. President of new resort acquisitions, six-figure starting salary, use of the company jet.

He had money from his trust fund and his job with Wellington, Inc.—damn, he'd been so naïve back when he'd started in the family business. Cheerfully grabbing his shiny new briefcase waiting by the door, kissing her lips good-bye, waving to the neighbors, contemplating buying a dog.

It had been a fantasy. One that had been ripped away from him without warning.

The last time he'd been truly happy he'd been sitting behind a desk, earning money for his family.

The family he no longer had.

His chest ached as the anger returned swiftly and violently—like it always did. God, he just wanted to be numb.

For a brief moment, he closed his eyes, his body tensing as he shoved the smell of her perfume, the taste of her tongue, back into the darkest recess of his mind, and focused on whatever trick Nadine and his grandfather were trying to pull.

Was his grandfather really giving up on him? When he'd fought like hell for both Brock and Bentley to get their shit together?

It made no sense. Maybe he really was a lost cause if his own flesh and blood was giving up on him.

Just like you gave up on yourself.

On her.

He shook the dark thoughts away. "What's the catch?"

"No catch," Grandfather said quickly, while Nadine sashayed to the front of the desk and leaned against it.

"You like bluntness, right? Honesty?" Her voice rose an octave.

Why the hell did it feel like he was getting scolded? He opened his mouth to respond but she beat him to the punch.

"You're killing yourself, you're angry ninety percent of the time, and you're about to beat your own grandfather to the grave by way of the clap!" Brant jerked back as she took a menacing step toward him, hands on hips. "You refuse to do the charity weekend you promised you would do, making both of our companies look bad, and you refuse to listen to your grandfather." A slow, satisfied smile crept over her face. His stomach dropped. "So now? You're all mine."

"Hate to break it to you, sweetheart." He gave her his most charming smile. "But you can't *make* me do anything." Yeah, apparently he was six again, and losing the pissing war to a woman who had lived through the plague.

"Oh, I'm not making you." Her smile was way too cheerful for his liking. "I'm presenting you with a challenge... and you'll take it."

"What makes you so sure?" His heart leaped in his chest as he said the words. It was either excitement or terror, he wasn't sure which.

Her eyes softened. "Because you need distraction, and the bottle only lasts so long before it's empty and you have to start all over again. You graduated from Stanford with honors—double majored in international business and resort management."

"You've been stalking me." He winked. "I'm flattered." *Keep smiling, don't let her see that she has the upper hand.*

"I need you," she added. "And I think you need to be needed."

The missile had been aimed perfectly—sailing toward its mark, stealing air from the room, making it hard to breathe as his chest tightened with the rightness of her words.

Damn it, she'd chased.

Pounced.

Won.

Because she was right. He'd been needed once. He'd failed.

There had to be a catch, a reason that Nadine was offering him a job that years ago he would have sold his brother for. He didn't need money. But if working for Titus Enterprises got him away from every damn reminder of her, of his past, of the money he kept sending back and the promise he skipped out on, then he'd do it.

Driving by the hospital in order to get to his penthouse apartment, passing restaurants they used to frequent. Reminders of her were everywhere—of them, when they were an *us*.

Who was he kidding? Nadine was offering him an escape from the very woman who still haunted him while dangling a challenge in front of his face.

She'd found his kryptonite. The need to be needed. To have someone rely on him and only him.

Her eyes narrowed in on him with keen intelligence.

He hesitated to speak.

Because Nadine Titus was Satan with cherry-red lipstick. She was up to something, and yet the thought of driving back down that street, glancing up at the apartment with its smoke-stained siding, or passing the office he used to walk to one last time...

Well, it made him feel all over again. It took away the numbness he was so desperate for.

And the cycle started again.

"You." Nadine's lips curled into a menacing line. "Owe. Me."

He leaned back in his chair, feigning a casualness he sure as hell didn't feel. "That's it...I work for you and the whole auction goes away, the date weekend with..." He couldn't even choke out her name.

Though his heart did a killer job of pounding out *Nikki, Nikki, Nikki*, with every fucking beat it made against his rib cage.

"No more auction. I won't even talk about it." She shrugged. "It will be as if it never existed. It's a win-win. What could you possibly lose?"

Nothing.

He'd already lost it all.

Slowly, he reached into his pocket. *Click, click, click.* His thumb went wild on the end of his pen before, with one last *click*, he signed the paperwork.

"What time do I leave?"

CHAPTER THREE

I love you," he whispered, kissing her cheeks. His lips stopped each tear before they fell from her face. He'd always promised that he'd stop her tears, never be the cause of them.

And she had believed him.

Who wouldn't?

His rock-hard body felt like granite beneath her hands as he moved inside her, each kiss a promise, each caress a memory burned into her soul. They were forever. It would always be Nik and B.

Always.

She shattered beneath him as his mouth fused to hers and his hands grabbed her hips. He drove into her once more before he fell next to her and sighed. "I'm sorry—we'll get pregnant, I promise."

"Or die trying?"

He shrugged, offering her a sly smile. "So we'll buy stock in Gatorade once I have my trust fund."

Brant reached for her again.

She met him halfway.

Mouths fused.

Tongues tangled.

"Round two?" he whispered.

"Yes!" A sense of dread washed over her as he slipped away. What the hell? "Brant! Brant!" She reached for him but she wasn't fast enough, and he disappeared into thin air as she clutched the white sheets and then burst into tears.

* * *

Alone. In her apartment. Without Brant.

She should have been used to it by now. She wasn't.

Be brave, Nadine Titus had told her the night of the auction, squeezing her hand until Nikki thought it was going to fall off.

With a sob, she turned into her pillow and let the tears fall freely—she hated pity, hated thinking about the past, but ever since bidding on that man at the auction, ever since having to mail back every damn check he sent to her, she'd been dreaming of him.

Most of the dreams were sad.

Most of them left her emotionally spent, but she needed to allow herself to cry.

Damn him for being so unreasonable! Did he think it was easy for her? To blindly walk into that auction with her head held high? Did he think she did it out of desperation? Guilt? No. She'd been given no choice. Nadine Titus, owner of Azul, the boutique hotel she worked at, had done a little digging and decided that the only woman capable of straightening out Brant Wellington—

—was her.

Add that to the fact that Nadine wasn't a woman you said no to, especially after she dropped several hints that it would be in Nikki's best interest to bid on Brant at the auction if she wanted to keep her job.

All she had to do was show up. And so she had. And what had that gotten her?

Nothing but more heartbreak and another reminder of all the reasons things hadn't worked out with Brant in the first place.

He was a self-absorbed asshole.

He wasn't always.

She punched her pillow and laid her head back down. Reminders were everywhere; whether her eyes were opened or closed, she still saw his face even if she couldn't actually see.

Loneliness washed over her. On the outside, things looked great, but on the inside, on nights like this, when she allowed herself to cry—and be bluntly honest with herself—she was heartbroken, angry.

Then again, that was what happened when you fell in love with your soul mate. It was rare that you ever got that piece of yourself back again.

And most days, she didn't want it back—not unless Brant came groveling with it. And considering he kept chucking money in her face so she'd disappear, she highly doubted that would ever happen.

It wasn't even her money.

It was bribe money from Nadine Titus, to get him to, what? Reconcile? And he'd taken one look at it and rejected the money, rejected her, rejected everything.

A shudder wracked through her body.

She'd always been optimistic.

Happy.

But on nights like this it was hard to be optimistic when the hollow ache might as well be a giant chasm in her chest.

Two more tears.

One.

"Done." Nikki breathed out a shaky exhale. "No more tears."

"Brave," she repeated, fighting for sleep the rest of the night.

* * *

As far as Mondays went, Nikki's was quickly going to hell. Another one of the masseuses had up and quit, leaving her with two extra clients. Her feet ached, and she was starving.

"Should have packed a protein bar." Her stomach grumbled as she quickly washed the almond oil from her hands and dried them off. Five minutes. She had five minutes until her next client.

Please, God, let it be a nice elderly gentleman. Her day had started with an NFL rookie, only to be followed by a guy who used to fight for the UFC. Then again, what did she expect? That was the type of clientele Azul catered to.

"Nikki?" A rap of knuckles sounded across her door, followed by a swift breeze as it opened.

She quickly turned to the sound. "Cole?"

No matter how hard she tried to get her tired eyes to focus on the blur of colors in front of her, it never happened, and she ended up getting headaches. Sometimes it was just easier to keep her eyes closed or put on sunglasses and pretend that she was a movie star—given her size they'd probably just assume she was on Disney Kids or something else equally as embarrassing for a twenty-four-year-old woman.

"Don't hate me." He moved toward her, his gait slow.

"I'm not going to like this conversation, am I?"

"If I mention key words like *chocolate* and *wine* you might."

She smirked. "That doesn't work on me anymore. You can't just randomly interject words in a sentence that don't make sense just to calm me down."

"Wine." His raspy voice dipped. "Hot..." He paused. "Cake."

"Cole." She tapped her foot. "Seriously, just four minutes; I have to make it all the way down the hall."

"I'll give you a piggyback ride."

Her lips twitched as she imagined him carrying her down the hall in front of the staff. They'd seen worse from Cole but still she'd always tried to keep it as professional as possible at work, much to Cole's dismay. "You're my boss."

"Also your best friend and knight in shining armor. Why don't you just marry me and get it over with?"

"Probably because this is the first time you've proposed today, and you still haven't brought me food."

He was always fake-proposing and a completely harmless flirt when let loose on the female population.

"So you're saying if I bring you pasta?"

"I may think about it."

"And then reject me?"

"Pretty much."

His laugh was deep, infectious, and she knew firsthand from the rest of the staff that the guy was drop-dead gorgeous, like John Stamos's long-lost twin. Sometimes it was more fun imagining what he looked like then actually seeing him—at least that was what she told herself when the pity parties started, but she did a good job of looking at the bright side.

Like the fact that she was alive.

Bright side.

Plus, she had a great job, a best friend who was also her boss, and look! A marriage proposal. Things were looking up.

"Three minutes," she reminded him.

"Sometimes," he whispered, a hard edge to his voice, "I wonder what goes through that head of yours when you get that lost expression... and other times, I don't want to know, because I wonder if you're thinking of him, and that just makes me want to commit a crime."

Unwelcome tears blurred her vision further as she jerked her head away. One bottle of wine was all it had taken for Cole to pry out every piece of Brant information. "That was four years ago. I know that's not what you came in here to talk about."

Sometimes she hated how much he knew about her past—and how desperately he always seemed to want to fix it.

"Oh?"

"Cole." Her voice caught. "Out with it."

"Sara had a few clients I didn't see on the schedule this morning. I think they were late additions, and with

Nadine Titus arriving later this afternoon, we can't risk moving them around and having them complain." He paused. "So I'm going to need you to stay a little late."

"I'm starving."

"So you'll stay?"

"If you bring me food and cut the appointments short enough to give me time to pee and eat, then yes. This isn't prison, Cole, I need to be able to eat!"

"And pee. Don't forget basic human functions."

She smirked. "You know I can never say no to you anyway."

"And yet, you do." He took a step toward her. "And quite often. If I were any other man I'd stop asking and cut my losses."

"Please, you get enough ass without adding mine into the mix. Plus there's that whole pesky employee-relationship rule." He was standing so close she could feel his body heat.

"Oh, that one." He chuckled. "I'm pretty sure I've already broken that one numerous times."

"We know, Cole. All of us. The entire staff." She groaned into her hands. "Please tell me that's not why Sara quit."

"Sara? Of course not. I think she just hated the hours."

"Gee, I wonder why."

Between our celebrity clientele and the buzz surrounding the hotel being bought out, lunch breaks had become a thing of the past.

"It will get better. The people from Titus have promised that they'll not only keep all the staff but double our employees and take a good, hard look at our bonus structures. I know it's hard now, but things are looking up. I mean, it could be worse, we could have the opposite problem and be going under, right?"

She hung her head. "Yes."

"Thank you." He reached for her hand and squeezed. "And I promise I'll bring you food, all right? Even prisoners get a phone call."

"So I get a phone call too, now? Wow, what kind of establishment is this? Best. Job. Ever."

"Shhh, you'll ruin my reputation as a hard-ass. Now, go massage the hell out of that NFL player in there."

Nikki ground her teeth. "Why can't they send me a soccer player?"

Cole laughed and ushered her toward the door, looping her arm in his as he led her down the hall and away from all major catastrophes. He always found time to help her to her next client even though she had the hallways memorized—it was the restaurants at the resort that gave her grief: all the tables, chairs, glassware.

Shivering, she suppressed the memory of the last time she'd attempted to go to dinner on her own, only to run into the buffet and end up with spinach in her hair—but hey, at least it wasn't between her teeth.

See? Silver lining.

Optimism.

"He's huge," Cole whispered once they stopped at the door. The sound of him grabbing the clipboard had her straightening her back for another grueling workout with her hands. Clients had to fill out forms for legal purposes, but she much preferred having a discussion about their needs, not just because she couldn't see the chicken scratch but because it seemed more personal. "No injuries or allergies." Paper rustled. "And he's had a massage every day since his arrival a week ago. See? Easy. Oh also, he's three hundred pounds of muscle, so have fun with that."

She elbowed him in the ribs and knocked on the door. "Are you ready?"

"Thanks, Nikki, I owe you," Cole whispered before sauntering off. The man didn't know how to walk in straight lines, couldn't if he tried. A part of her wondered if Cole did it for her—refused to walk straight and nearly ran his body into walls.

She sighed.

Too bad he was her best friend.

Too bad her heart was still broken.

Too bad even if it was whole—it would still completely belong to someone else. Even if that someone else didn't even really exist anymore.

"Ready!" a deep voice called from inside.

Quietly, she closed the door behind her and tried to mentally prepare herself.

It was always a bad idea to dig up the past during a massage. It wasn't fair to the clients; they didn't deserve to be on the receiving end of her anger—and strangling the man in front of her was probably a good way to get fired.

Or sent to prison.

"Where would you like me to focus our session?" she asked in a soothing voice as she slowly ran her hands up and down the sheet, pressing her palms against his skin.

"Hurt my back in the last game of the season, so if you could fix that I'd love you forever." His southern drawl was thick. "I think my IT band is ready to snap too, but that's nothing new."

Nikki took a deep breath and ran her hands down the man's back. A violent memory surged forward the minute her fingers came into contact with his warm skin.

Hands. His hands on her body.

His hips. Driving into her.

"Miss?" the guy grunted.

"Sorry." She shook her head and rubbed the oil down, massaging it into his skin.

There was something very wrong with the fact that for years she'd been able to exhume him from her daily thoughts—he was her past, not her future.

Maybe it was the hours. The stress. The rejection.

A man who didn't even care that she existed was prying his way into her only safe place—her job.

And instead of leave her wanting or sad, it pissed her off.

She dug her fingers, massaged, kneaded, and the more she thought about the power Brant had over her, the deeper she dug, until a bead of sweat ran down her temple.

Done.

She was done.

Brant Wellington could go to hell for all she cared.

CHAPTER FOUR

The familiar burn of whiskey trailed down Brant's parched throat as he stared out the window. Rain slammed the glass and blurred his reflection, making it look as if tears were staining his face.

But his cheeks were dry. Just like his throat.

He learned four years ago that crying didn't fix things. It didn't change the fact that he'd walked away. It didn't make the dead live again.

It was easier to hold on to anger and ignore the sadness.

He sucked in a breath and dropped the empty glass on the floor; it shattered around his bare feet. Reminding him of that night. The night his life had been changed forever.

"Sorry I'm late, baby." Brant had been watching the sexy brunette for the last hour—it was

bordering on creepy, so he needed to make his move. The only problem? He wasn't sure what to say other than hi.

Hi?

Did that work on a woman so attractive that the minute he set eyes on her his entire world had tilted?

He'd watched her turn down the last five guys without as much as blinking. What made him any different? Sure, he was good-looking, and eventually he'd be rich thanks to his trust fund—but right now he didn't have anything more to offer her than any of the other sad, pathetic guys who'd tried to stake a claim; in fact he probably had less. He'd been working his ass off just to get through his junior year, and at this rate he was so stressed that most of the time he didn't even sleep.

He had dark circles under his eyes to prove it.

When he was stressed, he couldn't sleep—even medicating himself didn't work.

Yeah, he was a real winner.

"Um, hey." The gorgeous woman's face broke out into a smile before she glared at the guy currently hitting on her and said, "As you can see, my boyfriend's here."

"Right." The guy sized Brant up and must have decided she wasn't worth it, because he walked away.

"First things first." Brant turned back around to face the woman. "If a guy isn't willing to punch another guy in order to have a conversation with you—he's an idiot."

"And you aren't?"

Brant grinned. "Of course not, because I was completely ready to break his nose—just so I could say hi."

Her eyes lit up. "That's a good line. Does it work often?"

"You know, this is the first test run I've done with it, so I'll have to give you my conclusive results later." He winked.

"So you're saying there's going to be a later?"

"Oh, absolutely." Brant pulled out a stool. "I'm actually from the future, so I know everything that's going to happen from here on out."

"Fine." She crossed her arms. "I'm game. Hit me with it."

Brant waved over the bartender, took one look at her, and guessed. "Beer?"

"IPA."

"Done." He pulled a bar stool toward her and sat. "We don't go home together."

He must have shocked her, because she jerked back from him and frowned. "We don't?"

"No. Because I don't just let any woman take advantage of me on the first date." He grinned at her stunning smile. "But we do exchange numbers, I send you some flirty texts, and you respond with a terrifying amount of smiley faces."

She laughed harder.

"And we go on a date. It's horrible, because even though I'm from a very wealthy family, my grandfather thinks its comical to only give me enough money to eat fast food and fill my gas tank." He sighed. "So I buy you a hot dog."

"And I like this hot dog?"

"Nope." Brant sighed. "You choke on it. I save your life, and you thank me by giving me a kiss."

"And this is after I'm done choking up food?"

"You brush your teeth. I offer floss, silly details, can I go on?"

"Please." She leaned in. "So how's this kiss?"

"You say it's the best kiss of your life, and I tell you that I plan on making the next one even better."

"And do you?" she whispered.

"What do you think?"

Her gaze sharpened. "I think a man who likes to talk as much as you must be good with his mouth."

"I love it when strange women compliment me."

"Now I'm strange?"

"Can I finish my story?"

"Sorry." She covered her mouth with her hand and giggled. "Please go on."

"We date for at least six months. You fall in love with me despite my twin brother's best efforts to steal you away. We get married, have ten kids and a dog named Fido. I inherit my grandfather's multi-million-dollar fortune, and with you by my side, we solve world hunger." Brant took a long sip of his beer and waited. "That being said, you should probably give me your number now."

She hesitated and then reached for his hand. "I'm too intrigued not to."

"Oh, yeah?"

"Yeah, but… " She pulled a pen out of her purse and scribbled a number on the palm of his hand. Then she blew across the wet ink on his palm,

causing his entire body to go up in flames. "There's one part of that story that's wrong."

"You sure about that? I mean I did live through this once already."

"Yup." She stood. "It's just a slight alteration."

"Rewriting history. I like it."

She wrapped her arms around his neck and leaned in. "I give you the best kiss of your existence." Her lips pressed against his, then her mouth slightly parted as her tongue slid into his mouth only to pull back. "And you lose sleep wondering if I'm going to call you back." She shrugged. "Everything else . . . spot on."

"Yeah." Brant didn't know what else to say. He was still thinking about the kiss when she walked out of the bar, just as Bentley tugged open the door, checked her out, and rolled his eyes at Brant's expression.

"Who the hell was that?"

"Your future sister-in-law."

Brant squeezed his eyes shut. He never forgot that kiss. And she didn't call right away, but when she did . . .

When the first date happened.

When a second date followed.

Life clicked into place.

Brant's focus shifted. His world was altered because suddenly everything wasn't about him, it was about *them.*

And just like that, the sadness of the memory, the burn of her lips, quickly switched to anger.

At her. At himself. At the world.

Twelve hours. He had twelve hours before he had to report to the resort, and he was already drunk and well on his way to breaking something else in his apartment. With a curse, he picked up the documents and started to read, only to throw them back down and walk into the kitchen to make a pot of coffee.

It was going to be a long night.

By the time the limo picked him up, he was exhausted. The seventy-minute ride was too short. When they pulled into the massive driveway with its twenty-foot water features and hacienda-style architecture, his eyes burned and he was shaking.

Unsure whether it was nerves or the fact that he'd gone through a twelve-hour period without drinking anything but coffee, he bit back a curse and cracked his neck.

He was staying at the resort for one week, and he had only that week to assess operations and give his suggestions to the team at Titus before they made any big decisions with the resort and its staff.

And even though he was exhausted, he was also excited.

And a hell of a lot relieved. He'd escaped his grandfather's clutches and joined forces with the one woman in the world who could probably rule and unify every nation out of fear alone.

Funny how things worked out.

His lips twisted in a satisfied smile. It was like a working vacation.

Every guest was given a printed itinerary, from the minute they arrived until the second they left. Then again, Azul was known for four things.

Their exceptional service.

Their high-end clientele.

Food.

And last, their spa.

The resort was part of a twelve-chain boutique that was newly acquired by Titus Enterprises in order to expand its rapidly growing luxury hotel brand.

Brant covered his mouth with a yawn and glanced at his watch just as the car was put into Park. The door was jerked open after four seconds.

Not bad. Anything under six was acceptable. He made a mental note and took a step out onto the Spanish-style blue tile.

Interesting.

The minute he locked eyes on the staff he knew something was wrong. One woman's eyes widened, while the man next to her stiffened.

All in all, four employees were staring at him like… they were afraid.

Of him?

The guy who'd lately been doing nothing but sleeping around, drinking, and eating leftover pizza?

Sure, four years ago he'd had a reputation as a hard-ass, but he didn't think it would precede him, not after all this time. Besides, he'd been young, stupid, and out to prove to his grandfather and everyone else in his life that he could take care of himself—and his family.

His chest tightened.

"Good afternoon, sir." A tall man with broad shoulders and dark, slicked-back hair held out his hand. "Pardon our…shock, we just—" He cleared his throat, and was it Brant's imagination, or was the guy sneering? "That is, we were expecting Nadine Titus."

"Too bad." Brant gripped the man's hand tightly. "Because you've got Brant Wellington."

He could have sworn he heard swearing from the staff. His eyes darted in the direction of the valet. Nobody moved an inch.

In fact, it didn't look like anyone was breathing.

Why the hell hadn't Nadine called ahead?

And why hadn't he thought to at least try not to look hungover?

That same apprehension that gripped him in the office was back full force. No catch. She said there was no catch. He had a job to do. This wasn't personal. It was business.

"Well?" Brant's eyebrows shot up. "Are you going to hold my hand all day, or should we get on with it?"

The man's teeth clenched before he dropped Brant's hand and forced a smile. "Of course, sorry. As I'm sure you already know, we're very understaffed. *Your* presence must have slipped through on our end." He emphasized *your* as if to say Brant's presence was unwelcome.

He had to give the man credit—it was always the resort's fault, never the client's. He was off to a good start.

Though something about the man seemed off. He seemed... angry.

Brant would know—anger recognized anger. And he was the angriest of them all.

"My name's Cole Masters." The man led Brant through two large double doors, pulled open by white-gloved staff members who made eye contact with the air right in front of them. "And I manage both the spa and the concierge service at Azul. I'll be in charge of your daily itinerary as well as anything else you may need during your stay." He swallowed convulsively and forced a blinding smile. "Why don't you sit at the bar?" He led Brant to a small, chic lobby bar with leather wingback chairs and small glass-topped tables with lanterns. "And I'll grab your room."

"Thanks, Cole." Brant tried to keep eye contact with the man, but he quickly stomped off like he was seconds away from firing whichever asshat hadn't known Brant was coming.

"What can I get ya?" An elderly gentleman with bright white hair and a wrinkled face wiped the bar in front of Brant and dropped a napkin on the table with a small leather-bound menu. "Our specialty is a whiskey margarita."

Brant's stomach rolled. Yeah, still hungover. How the hell was that possible?

"How about soda water and a lime?" Those words. They actually came out of his mouth. Bentley would shit himself and probably look over Brant's shoulder just to make sure the zombie apocalypse hadn't in fact just started.

"Coming right up." The man's knuckles tapped the glass bar before he quickly made the drink and set it in front of Brant.

Brant stared at it. For longer than necessary.

Water. He was basically drinking water.

With a slight shake of his head, he picked up the cool glass and brought it to his lips, surprising himself when he nearly chugged the whole thing and asked for another.

Embarrassment washed over him when he tried to recall the last time he had a drop of anything nonalcoholic.

"Shit," he muttered.

"Sorry?" The bartender leaned in. "What did you say you wanted?"

Brant's eyes flickered to the bartender's name tag. "Well, George, I sure don't want shit even though that's what I just said, so how about another soda?"

With a chuckle, George grabbed a new glass. In Brant's experience, the talkers were always the bartenders; they were like therapists but better, because they gave you alcohol when you poured out your feelings, whereas a damn psychiatrist just tapped a pen against a legal pad and charged three hundred dollars for heavy sighing and a few *Uh-huhs*.

The point was, he'd probably get more out of George than he would from Cole...speaking of, shouldn't his room already be ready by now?

Brant glanced over to where Cole had disappeared. There was only one desk at reception. It was freestanding, with several iPads and a few staff members tapping away while guests checked in. But no Cole.

"How long have you worked at Azul?" Brant asked, bringing his attention back to the bartender.

"Ah, 'bout fifteen years. Best job I've ever had, though lately the hours have been a little rough. As you can see, we're at capacity, and it's like that all the time now. It will be nice to have more help."

"Hmm." Brant sipped his soda. More help would be nice. It would also be costly. And even though the hotel was raking it in, they were able to do so because their employees worked long hours. Folks weren't given overtime, but they did have a bonus structure that kicked in once employees worked a certain amount of extra hours.

Expensive.

Brant made a mental note to look at the books to see where they could cut costs, especially since Nadine was hell-bent on keeping the same staff rather than restructuring and starting the hiring process over again—which typically saved a newly acquired business a lot of money. There was always someone willing to do the same job for less—always.

"Mr. Wellington." Cole approached in three long strides. "My apologies, I had to"—he coughed—"alter your itinerary a bit. I figured a bikini wax probably wouldn't intrigue you."

Brant nearly spit out his drink. "Thanks for that mental picture."

The old bird still waxed? He shuddered.

Colt pressed his lips together in a smug smile. "Yes well, we're completely booked, though I was able to get you a massage for later this evening."

Brant stiffened. The last time he'd gotten a massage had been from Nikki. God, those hands. He suppressed a shiver and begged his body not to betray him as his memory conjured up images of her hands on his stomach, straining lower, a giggle, and then her hands gripping him.

"Mr. Wellington?" Cole tilted his head. "Are you okay?"

"No." Brant stood and unfortunately found himself thinking about bikini waxes and eighty-nine-year-old women in order to stifle his obvious arousal. "And Mr. Wellington is my grandfather; please, just Brant."

"Great." Cole's nostrils flared. What the hell was his problem? One minute he was polite, the next it looked like Brant was about to get strangled. Whatever. "Your printed itinerary." He gave Brant a thick packet. "And your room key to the ultimate luxury—the presidential suite. It's on the top floor, includes twenty-four-seven room service, and boasts one of the best views in Arizona."

Brant slid out the room key and flipped it over. It was shiny blue with a giant black *A* on one side.

"Now." Cole cleared his throat. "If you'll excuse me, I have a staffing matter to attend to. If you need anything please don't hesitate to call. As you know, you have free rein of the entire resort. Welcome... home."

He turned on his heel and walked off, without a clue as to what those words did to Brant.

He hadn't had a home in a long time.

Home meant family.

Home meant her.

"You sure you don't mind?" He kissed her rounded belly. "That I can't access my trust fund yet?"

"I didn't marry you for your trust fund, Brant." Nikki's smooth skin broke out into goose bumps. "I married you because you're my home."

He smiled against her skin. "You're just saying that because we're living in a one-bedroom apartment overlooking an alleyway where I'm ninety percent sure an orgy takes place every night."

Nikki's laughter danced around the room as she tugged Brant by the arm and pulled him closer. "Hey, at least they're having a good time."

"By the sound of it, they're having a great time."

"Just like us." She kissed the tip of his nose. "You're my happiness, B."

Emotion clogged his throat. "God, I would die without you."

Her smile was sad. "You can't say things like that. It scares me."

"Why?"

"It's a lot of responsibility, keeping such a risk taker like you alive." She winked.

"Are you making fun of me?"

"Be careful not to trip over your briefcase on the way out the door. I put a note in your lunch next to the apple and pocket protector."

"Really? A backup pocket protector?" He grinned. "So the riskiest thing I've ever done is marry you in my senior year of college. I'll take it."

"I like being your risk."

"I love it." He kissed her into silence, as her hands began massaging the stress away from his skin.

"Brant."

Huh? Who was saying his name?

George waved a hand in front of his face. "You doing okay, son? You've been staring at the wall for the past few minutes, and you look pretty pale."

"Yeah." Brant cleared his throat. "Elevators?"

George tapped his fingers against the bar top. "Why don't I show you?"

"No need, seriously, just point me in the right direction." Why was it that he did life better drunk?

That's right. Because when he was drunk, he usually blacked out between a woman's thighs, forgetting all the memories that haunted him when he was sober.

Shit, it was going to be a long week.

He'd been living in a drunken fog for so long that he'd forgotten what it actually felt like to have a clear head.

"You sure?" George asked.

"Positive. You've already got a few new customers." Brant pointed at the couple approaching the bar. They couldn't keep their hands off each other—honeymooners, if he had to guess.

A very long week...

"Elevators through the lobby, to the left." George held up his hand for Brant to wait and quickly made another soda with two limes. "For the road."

"Thanks, George." He lifted the drink to the bartender and made his way through the dimly lit lobby. Candles hung from the ceiling as if they were floating; the décor was a mixture of Gothic and Old World Spain. It was haunting yet warm.

Brant breathed a sigh of relief once he found the elevators and hit the penthouse floor.

The elevator doors opened wide to a private entryway with a dozen or so lit candles spread on a high glossy black table. A note rested on a silver tray in the middle of the table: WELCOME HOME.

The words were typed out in perfect square letters. He picked it up and tapped the small card against the table before sliding the key card out of the packet Cole had given him and tapping it against the black sensor.

Nothing.

Not red.

Not green.

Just nothing.

He tried again.

And then, like an idiot, he flipped the card over so the *A* was pressed against the black, and bingo, the door slid open.

No hinges.

Just a sliding door that quietly went from left to right and then slid shut behind him.

Huh. He needed a hands-free door like that. His brother would lose his mind.

A hollow feeling spread through him.

His brother.

Which one?

Ever since they'd found their soul mates (the term made Brant shudder), both Brock and Bentley had been basically nonexistent in Brant's life, except for the other morning when Bentley charged into Brant's apartment with guns blazing.

He set his briefcase down on the nearest table and sucked in a breath. The room was perfect.

And completely unexpected.

The balcony was as large as the room itself, with a pool and a hot tub, a private bar, and a bed with white fabric strewn around bamboo-style bedposts.

And because he was sober, his first thought was *Nikki would have loved this.*

He would have loved to give her this.

Fuck.

He ran his hands through his hair and bit down on his bottom lip, about five seconds away from throwing every piece of glass within a one-foot radius against the wall.

This. This was why he drank. She was his past. His very painful past.

Concentrate on the resort, asshole.

He grabbed the portfolio with is itinerary and checked his watch. He had a massage in an hour.

It was exactly what he needed to relax.

Well, it was either that or get drunk and ask good ol' Cole if it was against hotel rules to send up any single available women.

Yeah, he highly doubted that was part of the 24/7 service, though could it hurt to ask? His dick twitched, as if he needed another reminder that it had been at least fifteen hours since he'd had sex.

And sex, just like drinking, did a damn good job of making him forget about all of the reasons he was still so angry with himself.

And at the universe for taking the one good thing he'd had and ripping it from his fingers.

"Enough." Oh good, now he was talking to himself. Sober, Brant? Slowly losing his damn mind.

Well, at least nobody was there to see it happen.

CHAPTER FIVE

Whoa there!" Nikki held up her hands to keep Cole's blur of a body from slamming into her. "In a hurry?"

Cole pressed his hands against his knees and exhaled a curse. "New. Client."

"Aren't you a runner?" she wondered out loud. "How are you out of breath?"

"Running." He heaved, holding a finger in the air. "Sprinting." Another curse as he exhaled. "Two very... different...beasts." Standing to his full height, he gripped her by the shoulders and spoke slowly. "He's deaf."

"Huh?"

"He. Your next client. Horrible, um, train accident, he was a conductor, and you know how those careers are. Trains. Loud. Deafness."

No. No, she didn't know because he wasn't making any sense. "A train conductor? Wow, now I'm curious, I wonder if—"

"Pay attention." Cole cupped her face with both hands. "He's extremely... sensitive about it, so don't try engaging in conversation. Besides, he won't be able to hear much except for mumbling, and mumbling makes him—"

"—sad?" she offered.

"Yes." He sounded so relieved, she patted his shoulder. "So very sad. His poor wife just wants a nice vacation with him. Your job is to relax him, and do not, under any circumstances, speak."

"Okay." She drew out the word. "Can I head in there now? Or is there something else you aren't telling me? Because you don't sound like yourself."

"How was the burrito?" His words tumbled out on top of one another.

"Burrito?" She frowned. "You mean the pasta?"

"Shit, pasta, yes, how was the pasta I sent you? Ha-ha, I must have had the burrito." He coughed.

"Cole, seriously, what's going on?"

"Busy afternoon." He took a step back. "Remember, you're mute."

"Right. I'm mute, he's deaf, if only I were blind. Oh, wait!" She snapped her fingers. And offered a sad smile.

"Very funny, now get in there." He grabbed her hand and placed it on the door. She was surprised he didn't slap her ass and say something like *Go get 'em*. Cole was acting weird. Very weird.

With an eye roll she knew he had to have seen if his snicker was anything to go off of, she opened the door and let it quietly close behind her.

And immediately she knew something was wrong. Her

body went on high alert as a familiar scent invaded her nostrils.

With shaking hands, she willed her body to calm down. What were the odds? Besides, Cole would have said something—it wasn't like he didn't know every painful detail of her past.

And he'd been odd, but not pissed.

And if he'd seen Brant, talked to him, well, the cops would probably already have shown up, right?

She shook her head at her own idiocy and the stupid fluttering in her stomach at the thought of touching Brant again.

Running her hands down his smooth body.

Suddenly hot and aching in all the wrong places, she gritted her teeth and ran her hand along the arch of the man's foot, before sliding it up his strong calf and pausing on the tightest ass she'd ever felt—and it was her job, touching bodies.

Would she get fired if she squeezed? Just once?

Bad Nikki!

She shook the errant thought away.

And just like that, the memory of Brant transformed into the feel of the man beneath her. What the hell was wrong with her? She'd never been tempted by a client.

Ever.

Clearing her throat, she worked her right hand from his ass to the dip of his lower back. What did the guy do in his spare time? Run until his shoes fell off? His muscles were lean, defined, toned.

And suddenly she found her treacherous bitch of a right hand sliding back toward his ass.

It was going to be a long massage.

* * *

She touched his ass.

Twice.

The second time wasn't a mistake, was it? He sucked in a breath when her fingers dug into his already overheated skin. The sheet did nothing to protect him from the erotic way her fingers spread across his body.

Too bad his masseuse was mute; he'd at least tell her he didn't mind if she lingered in those places if she kept touching him like that. Cole had written specific instructions in the itinerary, which Brant thought a bit weird, but who was he to judge? The poor woman could hear him but not respond, and even though she could hear, according to Cole she only understood some obscure Japanese dialect he had never heard of.

Which was fine by him.

Her hands flexed over his back and slid down his ass a third time. He wasn't sure if he should laugh or wonder if he had a sexual harassment lawsuit in his future. Great. That was just the news Nadine would want to hear about his first day.

Cold air hit his back as the sheet was pulled down and tucked beneath his hips. He flinched when the tips of her fingers nearly had a shaky first encounter with his dick.

He barely suppressed a moan of pleasure as she worked out every damn knot in his upper back, pulling her hands down his sides until he thought he was going to experience an honest-to-God orgasm from her touch.

It was...magic.

His eyes jerked open as he focused in on the simple black-and-white Nike shoes in his line of vision.

He froze.

No.

Nope.

Hell, no.

Rejecting the idea as soon as it popped into his head, he closed his eyes again.

Her fingers dug deeper, harder, and suddenly what had started out amazing quickly took a turn toward hellish and spiraled into *What the fuck do you eat for breakfast? Wheaties?*

Brant squirmed under the pressure of her elbows as he gripped the massage table with both hands and tried to breathe in and out.

What the hell was he supposed to do? Flip around and wave his hands in the air?

What was the universal sign for *Bad touch, make it stop or you'll see a grown man cry*?

He bit back a curse when her fist dug into his ass and twisted, then he nearly leaped off the table when her elbow replaced her fist, right underneath his ass cheek.

Five minutes went by. Then ten.

He counted. It was the only way to keep himself from strangling the woman or making a run for it—naked—down the hall.

Finally, the woman removed her hands and slid the sheet away from his leg, tucking it suspiciously close to his junk—again. His treacherous body perversely seemed to respond to her abuse, since he had a hell of a time keeping his dick from leaping into her hands. What the hell?

She ran her hands down his thigh muscle and then dug into his calf.

Minutes whizzed by, and suddenly he was getting tapped on the shoulder.

"Huh?" He pressed his palms to his eyes and rubbed, then blinked, then rubbed again. She held the sheet up high like she wanted him to turn over but he still couldn't see her face, not that it was important that he put a face to the woman who'd copped a feel and nearly killed him.

With a grunt, Brant flipped onto his back and stared up at the ceiling as a flash of dark hair entered his line of vision and then a hot towel was placed over his eyes. It smelled like lavender.

She worked out every knot in his hands, every single muscle strain in his arms. When the door clicked shut behind her, he jolted awake, feeling as if he'd just been taken advantage of, but in the best way possible. A little violence, a little pain, a lot of ass touching, and apparently a raging hard-on.

Huh. So her hands got him that turned on? Interesting. Maybe she was single? With a groan, he moved to a sitting position, an uncomfortable sitting position, and froze.

The air—he could have sworn he smelled her.

Damn it. Brant's mind always had a way of playing tricks on him. How many times had he woken up from a drunken stupor to smell her against his pillow? Even though she'd been gone for years?

You'd think after a few years the vision of her would fade, the feel of her, the scent of her. If anything, his memories of her were stronger than ever.

He gripped himself in his hand and let out a moan.

Jet-black hair.

Red lips.

Dimples.

Soft laughter.

He pumped harder.

I have everything.

I've lost everything.

"Fuck." Rage replaced every lust-filled thought, and then shame. Shame that he'd left, shame that she'd let him, shame that he'd had it all—and allowed it to slip through his fingers.

Brant slammed his hand down on the bed and stood on shaky legs.

Bikini wax, Grandma Nadine, Grandfather Naked. He looked down. Problem *almost* solved. With an exhausted yawn he reached for his clothes and slowly put them back on, then made his way to the door only to backtrack, pull a hundred-dollar bill out of his pocket, and drop it on the table. The least he could do was tip, right?

For some reason he was lingering. He inhaled. Exhaled. Closed his eyes, and tried to even his breathing. It was just a massage, and this? This was just another job.

His eyes flashed open. He glanced around the small room and slowly took stock of the candles, the oils that weren't labeled. His eyes zeroed in on the table; dust had collected across the wood grain.

Frowning, he ran a finger across the table, and it came back dirty.

He immediately grabbed his cell, took a few pictures and wrote down a few notes, then jerked open the door.

Room five.

Best massage of his life or not—the woman clearly didn't understand how important it was to have a work space that adequately represented a luxury hotel, and it was his job to make sure she did.

And if she refused to listen, he'd just fire her.

CHAPTER SIX

Nikki took a giant gulp of water and sat down in the empty break room, then ate the rest of her pasta in glorious silence. No soft classical music, and no tempting man with muscles made for sin bulging beneath her fingertips.

She'd touched his hips twice, both times accidently brushing against—well, it clearly wasn't his cell phone!

At first, she'd been pissed that he'd reacted that way to her touch.

But that feeling lasted for maybe two minutes—was it a simple chemical reaction, or was he thinking of her? Did her touch do something to him?

She shivered, a whole lot more turned on than she had a right to be. Damn it, she was a professional!

If she closed her eyes she could still feel his muscles beneath her fingers. Every inch of him was hard—*every inch.*

It had happened before, men getting aroused during

the massage, but she'd always attributed it to blood flow. This felt different.

Hot.

Good.

She slammed her hands down next to her leftover pasta. "Ugh!" What was wrong with her? She never acted like this. Ever.

Exhaustion. That's what this was. She'd been on her feet all day—what she wouldn't give for a nice foot rub.

Bet her client would have liked a rub.

Okay. too far.

Low blood sugar and exhaustion. She needed more than a few bites of pasta and a bottle of water. Stretching her arms over her head, she felt muscles her tense and relax. Then she grabbed her white cane and stood. The cane was wrapped in white leopard print, her way of feeling better about the fact that she had to use it to get around. *It could be worse, though, it could always be worse.* At least she saw shapes, colors, blurs. *Tap*, *tap*, she moved the cane in front of her.

Nikki's dream was to be able to afford a seeing-eye dog. The idea of having a dog with her at all times and living with her in her small apartment across from the resort sounded like a dream come true.

Someone to spend time with.

She swallowed the sudden sob in her throat and focused on the future. Because every time she thought of the past, a deep sense of hopelessness would threaten to overtake her, and she didn't want to be one of those people. The ones who felt sorry for themselves, who refused to leave the past where it belonged.

What good would it do her to focus on something she

couldn't fix? None. Forcing a smile she didn't really feel, she picked up her pace, tapping left to right, as she went down the hall.

Low voices buzzed around her.

Ahead was the main lobby, to the right was one of the staff meeting rooms, and as she passed the buzz grew and then went completely silent as staff members exited the room in a flurry around her.

Cole stopped in front of her. His scent was always a mixture of spicy cologne and spearmint gum, and his height always seemed to tower over her, casting a shadow over her small frame.

"Did I miss a meeting?" She frowned. "Why didn't you tell me?"

"Oh that?" Cole's warm fingers brushed her arm as he pulled her into step next to him. "I was just reminding them to be on their best behavior while, uh... Nadine Titus visits. VIPs deserve the best treatment, and since she's the boss now, it's important to make sure that everyone works hard to..." He coughed. "Make his—" He sputtered. "Her, make *her* stay... busy."

"Isn't she in her eighties?"

"She's young at heart. Spunky. Hell, her itinerary included skydiving."

"We don't offer skydiving."

"Exactly." His breath tickled her ear as they walked toward the hotel lobby, which was busy as always, a flurry blur of action in front of her as valets took suitcases to their rooms and people met over drinks in the main bar.

"So..." They stopped walking. "Is that all I missed?"

"Yup. Totally." Cole was acting weird again; his voice sounded—strange.

"Cole?"

"Yes?"

"What's going on?"

"Why would anything be going on? Hey, here's an idea..." He grabbed her by the arm and led her away from the hustle. "You should go home."

"Wow." Nikki patted his hand and smiled. "What a great idea. Why haven't I thought of that?"

"See? Go, you should...do that. Do what you feel."

"You must be really stressed." She let out a relaxed laugh and inhaled. "That smells amazing, what's on the menu for tonight?" Already, she was leaning toward the restaurant and the delicious aroma coming from its direction.

"Sushi," he blurted. "You hate sushi. Where are we on that whole going-to-bed thing?"

"My bed," she corrected. "Not yours."

"Can't kill a man for trying."

"Also, you're a liar," She poked him in the chest and tapped her way toward the smell. "That's not sushi."

"Yes it is."

"No, it isn't."

"Look, why don't I have one of the guys walk you home?"

Nikki snorted, "Because I can't manage to cross the street on my own? Chill. I'm not going to get hit by a car, I'm not *that* blind."

"Sorry, Nik, I didn't mean—"

"Shh." She took another step as her stomach grumbled. Clearly the pasta hadn't been enough. "Why don't you feed me? You've been asking me to have dinner with you all week—the least you can do after forcing me to work until eight at night is give me food."

He was silent.

Cole was never silent.

"Cole?"

He cleared his throat and pulled away from her. Since when did they ever have uncomfortable silences between them?

"Sure." He choked out the word like the absolutely last thing he wanted to do with his life was spend an hour in her presence.

"Wow. You sound elated." Something was up, but she was too tired to pry. Maybe the stress surrounding the resort's acquisition really was getting to him. He worked twelve-hour days and was constantly trying to please every guest that stayed there. Catering to them hand and foot wasn't easy; he'd said as much before.

"You know what?" Nikki turned around. "I'm more tired than I thought—I'll just head home."

"No!" Cole blurted, turning her around so fast she nearly fell against him. His bulky arms wrapped around her from behind, his breathing heavy in her ear. "Food. You're starving. I'm starving. This way!" His panicked voice wasn't helping his case at all.

"Remember, I'm not deaf," she sang in a teasing voice as he jerked her toward a table, grabbed a menu, and shoved it in her face. She recoiled from the intrusion with a jerk. "Um, I can't read this."

"Right." He swore. "Sorry, wasn't thinking. Say, speaking of thinking, here's a totally random thought. Hats."

"Hats?" she repeated. "That's your random thought? Hats?"

"How do you feel about hats? I think they're making a comeback."

"When did they leave? Be honest, are you having a nervous breakdown?" She groaned. "You slept with one of the maids again, didn't you? That's what this is about! And you're avoiding her?"

"Ha, maids, classic!" He laughed loudly and then leaned down to whisper. "You'd look sexy in a hat. We should get you one, or say, five, for each day of the week—sunglasses, a makeover might be fun?"

Her eyes narrowed in on his blur. His body was hunched forward, and something was blocking her view of the other blurs in the room. "Cole?"

"Should we order?"

"We just sat down, and then you started yelling about hats. Are you sure you're okay?"

"Completely fine. Never been better. You like steak? We'll get a few steaks, salads, alcohol—"

"You're on the clock."

"Today I don't give a shit."

"Whoa." Nikki leaned back. "She must be horrible."

"Huh?"

"Nadine Titus. Granted, I've only met her a few times, but she's clearly got you ready to nosedive off a cliff into a pool of tequila."

"God, that would be amazing right about now."

She burst out laughing. "Every time I've spoken to her she's been incredibly sweet." Except for that one time when she blackmailed Nikki into bidding on Brant. But she kept that information to herself. "I think you're just stressed."

"Not sweet." He swore. "A nightmare. He's a total nightmare."

"He?"

"*She*, sorry, stressed."

"So order your drink." Nikki folded her walking stick and tucked it next to her purse. "And tell me all about it."

He was quiet. Too quiet.

"Cole?"

"Well..." He was fidgeting so much she almost reached across the table to hold his hands still. The constant blurry movements were giving her a headache. "He, uh, sorry, *she* was... hungover."

"So?"

"So, she looked hungover."

"And that's stressful because...?"

"No reason." He cut loose with another curse. "I had to change her entire itinerary in a span of five minutes while warning every single employee to be on their best behavior while simultaneously begging them to—"

She waited, and then when he didn't continue she prompted, "To...?"

"Keep an eye on her." He reached for Nikki's hands and squeezed. "Because the last thing we need is for anyone to get hurt." His voice softened. "Right?"

"Cole," she whispered, and he leaned in. "Why would an eighty-nine-year-old woman who likes skydiving hurt anyone?"

"I think..." Cole cupped her cheek and his large hand engulfed half her face. "You'd be surprised what some people are capable of and what some people are willing to do for those they love."

His hand dropped.

"Hey, Cole." A man stopped at their table. "Nikki, good to see you. What can I get you guys?"

"Fuck."

"Uh, I think you're at the wrong restaurant for that, Cole," Nikki teased. He didn't say anything for a good two minutes while his arms shot into the air in front of the waiter, who shook his head and then stood directly in front of her.

The waiter completely blocked her view, not that she'd be able to see anything but shots of color and blurry movements.

"Stay!" Cole barked at her. "Just don't…Stay right here, I have to take care of something really quick."

"Staying." Nikki lifted her hands. "But don't get mad when your drink's empty!"

"Ha!" His laugh was forced as he bolted away from her like she was diseased. If she didn't know him better, she'd be insulted.

She shrugged and looked in the general direction of the waiter. "Put his drink in my hand and nobody gets hurt."

"Are you sure you shouldn't wait for Cole and—"

"—And?"

A cold drink was pressed against her palm. "Nothing, never mind, Cole's probably just having a rough time dealing with Nadine Titus. Two employees got written up this morning already."

"Two?"

She cringed. Good thing she was stuck in the spa or she would have been nervous. That didn't sound at all like Nadine. Then again, the woman had forced Nikki to do something that wasn't only painful but embarrassing. And Nadine was above all else a businesswoman.

"Did you want anything else?" he asked.

For some reason she felt embarrassed, again, and Brant wasn't even there. How was it fair that even from miles away, he made her feel angry, resentful, and still hopeful that one day she'd be rid of him and all the memories that came with him?

CHAPTER SEVEN

Brant's itinerary was specific.

Sushi bar by the pool at eight thirty, followed by dessert in his room at ten, with turn-down service at ten thirty.

Cole had thought of everything.

He was surprised the man didn't add in bathroom breaks. On one hand, his attention to detail was impressive. On the other, Brant was never good at following directions. Besides, how the hell was he supposed to assess the resort if every staff member knew where he was at all times?

The food in the main lobby restaurant had smelled incredible. His stomach growled when a waiter passed with a tray bearing filet mignon and the biggest bread basket he'd ever seen, so he made a small detour.

And nearly ran into a passing waiter.

It didn't matter that it was most likely Brant's fault—

the waiter didn't even apologize. He wrote the guy up immediately, threatened him, and then asked to be seated at the best table.

Once seated, he cracked his neck. Guilt gnawed, the same guilt that told him it was unfair to take out his anger and frustration on the staff. Hell, he was just doing his job, making them better. At this rate he'd need another massage in order to deal with the stress.

But not with the same masseuse.

Although his muscles *did* feel looser, even if his pants felt tight. Damn it.

"Brant." Cole approached the table, fists clenched, face grim. "What are you doing here?"

Cole bothered him. Maybe it was the cocky stance he seemed to always take in front of Brant, as if they were part of a pissing match he never even asked to participate in. And Cole seemed constantly...angry. Nothing like calling the kettle black.

"Eating." Brant stared him down then returned his attention to the menu. "What's the special?"

"I'll send the waiter right over."

"I'm asking you." He was being a jackass, but Cole needed a reminder that regardless of whatever problem he had with him, Brant was still his boss, and he deserved his respect.

"I believe the special is a pan-seared rib eye with pineapple glaze set over a bed of asparagus and scallops..." He paused then added, "Sir." Though that sounded more of an insult than anything.

Brant snapped his menu shut and handed it to Brant. "You'll let my waiter know?"

Cole's eye twitched, his teeth clenched, and then he

nodded once as he took the menu. "Did you need anything else, Brant?"

"The massage was great." He changed the subject. "She was very...thorough."

Cole exhaled, his face softened. "Good, she's...the best we have."

"Really?"

Cole's eyes narrowed. "Yes, why?"

Brant smiled politely. "Her room was a mess. I wrote her up, and if she doesn't start taking care of her work area I'll be asking her to leave. In fact I've found a few areas where you've been"—he shrugged—"lenient. I'll be sure to give you my notes later."

Cole grit his teeth together.

Brant had to give him credit—he was angry but he wasn't lashing out.

Brant smiled politely and handed the menu to Cole. "You know, a few times I thought she was going to kill me."

A smug grin flashed across Cole's features. "Oh, I wouldn't put it past her."

"Well, I made it out alive."

"Yup." Was it Brant's imagination or did Cole look disappointed? "If that's all?" He started to walk away.

Brant waited until Cole was a few feet from the table before he called out to him. "Actually, there was one more thing."

Fact: Being an asshole was way more fun sober.

"Yes?" Cole clenched the menu so hard his knuckles turned white.

Brant unfolded his itinerary for the day. "Twenty-four-seven service, right?"

"Right." Cole's eyes narrowed.

"I noticed that guests can request an in-room massage with turn-down service?"

"If we have enough time to plan for it, yes."

"Great. I'd like that."

"Okay." Cole pulled out his cell phone. "I'll just take a look at the schedule."

"Tomorrow night."

Cole's fingers paused over the phone. "Actually, you'll notice that the masquerade-themed cocktail party is tomorrow night. We'll have every staff member working there."

Brant shrugged. "So you're saying you can't make it happen?"

Cole's jaw clenched until a muscle flexed and popped on the right side of his face. "I'll make it happen."

"Thank you, Cole."

"Will that be everything?"

"Yup."

"You sure?"

"Of course."

"Positive?"

"You can go now. It's not like I need you to fluff my pillows."

Cole nodded once and walked off.

With a shaky hand, Brant motioned for a waiter. Any waiter. Somehow the minute Cole had left, the scent of Nikki had returned.

Son of a bitch.

He needed to either get drunk or get laid.

"Yes, sir?"

"Whiskey." *All of it.* "Two fingers, splash of water."

"Any preference for—"

"Fast. I want it fast," Brant said in a condescending tone, all the while feeling trapped, angry, that even though he was still running, the pain refused to go away.

Numb. He needed to be numb again.

Because even though he had a job to do, he was pretty sure if he kept smelling her everywhere he went in this damn hotel, he was going to do something stupid.

CHAPTER EIGHT

I lost my appetite," Cole mumbled once he came back to the table. Nikki had already eaten two pieces of buttery bread and downed his entire drink. Maybe it was the alcohol or the carbs, but suddenly she was so exhausted, it was hard to keep her eyes open.

"I don't think I've ever heard you turn down food."

"Yeah, well..." His voice was hoarse. He sounded as exhausted as she felt.

"That's okay." She waved him off and started to slide out of the booth. "Let's just get things to go, and you can walk me to my apartment."

"Done." He sounded pissed but relieved.

"Unless you want to stay? Sorry, I can't exactly read your expression, but you sound angry."

His sigh was long and hard. "Sometimes I hate my job—the forced kindness when people are complete assholes and deserve to be punched in the dick."

"Whoa."

He stood and offered his arm. "I'll grab our food and meet you in the lobby, all right?"

"I can wait here—"

"I know you can," Cole interrupted. "Just... please?"

"Wow, Cole Masters just said please..." she teased. "I guess I'll go wait in the lobby."

"And to think, all it took was good manners," he said.

"Good manners still won't get you a yes on that marriage proposal."

He whispered a quiet "We'll see" before kissing her forehead and pointing her toward the lobby.

Why couldn't she love a man like Cole?

Other than the fact that he was her best friend.

And a complete manwhore.

And held her job in the palm of his hand.

Groaning, she tapped her way to the main lobby and plopped down on one of the plush leather chairs. When she closed her eyes, it wasn't the vision of Cole that filled them, or at least what she thought he looked like.

It was Brant.

Always Brant.

Maybe that was because they'd never had any real closure. Just fighting, yelling, and then silence.

God, she'd hated the silence so much more than the yelling.

The silence crackled with tension—it was always filled with more meaning than when words were actually spoken.

It wasn't the yelling that had killed their relationship.

It was the silence that had followed. When he had every opportunity to fix it—and didn't.

Why was it so hard to move on? Probably because she hadn't tried.

Instead, she'd worked. Tried to stay positive. And hoped.

Damn hope. Stupid hope.

Hope flickered away the minute he sent back the check the first time. And every single time after that, hope died a bit more until all she was left with was darkness.

"He's not coming back for me," she whispered, knowing that if she finally admitted he wasn't coming, she would have to take her part of the blame as to why. Because it wasn't just on him to come running back. A small part of her knew that it was her job to meet him halfway. Instead, she'd ignored the need in his eyes, the desperate plea in his voice, and allowed grief to swallow her whole. Because at the time she'd needed someone to blame, and it was easier blaming him than herself. "It's over, he's gone," she said under her breath. Great, now she was talking to herself in the hotel lobby like a depressed psycho.

"Who?" Cole's voice interrupted her emotional breakdown.

Well, it was now or never.

And what better way to try to forget about Brant than with her best friend, the one who had been there to help pick up all the pieces all those years ago when she'd begged for a job? When she'd needed someone to listen to her? At least he wouldn't hurt her—he needed her heart to do that—and she'd never gotten it back from the man who took it first.

Maybe a date would at least distract her from the pain,

from the stupid hope that she still had in her heart that one day she'd open the door and Brant would be standing there.

She shuddered. Her throat tightening, she stood and held out her hand to Cole. "One date."

He didn't move.

"Cole?"

"Sorry, I think I just had a stroke—did you say one date?"

"Y-yes." She cringed. "Maybe?"

"That face you just made does wonders for my self-esteem. Seriously, you look like you just ate an entire plate of sushi."

"I hate sushi."

"I'm not sushi."

Sighing, she placed her palm against his solid chest. "I just...I know I need to move on. Maybe this will help, you know?" Besides, even though Cole had been after her for years, she knew the truth. They teased, but he was just a friend—he wasn't seriously interested in her.

"It's been four years, Nik." Cole's voice was soft, concerned. Gah! Why did he have to be so amazing? And why did she have to be so...sad?

"Well, when you put it that way I sound....damaged." Her lips twitched into a smile that probably looked more helpless than hopeful.

"Not damaged." He cupped her face with his massive hand. "Just...a bit lost."

"Yeah." Her voice cracked. "It's a stupid idea, although I'm sure you're a great dater."

He laughed.

"It would never work."

"It would if you actually wanted to try, but part of me thinks that this is a desperate attempt to fuck him out of your system."

Embarrassed that he'd seen right through her, Nikki let out a little gasp. "I never said—"

"Trust me, it would happen, and then you would hate me and yourself in the morning. God, listen to me…I've wanted you for four years, you finally offer one date, and all I can think about is the fact that I'm a greedy bastard who wants all of you—not just the pieces."

"See!" She spread her arms wide. "This is exactly what I'm talking about! Why isn't this working?"

"Huh?"

"You say all the things, the right things, and everyone says you're sexy—"

"You know I'm sexy."

"I said your voice is sexy."

"All of me is sexy."

"Fine!" She dropped her arms. "You're sexy and I—"

"Nikki." He wrapped an arm around her. "You're exhausted, you need sleep. If tomorrow morning, after a full night's sleep, you still want to try a date, we'll go on a date…all right?"

"I convinced you?"

"More like I feel sorry for you."

"Such a good friend," she grumbled. "And I'm warning you now, I won't sleep. I keep having dreams about—"

Cole tensed. "About him?"

"Yeah, and—okay, you're officially back into best-friend territory, since I don't know who else to tell this to and you can't fire me."

"What the hell did you do that would make me fire you?"

Nikki chewed her bottom lip as they walked out into the dry Arizona air. "Well, I may have"—she rolled her eyes—"touched a client's ass."

"Hate to break it to you." He laughed. "But you're a masseuse, kind of part of the job there, sport."

"I hate you."

"Is that what has you all freaked out? Or is this about getting written up?"

Nikki paused. "Wait, *what*? I was written up?"

"It's getting taken care of, it's not like you can even see your workstation well enough to find dust mites."

"Huh?"

He wrapped his arm around her. "Subject change. Tell me about the ass touching."

"It was the deaf guy!" She slumped against him. "I touched the deaf guy's ass. What sort of person does that?"

Cole went completely still, then roared out, "*What?*"

"You just said it was my job! You said you wanted to know!"

"*He* is not your job!"

"Why are you yelling at me?"

"He's bad news." He let her go and moved away. "Shit, shit, damn it, shit!"

Nikki reached out and gave his arm the slightest touch. Maybe he'd snap out of whatever psychotic breakdown he was having.

"Sorry, I'm sorry, I just…no more touching clients' asses, especially that little shit," he snapped.

"Little?"

Cole groaned. "Please, God, tell me you didn't touch anything else."

"Er, no, not exactly, I mean there was..." She took a step away. "Worst conversation ever."

Cole grabbed her arm again as they crossed the street. She could tell he was angry because his body was shaking. "Tell me he didn't hit on you, or grab your ass, or force you to give him a happy ending, swear to all that's holy, because if he did any of those things I'm going to prison for murder."

"Of course he didn't!" She laughed. "And I thought you said he was married."

"Well..." Cole was quiet for a moment and then said, "Even married guys can be pricks, you know?"

"Good talk." She nodded her head and wrapped her arms around him for a hug. "Thanks for not firing me for the ass touching or for getting written up. Why was I written up again? You said something about dust mites?"

Cole ignored her and returned her hug. "Best behavior," he grumbled, hugging her tighter. "I mean it."

"Of course!" She lied, she totally lied, because all she kept thinking about was the man who smelled like sexy cologne and had the body of a god, and she wondered if he was going to be on her client list again tomorrow.

She'd date him.

The thought almost knocked her on her ass.

Cole was right. She needed rest.

"See you tomorrow, friend." She waved in his direction. He grasped her hand and pulled her to his chest, but not before brushing a kiss across her mouth. "Dream of that."

Her throat tightened. Maybe she was wrong about him just wanting to be friends. "Cole—"

"Good night."

CHAPTER NINE

One drink.

Two.

Three.

Not drunk. Hell, not even close.

Apparently, a fun side effect of partying for the last four years meant it was going to take a hell of a lot more whiskey to make him numb.

"Drinking to remember, or drinking to forget?" George wiped the sparkling bar top then filled a tall glass with club soda and a lime.

With a nod, Brant shoved his half-full drink toward George, trading it for the club soda that for some ungodly reason sounded better.

It tasted better, too.

Damn it.

What was with this resort?

"Forget." Brant cleared his throat. "Who drinks to remember?"

"Old folks." George grinned. His wrinkled face looked so much younger when he smiled. "Folks like me who drink bourbon to remember the good old days, or toss back a nice rosé to remember the wives."

Brant sputtered out his drink. "Plural?"

"Four."

"You dog." He couldn't keep his smile in. "Are you going to expand on that particular memory or just let me assume?"

George winked. "You enjoy that club soda. Let me know if you need another whiskey."

"No." Brant stood. "There are some things...even whiskey doesn't fix."

"Blasphemy." George made a cross over his chest and chuckled. "Sleep well, Brant."

"Keep remembering, George." He tipped his drink toward the bartender and turned around.

As he walked off, he could have sworn he heard George whisper, "You can't forget forever."

The words hung in the air.

Haunting him.

Following him all the way into his room and into his bed. When he closed his eyes to sleep, the words hovered beneath consciousness as he struggled to remember all the reasons he'd been trying to forget about the best years of his life in the first place.

Sometimes it was just easier, not acknowledging the pain. It didn't make it go away. But it did lessen the blow.

He fell asleep to the vision of dark hair, Nike shoes, and a masseuse with hands of gold.

It was the first time he'd dreamed of a woman who

wasn't Nikki, and when he opened his eyes the next morning, guilt followed him around just as George's words had the night before.

His itinerary had him visiting the five-diamond spa again for another massage and a tour. What if he ran into her? What if he just randomly asked for the name of every employee who had dark hair and then followed them home?

Yeah, Brant, good one. The lady touched your ass, then you wrote her up for having dust in her room, and now you're going to stalk her.

With a curse, he walked toward the spa and stopped when he saw a flash of dark hair.

"Damn it." He tried following her, but Cole Masters suddenly appeared out of thin air.

Cock blocked. He was literally out to ruin Brant's life.

"Need something?" Cole asked. Hands folded behind his back, posture perfect, straight, blindingly white teeth, and irritating smirk.

Brant had to remind himself not to strangle the man in an effort to shove him to the side so he could stalk—*follow*—the woman he assumed had massaged him.

He'd seen a flash of Nike. She was wearing all black. And dark hair had peeked out from underneath a giant hat that looked ridiculous perched on her head.

"Hats," Brant blurted. "Isn't that against company policy? I vaguely remember a strict black-and-white dress code; I would hate to write up someone, especially if that particular someone has already been warned."

Cole flinched. "Yes, well, when an employee is allergic to the sun they're allowed to wear hats."

Brant crossed his arms. "Inside?"

"It's an open resort." Cole wasn't backing down. "Sun at times does filter in through the... air."

"The air," Brant repeated. "I can't decide if you're an idiot or a jackass."

Cole's smile fell.

"Or maybe a bit of both?"

Cole flexed his fingers into fists.

Brant was having the time of his life. "So." He rubbed his hands together. "How about that tour?"

Cole opened then shut his mouth. "You don't make it easy to like you."

Brant frowned. "What the hell makes you think I give a shit if you like me? I'm your boss—you don't have to like me."

Cole gritted his teeth. "Well, boss, maybe people would react better if you didn't have a stick up your ass....sir."

Well, at least now they were getting somewhere. Cole had been reserved up until then, keeping his thoughts to himself, though his expressions always gave him away.

Brant stopped walking. "I've given you no reason to hate me, I've just been doing my job. No reason to disrespect me. This can be painless. You just need to pull your head out of your ass long enough to realize this is going to be best for the employees—best for you, in the long run. But I can't do my job when you linger around every damn corner. Let me do my job. And I'll let you do yours. And if I for one second don't think you're the fucking best at what you do, I'll fire your sorry ass, understood?"

Cole muttered a curse. "Fine."

"Wow, don't piss your pants." Brant shoved his hands into his pockets. "Now you can show me the spa."

Cole was quiet as they walked down the luxurious hallway. A stream ran down the side of the building over rocks and different pieces of metal sculptures.

They stopped in front of a wooden door. Cole opened it, and steam billowed out around Brant's feet. He took a step in. The air was thick.

"You've been to the massage area," Cole said in a seminormal voice. "This is what we call the Zen room."

Brant did a small circle. "It's too quiet."

Cole rolled his eyes. "Zen. It's a Zen room."

A guest walked in, unwrapped her bathrobe, and lay down on one of the lounge chairs. Two staff members immediately brought her tea and hot towels for her face. Her white bathing suit had the hotel's emblem stitched in gold around the center.

"Huh." Brant nodded. "You couldn't pay me to sit that still, in the quiet, with all the tea."

Cole shrugged. "Some people actually enjoy relaxing. And this is the best place to do it." He pointed to a far wall. "Through that wooden door is the sauna, a steam room, a plunge pool, and a hot tub. It's all private, for the guests only, of course, but any guest can use this area if they are paying for spa services."

The rest of the tour went better. If "better" included Brant and Cole not killing each other.

"All right." Cole rubbed his hands together. "I think that's it. I'll see you later tonight at the masquerade cocktail reception. A mask will be brought to your room, and I believe that your tux has already been delivered."

"Thanks." Brant held out his hand.

Cole stared at it. Angry again.

"Seriously?" Brant exhaled.

Cole shook Brant's hand. Hard. So hard that Brant was surprised his fingers didn't make a popping noise.

"Where are we on that massage?" Brant asked.

They were standing in the spa lobby, with its choking incense and beauty products.

"Everyone's booked," Cole snapped.

"Oh! Actually..." said the receptionist, beaming at Brant.

"Annie," Cole warned.

"What?" She shrugged. "We just had a cancellation for—"

"Great!" Cole yelled, running toward Brant like he was about to dive over a grenade. Was he sweating? "Why don't I go back and check to see if she's..." His eyes were darting back and forth over the computer monitor that he'd jerked toward him. "Yup, okay she has an opening in fifteen minutes, how"—he choked—"awesome."

"Are you gonna make it?" Brant whispered. "Seriously? What's wrong with you? Do I need to do a drug screening for all employees?"

"Ha." Cole had a look that said, *I wish I were on drugs right now*. The hell was his problem? "I'll just go...help her get the room ready, since you wrote her up last time, I would hate to see her get into trouble because you find a microscopic piece of dirt in a potted plant or something." He glared at the receptionist, who paled.

When he was gone, Brant turned the monitor back toward Annie and shook his head. "Don't worry—he can't fire you."

"Cole?" She gave a half shrug. "He's the nicest boss

ever. Seriously. He wouldn't hurt a flea, let alone fire me for doing my job. He's just"—she swallowed slowly—"protective."

"Of his employees?"

"Right." She chirped and flashed a smile. "But, sometimes...men don't know everything, you know?"

"You get that I'm a man, right?"

"She's ready for you." Oh good, Cole was back. Insert sarcasm. "Just remember, she doesn't speak."

"How could I forget when you keep reminding me?"

Cole stomped off.

Brant shook his head and made his way to the massage room, slowly at first, only to end up half-running. Something was seriously wrong with him if he was that excited over a damn massage that had nearly killed him the day before.

She'd been so rough he'd nearly died on the table. And then he'd been so turned on he almost preferred the roughness.

He went to room five, stripped, and laid facedown on the bed. A minute or so later, a soft rap at the door broke the silence, and then it opened, closed.

Alone. He was alone with her. The woman who had haunted his dreams the night before.

She could be an eighty-year-old troll with a lazy eye, and he'd have no idea. Hell, she probably had a unibrow. And yet, no matter how many times he tried to convince his body of all those fun possibilities—it still reacted to her scent, her touch.

He inhaled as her hands rubbed together. He tensed, stopped breathing, waiting in anticipation.

Rub, rub, rub. The sound of her hands slicking oil all

over each other had to be one of the most erotic sounds he'd ever heard.

Rub, rub, rub.

Okay just how much oil did she need?

Rub, rub.

He was going to die on that table. Die from anticipation. Die from want.

Rub, rub, rub, rub.

Fucking hell!

And then, the barest of touches across his neck, and the sheet slid down. He froze. Her hands slid down the middle of his back, then spread wide before going down his sides.

Bliss.

Heaven.

Hell.

It was torture. The last thing he should do was respond, moan, do anything that showed her how he felt, but not reacting was almost as painful as whatever the hell she was doing with her damn elbows.

The first part always felt good.

The middle hurt like hell.

The end.

Sweet God.

The end.

His eyes strained to make out the size of her shoes, like a freak, as she walked toward the front of his head.

She was short. But those hands—yeah, her nickname should be Mighty Mouse.

A knot twisted beneath her elbow. "Hell," he breathed.

Feet. Look at her feet. Focus, Brant! Her Nikes couldn't be any bigger than a size seven, maybe a six and a half? Small feet. Delicate.

His vision blurred as she worked that same knot, and he grabbed the edge of the table and tried to control his breathing. She went up on her tiptoes and shoved him down against the table like one of Satan's minions.

He hissed out a curse as the knot finally released, only for her to move on to the next one.

What the hell was wrong with having a relaxing massage? Should he say something?

Oh wait, she was mute. Not deaf. He mentally slapped himself. The massage would be a lot better if she could communicate with him—then again, his constant squirming was probably enough of a clue to the pain he was in.

He was dripping with sweat, and she was just massaging his back. Yeah, it was going to be another long hour.

CHAPTER TEN

The poor guy was sweating.

Then again, it wasn't like she was being gentle—she was terrified that if she actually spread her fingers wide across that gorgeously muscled back, she'd hop on the table and mount him. It was bad enough that she'd heard him trip when he entered the room—but she needed it dark; otherwise it was hard to focus when she could still see moving colors and parts.

Pitch-black except for the small crack of light from under the door that at least allowed her clients to focus on silly things like her feet as she moved around the table.

And yet she'd give anything to actually be able to see him, to see if he really looked as good as he felt. Her body shivered.

What the hell was wrong with her?

Pain. Pain was the only way she was going to get through this massage, and while she did feel a bit bad that she was making him more tense, the only way she was able to control herself was by using her elbows instead of her hands. Hands felt too personal for him, but elbows felt....technical.

It took her minutes to rub her hands, because every time she thought of touching him again, she wanted to do more than touch.

Bad Nikki.

She tried thinking of Cole's good-bye kiss. It had left her cold.

And right now? Touching this strange man? She was searing. On fire. Dying inch by inch as she spread her fingers wide and pressed deep into his muscles.

How could a complete stranger elicit such a sexual reaction from her?

Focus. She ran her hands down his back and stopped at his ass. Her hands shook. Cole's warnings sounded in her head.

She softly ran her hands over his perfection, and she bit down on her lip to keep from saying something stupid to a guy who couldn't hear her.

Keep it professional, she told herself.

She worked on his gluteus muscles with her elbows, then transitioned to her hands, using her palms against his thigh and sliding up toward one perfect ass cheek.

And then, the man, the man who could quite possibly have the face of a decaying hamster, barked out a curse.

She winced. Maybe she *was* being a little rough.

When she walked back toward his head and ran her hands down his neck, he trembled beneath her. She sucked in a breath, lips parted, as she leaned closer to his body. He tensed and arched toward her.

This was bad. So bad.

She should stop. Let go. Run.

Instead, she froze.

One hand moved from the table and gripped her right hip, pulling her close. Her mind screamed *run*, but her body screamed *hell yes*. If Cole walked in…she wouldn't just be fired, she'd be mortified.

She'd already been written up once. And this was way worse than having a semidirty work space.

She shuddered as he mimicked the way her hands moved over his neck, softly at first. Then, as she worked the muscles near the back of his head, his right hand dug into her ass while his thumb brushed across her hipbone. She bucked against his hand before her brain could tell her body it was a bad idea. He moaned.

It was a low moan.

Gravelly.

She felt that moan from her pinky toes all the way up to her flushed face.

Her hands slid down his back until she came into contact with his ass, only this time she was basically laying her body across him. His head was almost between her legs, and with their positioning, well, things would be bad if they were naked.

Both of his hands jerked to her hips, sliding up and down, up and down, and then he very slowly dipped his thumb into the band of her black leggings.

This was insanity!

He hesitated. Like he was asking for permission.

And like the hussy she was, she just kept massaging him, and then gave him her answer when she ran her hands down his ass, cupping it once, twice, and squeezing, only to dance her fingertips along the side of his hips and slide underneath.

He hissed out a curse that sounded like he definitely did not have a communication problem, and he shook when her right hand grazed down the front of his hips. She started to move toward the foot of the table, only to have his right hand jerk out and grab her by the wrist, holding her in place, his breathing heavy.

She felt him slowly start to turn onto his back.

What if he thought she was ugly?

What if he could tell she was blind?

Insecurity slammed into her, and she grabbed the hot towel she usually applied at the end of the massage, and dropped it onto his face just in case he had superhuman eyesight.

He made a choking noise.

Crap! Usually she let it cool down a bit.

He tugged her wrist and brought her closer to him, then reached for her hips, pulling half of her body onto the table. She placed her oiled hands on his face. Thank God the hot towel was still in place.

Slowly, with trembling hands, she lifted the towel and felt his lips.

The minute her fingers brushed his lips he parted them, slid out his tongue, and slowly licked the tip of her finger.

She moved her shaking fingers over his face, noticing that his face was perfect, at least from what she could feel—it was also—

Familiar.

Warm.

Sexy.

But familiar in a *I know I've touched this face before* sort of way.

Her fingers skimmed a freshly shaved chin only to return to his lips, his tongue.

With a bold caress of his tongue, he licked her finger again, then sucked it into his mouth.

Knees buckling, she had to brace herself against his rock-hard body to keep from falling over. She hissed out a breath when his teeth nibbled where he'd just licked, and then his mouth was on hers. Fused.

He was potent.

Igniting a desire in her she hadn't felt since—no. She pushed Brant—her past—away and clung to this sexy stranger for dear life. Brant had never been this built, not by a long shot.

Why was she thinking of Brant of all people? She hated him, right? He never came back, he didn't care.

This, this was real, this was someone who at least wanted her. Even if it was wrong. Morally. Legally.

She was acting crazy!

But he felt so damn good. And it had been four long years since she'd felt anything even close to this.

Pleasure rocked through her as his muscles flexed beneath her touch. Her palm pressed against his hard chest as one of his hands moved to her ass, hauling her against the table just enough for him to grab her leg and pull it over the side of his body—straddling him, she was straddling him! What was she thinking? His kiss deepened with frenzied aggression. His hand continued to move freely from her ass up and down the sides of her rib cage, like he was memorizing every inch of her for later.

How could something so wrong feel so perfect? So right?

She wiggled against him.

He sucked in a breath, breaking off the kiss, before gripping her hips and moving her body against his, the only thing between them the flimsy sheet and her leggings.

It would be so easy. Wrong. But easy.

He tugged at her shirt. She waited with breathless anticipation as his fingers grazed her skin.

A knock sounded at the door. Both of them froze.

Another knock.

With a squeal, she jumped off him, kneeing him in the balls in the process, causing the poor guy to make a whimpering noise.

"Sorry!" she whispered before slamming his body back against the table. She covered him with a blanket to keep whoever was knocking from seeing his tent-building skills. She righted herself, and then very calmly walked to the door and opened it. "Yes?"

It was Cole. She could smell his cologne.

"It was only a sixty-minute massage." Cole's voice was angry, holding on by a thread. He tugged her away from the room, closing the door behind them.

"Was it?"

"You know damn well it was."

"My alarm must not have gone off." She shrugged, and tried not to sound panicked. Was her hair mussed? Her lip gloss? "It probably needs batteries."

"It's digital."

"Computers these days." That? She was going with that?

"Damn technology quitting on us just when we need it the most," he countered. "Maybe I should take a look at it. Wouldn't want you to be late for our date tonight."

He said it loud. Too loud. Loud enough for anyone walking down the hall or quietly waiting in the room to hear.

She crossed her arms. "So now you want to go on a date?"

"I liked the kiss." He tugged her into his arms. She still tasted her client on her lips. And being touched by her client—and now being touched by Cole? Two very different things.

Like being set on fire. Then landing in Antarctica.

"You smell funny," he commented. "And your hair looks...different. Where's the hat?"

"Can't do my job with the hat." She shoved playfully at his chest. "And I probably smell funny because it's scorching in there and I'm sweating...but you're a jackass for commenting on it."

He was quiet.

"Cole?"

"Be careful, Nik."

"Huh?"

"Wouldn't want you...getting heat stroke."

"In my massage room?"

"Yeah, you could get hurt." He swore and then leaned in until his face was inches from her. It took everything not to step back. "You're booked until the cocktail party. Consider that our date."

"How exciting," she said in a sarcastic voice. "A date on company grounds. You better watch it—you're going to totally sweep me off my feet." She batted her eyelashes.

"Oh, trust me." He tilted her chin toward him. "I'd rock your world—but something tells me I'm not going to get that chance."

He walked off.

And she returned to the room completely shaken.

"Sorry," she said and then felt like an idiot. "I mean, sorry, ugh, why do I keep saying sorry when you can't even hear me?"

"Who says I can't hear you?"

The man's deep voice shocked her so much, she knocked over a small lamp, blanketing them in complete darkness. That voice. She'd heard that voice before.

It haunted her dreams.

But that was impossible. Right?

Damn it. Tears burned her eyes. Would the memory of Brant poison everything? Even what was supposed to be a fun, albeit illegal kiss?

He moved.

She could feel him.

But without light, she was lost in the dark—and a bit terrified, if she were being honest with herself. And a whole lot of disappointed that even now, even when she wanted this man—she wanted Brant more. Still.

"I thought you were deaf." She felt around for her stick and met something more muscular, bigger, definitely not a stick.

Leg. A man's leg. His leg.

Her hands inched up to a knee. It was a really nice knee.

Solid. Hard.

CHAPTER ELEVEN

Brant's hand shot out so fast he nearly fell off the table. "What the hell?"

Nikki didn't say anything at first.

Instead, she slammed her hands against both of his cheeks and very slowly ran her thumbs down his face until they came into contact with his bottom lip and froze. "B-Brant?"

He couldn't find his voice. Shaking, he very slowly grabbed her hands and pulled them away from his face.

"Are you really deaf?" she asked out loud. "Cole said your wife—"

That did it. He burst out laughing. "My *wife*?"

"Oh." Her voice sounded broken—sad.

" 'Oh,' what?"

"I just—Cole said you were deaf."

"Interesting, since he told me you were mute."

She glared at him. "No, just blind."

How was she standing there? After what the hell just happened? After the kissing? Touching?

The accident.

His body jerked.

Fuck.

The last time they saw each other there were so many tears, the yelling, the pain of his heart being ripped in two.

"No wife," he said harshly. "Just a steady stream of willing women."

Pain flashed across her face before she gulped and stared down at her hands. "If you lie down, I can finish your massage."

"No." The word was clipped, angry. "Did you know about this? About me coming here?" He needed something to blame, someone to take the blame so it wouldn't be on his shoulders, so he could deal with the violent hurricane of emotions stirring in him.

"What?" She took a cautious step back. "How would I know? Are you so arrogant that you think I spend every free minute I have stalking you?" Her eyes were guilty. "Besides, it's because of you that I'm still here. I haven't eaten since one and—"

"—you could have said no."

"It's extra money."

"Funny, I seem to remember sending you money only to have it sent back." Besides, it wasn't like she didn't get a shit-ton of his money after the divorce. She could own the hotel if she wanted to.

"Look." Her hands started to shake as she wrung them together. "If you just lie down I can finish the rest of the massage."

"Fine," Brant snapped. He tried to focus on the anger, the hurt, the betrayal, but it was like his brain had shut down the minute her hands touched him.

Story of his life.

"What are you doing here?" She moved her hands down his left arm, pausing only slightly when she got to his ring finger; was it his imagination or was she shaking? "Weekend vacation?"

"I'm your new boss."

She dropped his hand onto the table.

He leaned up on his elbow and drank in the sight of her stunned expression. "Just how many times did you cup my ass? Twice? Three times? And that kiss…I may have to write you up again."

Again.

Her eyes widened. "*You* were the one that wrote me up? Yesterday? You do realize I can't see dust, right?"

Outwardly he did nothing; on the inside, his chest pinched, just enough to remind himself that his heart was there and it still hurt whenever he was reminded about her blindness—and his part in causing it.

Fuck, at least now he knew why Nadine was so cheerfully ready to give him a job. He'd sent back the auction bid money. So she'd sent in the next best thing.

Him.

Son of a bitch!

Nikki snapped her mouth shut and glared at the table, her cheeks tinged a deep red. "I'm sure it's escaped your notice, since most important things typically do—but I'm legally blind, Brant, it's not like I can actually see your ass. Though I'm sure it's nice, and I do *full* body massages."

"You know it's nice." He just had to go there.

"Do I?" She smirked. "Because by the feel of you, you've let yourself go."

"Boss." The minute he said it, her smirk fell and her expression went pale. "Don't forget."

"You know what?" She licked her lips and backed away, one step, two. "I think maybe it's best if we cut this short."

"No." The word was out before he could stop himself. What the hell was he doing? He didn't want to be near her any more than she wanted to be near him.

Liar.

He lay back down and pretended a comfortable air he sure as hell didn't feel. "Think of this as your official employee assessment. Make it good—or you're fired."

Brant closed his eyes. He knew he was being a jackass but he was just so....angry.

And his anger at himself had a very irritating habit of projecting onto everyone and everything in his path.

He was going to have a serious conversation with Nadine Titus when he got out of this room. And then he was going to get a drink.

Guilt nagged at him. He shoved it away.

A drink and a woman. A woman whose touch wouldn't affect him like hers did, a woman who could see exactly what she was missing out on—a woman who didn't blame him for the death of her child.

Or for the fact that she would never see.

All his fault.

I have everything.

I have everything.

I've lost everything.

"Well?" he snapped.

Her hands were on him once again. He should have known she wouldn't be soft, tender.

Elbows. So many elbows dug into his chest. He hated elbows. Elbows should go to hell right along with women who managed to look sexy with bright red lipstick and little to no makeup.

It wasn't natural.

He gritted his teeth when she silently worked out another knot with her right elbow while pressing her left hand on his shoulder, basically holding him on the table with what little weight she had so he wouldn't jump and run.

His eyes flashed open when her breast came into contact with his chin.

"You're doing this on purpose," he rasped.

She frowned and pushed harder, causing his legs to jerk. "You asked for the rest of your massage." She paused and looked in his general direction, her clear blue eyes unfocused. "So I'm letting you have it."

A very sick part of him was so turned on he couldn't see straight. Then she pushed down again, and every thought of slamming his mouth against hers and tossing her against the table flew out the window, right along with his dignity, when he muttered a curse and said, "Fine! Stop!"

"Fine?" She kept pushing. "Stop?"

With a curse, he pushed her hands away and stood, completely forgetting that he was naked.

Until the white sheet floated softly to the floor, pooling at his feet.

* * *

"Have you had all you can take?" Nikki asked sweetly, loving the fact that she'd made him sweat after his hurtful words. Who was she kidding? Brant hadn't changed. She refused to look down. The sheet might as well have been a homing beacon, though. Her eyes betrayed her at least twice before she was able to focus again. Even though she couldn't see him, she knew his body, knew what it felt like, and her fingers itched to reach out, even though she knew it was a horrible idea.

He'd stayed bitter. While she'd allowed herself to live, to move past the past. Past the pain.

This man, the one in front of her, wasn't the one she'd fallen in love with, the one she at one point saw herself spending the rest of her life with. Having kids with.

She choked back a cry. With a sigh, she crossed her arms and gazed in his general direction. He was one giant, muscular blur, and then her eyes lowered. "I've never been so thankful to be blind."

"*Thankful*," he spat. "You're thankful?"

"Brant—"

"I'm leaving."

"Fine." She swallowed back the tears and felt her way to the door, tugging it open with both hands.

"Why?"

"What?" She didn't turn around. "Why what?"

"Why won't you cash the damn check?"

"For the same reason I made the donation in the first place," she said softly.

"What's the reason?"

He didn't deserve to know—he didn't deserve *her*, and

yet for all these years she'd held on to a sliver of hope. It was small, but it was hers, her cross to bear, that the man who had hurt her the worst would finally see himself the way she'd always seen him.

Because I'll always love you. Because no matter how many times you hurt me, I want you.

I crave you. I dream of you.

Because she lost the loves of her life in one fell swoop.

Her family had abandoned her the minute she said yes to him, and his family never forgave him for getting married so young. She was left with nothing.

She told him a half truth. "Nadine Titus. I owed her a favor."

"And she called in the favor by having you bid on me?"

"Yup." Let him believe what he wanted—it wouldn't change anything, nothing would. Especially not now. "Brant?"

"You should go." His deep voice was like a shot to her heart. She'd fallen for that voice first, the personality second, the body, surprisingly, third. His voice always reminded her of warmth, comfort.

Now? It was hollow, emotionless—dead.

"I'm not the man you knew, Nikki." She froze as warm hands suddenly pressed down on her shoulders from behind, tugging her against his naked, hot, body. His lips lowered to her ear as he whispered, "That man is dead. Make no mistake, I will fire you without hesitation. Our past"—his voice was shaking—"means nothing."

CHAPTER TWELVE

Brant stomped out of the spa area, a man with a mission. And his mission? Kill Cole, find Nadine Titus, repeat the process of killing, and take a cold shower.

His body jerked to attention. Maybe he should start with the cold shower.

What the hell had Nadine been thinking? Was she insane?

He snorted, making his way through the lobby.

"Watch it." He sidestepped one of the staff just in time to see towels go flying. With a sigh he stopped, turned on his heel, and glared. "Clean that up unless you want to get fired."

The employee hurriedly started folding the towels with shaking hands while Brant groaned and pinched the bridge of his nose. "Cole, where is he?"

The guy gulped. "O-outside."

"Can you be any more specific?" Brant said in a tense voice. "After all, 'outside' could be anywhere, you could be talking about fucking Antarctica for all I know. Want to try again?" He loomed over the guy, casting a shadow over the kid's face. Hell, the kid couldn't have been any older than Brant was when he first started working. His baby face had no lines of displeasure, no haggard look of too many late nights, still innocent.

Not for long. Nothing in this world ever stayed untainted. Not even the most pure. The most innocent.

"By the pool," the kid finally spouted. "Last I saw him, he was by the pool."

Brant shook his head. "That's better." When he looked up, Nikki was headed down the hall, her walking stick poking out of her right hand.

His body jolted violently as if he'd just been shocked. When Annie, the spa receptionist, met Nikki and pointed in his direction, he felt the sudden urge to duck behind a tree or run in the opposite direction.

He could smooth-talk his way out of any situation. Except with Nikki. He'd never wanted to. Because he'd just wanted her. Just her.

And because sadness was so often intertwined with the constant anger he felt whenever he thought about her or his past, he sneered even though she couldn't see the expression. He wanted her to feel the anger directed toward her, however misplaced it may have been.

"Stalking your boss?" he called out to her.

Nikki froze, and her grip on Annie's arm loosened. "No, actually I thought I heard my boss yelling at one of the college interns and thought I could intervene, you know, be the calm to his storm."

"Nobody asked for your help."

"And yet here I am." Her chin lifted.

"I'm fine." The kid finally had all the towels restacked. "Mr. Wellington, I was actually headed toward the pool, if you'd just follow me this way."

Brant shoved past Nikki.

Completely unnecessary. But in a sick way, he wanted to touch her, wanted to make her feel all the things he was feeling, even though he would die before he admitted it.

Her touch. He'd gone too long without her touch.

And he was pissed as hell that he'd been reminded what it was like to walk through life like a dead man and suddenly experience a single jolt of sunshine, like the clouds breaking apart and allowing him one minute of peace.

Too bad peace never lasted, because a natural effect of finally being at peace…

Meant it wasn't long before you experienced more war.

Fighting.

Death.

It always came back to that, didn't it?

"Great." He followed the kid down the hall and out the door, while little whiffs of Nikki's perfume danced around his nostrils.

Cole was in front of the pool, waving his arms around frantically at an employee who was shaking her head, and then he glanced in Brant's direction.

Cole took one murderous look at Brant. And charged.

It happened fast. As he got shoved into the pool, Brant pulled the angry bastard in with him.

"Pissing off employees!" Cole shoved Brant under the water then pulled him back up. "Taking advantage of Nikki!"

Brant fought for air then shoved his hands against Cole, pushing a wall of water between them. “It’s none of your fucking business!”

“The hell it is! I’m her best friend!”

“Is that what this is? A friend defending another friend’s honor?”

Cole splashed him. Mature.

Employees started filing in, their expressions horrified.

“Not here,” Brant said.

Cole nodded tersely.

“One reason.” Brant swam to the side of the pool, grabbed a clean towel, and wrapped it around his wet body. “Give me one reason not to fire your ass.”

Cole heaved himself up out of the pool. Cell phones were pointed at both of them.

“Back to work,” Brant barked. “Now.”

A few people grumbled. The rest flat-out ran back to wherever they were supposed to be, but not before looking at Cole as if asking for permission to listen to Brant.

Cole grabbed a towel and nodded.

A waiter asked, “Mr. Wellington, can I get you anything—?”

Brant glared.

The waiter cleared his throat. “More towels, maybe?”

“Two margaritas on the rocks, with salt,” Cole piped up. “Now.”

“Drinking during work hours.” Brant smirked. “You know that’s not really a mark in your favor.”

“Ask me if I give a shit,” Cole snapped.

“You’re fired.”

“You said that already.”

"And I meant it both times."

"Don't fire me. Not yet." Cole leaned back against the chair. "Especially since I saved your life."

Brant's mouth dropped open. "By pushing me into the pool and trying to drown me?"

"By cooling you off." Cole's eyes narrowed. "According to some of the staff, you seemed overheated after your massage. I was concerned about heat stroke. And your job." He leaned in with a sneer. "You're welcome."

Brant shifted uncomfortably in his chair. Damn it. Even though he was technically Cole's boss, the man had a point. The company policy basically stated that any sort of fraternization between employees was frowned upon. He suspected he wasn't the only one who'd been wanting to piss all over that policy.

"What do you know?" Brant asked.

"Too much."

"What the hell is that supposed to mean?" Vague. Great. Just what he needed after a near drowning.

"You hurt her, and I'm going to run you over with my cement-filled SUV."

Brant shook his head. "And there's cement in your SUV because?"

"Because I plan on running you over, and I need it extra heavy."

The waiter returned with their drinks. Brant sipped his, mainly because all he could think about was a certain masseuse and how he'd be seeing her in a few hours—finally.

His fingers itched to touch her. His body burned for her.

"Either you have a thing for margaritas or you're

thinking about her again," Cole mused, chugging his own drink. "You don't deserve her."

"You don't fucking know me," Brant snapped.

"I don't?" Cole leaned forward. "Hmm, let me see: Alcohol-induced orgies and the inability to keep it in his pants ring a bell?"

"What? You nearly kill me and suddenly you have no filter?"

"Or maybe I just don't give a shit anymore."

"You're that protective of your... *employee*, huh?" Brant waited for Cole to slip, for the guy to say something like *She's mine*. Cole shrugged and kept sipping his drink. Damn it.

"You run this hotel well," Brant said, trying a different tactic. "But don't think I won't hesitate to fire your ass if I see any reason to be concerned that you aren't the very best for business. You did just push your superior into the pool."

"And you've been getting massages ever since your arrival—two days now, is it? And each time you leave smelling like her—not massage oil, but her. So I guess we both get to keep our jobs, huh?"

He wanted to tell Cole that Nikki was going to be a problem, that she already *was* a problem. Hell, life would be easier if he just fired her.

But she'd said she needed the job. So why was she still sending back the check?

Not her money. Nadine's.

"You don't know shit," Brant muttered.

"I know everything," Cole said in a sad voice. "I have to get back to work... don't want to piss the boss off. I'll see you tonight."

He set his glass down and walked off.

Leaving Brant the impression that Cole had just started a war—which was fine with him. Brant didn't lose.

Not anymore. Not again.

He'd just have to avoid Nikki at all costs at the masquerade and do his damn job. There would be no more massages with happy endings from the one woman capable of breaking a heart he no longer possessed.

God, he did still have pieces of that heart, though. That was how he knew he was alive, breathing. Because when the drunken fog lifted—he felt pain.

Yeah, he still had pieces, all right. And girls like Nikki, they demanded every last one. She'd destroyed him once. She'd jump at the chance to do it again, right?

Because when he'd needed her most—when they'd needed *each other* most—they'd both fucked up. And never recovered.

That was where love got you. Soaking wet, alone, poolside, drinking.

Even now, he still smelled her. It wasn't fair that Nikki would haunt him regardless of where he was.

His phone buzzed on the concrete. Thankfully, he'd seen Cole charging him and had dropped the cell phone from his hand onto the ground before getting pulled into the pool. But when he saw the caller he almost wished it would have sunk to the bottom of the pool right along with his shoes. Either Bentley was in prison or something was wrong. There was a shit-ton of missed calls.

Sighing, he picked it up and swiped. "What?"

"You sound different," Bentley said accusingly.

Brant pulled a towel over his face and cursed, then

waved over a passing waiter and ordered club soda with lime. "Miss you too."

"Shit." Bentley chuckled. "Did you just order water?"

"Club soda. Totally different."

"It's sparkling water, bro."

"Is not."

"Hey, Red," Bentley shouted at his girl. "Is club soda water?"

"Yes!" Her loud response.

"I'm regretting answering my phone." Brant leaned back against the lounge chair. "What was so important that you called me seven times in a row and then left text messages with nothing but middle-finger emojis?"

"I'm pregnant," Bentley said in a deadpan voice.

"Physical impossibility."

"Right, but if I was, you were the first person I was going to tell, and you weren't answering your phone. Ergo, I would have been on national news and you would have had to learn via CNN. That's not how twins act, man."

"Stop lashing out." Brant laughed, probably for the first time all day. God, he missed his brother sometimes. Ever since Bentley had found his happy, Brant had been ignoring him more and more, mainly because what fun was getting drunk when your brother didn't encourage it? When his face went from happy to worried? Brant carried enough guilt on his shoulders. He didn't need to add Bentley's concern—or his judgment—on top of it. Amazing what finding an honest woman did to a man.

His thoughts lingered on that massage room. On her hands.

Because no matter how magical her touch was, how

incredible her kiss had been, he wouldn't go there, not again.

"You haven't returned any of my texts or phone calls since it was announced you were leaving Wellington to work for the enemy," Bentley said, interrupting his thoughts about Nikki. Thank God.

"We're on the same side, and why do you care? You're doing charity work with the zoo. You couldn't care less about Wellington."

"Let's talk about you." Bentley was always great at changing the subject. "I'll start."

Brant rolled his eyes. This. This was why he'd been ignoring his twin. Bentley was nosy as hell and refused to back down. Hell, he was the type who beat the dead horse, revived it, then beat it again. He didn't know when to quit. Ever.

"A week ago, I found you in an alcohol-induced haze, drunk off your ass, angry, smelling like cheap perfume and sex, and today you're ordering club soda? If you cut your hair I'm disowning you."

Brant guiltily tugged at his short, wavy hair and quickly changed the subject. "Weren't you the one worried about me?"

"Being worried is one thing—change is good. But you've done a complete one eighty, what gives?"

A certain masseuse.

The job.

A challenge.

Life.

The past.

So many things.

"Is there another reason you called?"

"I was thinking about visiting this weekend—especially since, when Grandfather told me where you were, he had a twinkle."

"A Twinkie?"

"Twinkle. Keep up. His eyes did that creepy twinkle thing. Are you sure this isn't a setup?"

"I just got pushed into the pool by the concierge, nearly got impaled by one of the hairstylists because she prefers two types of scissors, and had a massage that was so painfully deep I walked funny for hours. So no, I don't think it's a setup, though my reputation apparently hasn't faded in the last four years. The employees are either pissed off at me or they're too terrified to say hi."

Bentley chuckled. "You were a hard-ass when you worked for Grandfather. You fired two people for not getting coffee fast enough."

Brant groaned. "They were interns, and I was making an example. Plus they'd been lying on their time sheets for weeks."

"Right, but everyone thinks it was the coffee."

"Not my fault."

"You were good at your job."

Past tense. Brant didn't like the direction this conversation was going. He knew where it would end.

And the last thing he wanted to do was talk to Bentley about his feelings, about his sadness, about his hate.

God, it was hard enough living with it on a daily basis.

"Hey, I gotta run," Brant lied.

Bentley let out a long sigh. "I know you're lying, but since I heard you laugh at least once in the last few minutes, I'm going to let it slide."

Brant would probably regret his next words. "You

should bring everyone down this weekend...maybe even invite Brock and Jane. It would be fun."

"Damn." Bentley said in a stunned voice. "Was it the death massage or getting pushed into the pool?"

"Huh?"

"You sound"—Bentley hesitated—"nonsuicidal."

"Nice. Real nice, Bent." Brant pinched the bridge of his nose and shook his head. "Look, I'm fine, I've always been fine, just..."

He didn't want to say it.

But apparently, he didn't need to, because Bentley added, "Sad."

"I was going to say angry."

"Sometimes they're the same thing."

"I gotta go."

"You said that."

"Bye, Bentley."

He disconnected the call and tossed the phone onto the opposite chair.

Maybe the biggest step was just admitting that you had a problem. Even though you weren't so sure you wanted to even solve it.

"Shit." Brant tugged at his wet shirt and wrung it out. Two days, a few hours, and Nikki was twisting him up in knots.

Just like she always had. Just like she always would.

He squeezed his eyes shut, mentally preparing himself for later that evening. He had two choices. He could ignore the tension right along with the chasm of mistakes that separated them. Or—he braced his hands on the chair as pain sliced through his chest—or he could just kiss her again.

CHAPTER THIRTEEN

Holy shit." Cole ran his massive hands up and down Nikki's arms, finally stopping at her hands as he twirled her around and then pulled her against his chest. "You look amazing."

"Don't I always look amazing?" she teased, nervous that she had no idea what she looked like and had to rely on everyone else to tell her she was passable. But judging by the heat emanating from Cole, she was more than passable. Really, all she wanted was to look pretty. Anxiety washed over her whenever she thought about what she looked like.

Because sometimes it was hard to remember. Not the full picture.

She knew what color her hair was—a jet-black that was often shiny and bouncy. Her eyes were more golden than brown. And her Hispanic grandmother had passed down her amazing golden skin. Full lips, a petite curvy body. But it stopped there.

It was the little details that killed her, like what her teeth looked like when she was laughing. Did her eyes crinkle at the sides like they used to? Was her expression blank like most people's were when they were struck with blindness?

And why was it, when she thought of herself, that the image was blurry at best?

But when she thought about Brant, it was clear as day. As if she could actually see him.

She closed her eyes for a few minutes and gave herself permission to imagine the man she'd married—not the one who'd stomped out of her life yet again only to yell at the first employee he'd seen, and continue on his tirade.

Apparently Cole had pushed him into the pool. She wasn't sure if she should be concerned for Cole's job or give him a high five for knocking Brant down a few pegs.

This was for herself. The dress. The night.

And now, more than ever, the date. She was suddenly so thankful that Cole had basically demanded a date tonight that she could have cried. The last thing she wanted was to show up stag to a company party and have to constantly look over her shoulder and wonder if he was there, if he was staring, if he thought she looked pretty.

She bit down on her bottom lip, catching it between her teeth, piercing it until blessed pain took over. She had to remind herself that was what Brant represented. Pain. Loss. Bitterness.

Brant didn't just run when things got hard—he'd hurt her in the process and she pushed him away in order to protect them—or at least what she thought was left of them.

"Normally when I give girls compliments they reward

me with a kiss." Cole's rough voice jolted her from her thoughts, then his lips grazed her ear. "Maybe you're just fishing for more compliments, so in case you didn't hear, you look absolutely stunning."

"You're only saying that because you're my best friend." Why did her voice sound so pathetic?

"No. I shouldn't say that because I'm your best friend," he grumbled, jerking away from her, only to grip her hand and start the slow walk across the street and into the hotel.

Warm, dry air hit her in the face as they made their way down the sidewalk. "So what are you wearing?"

"Nothing," Cole said quickly. "I'm completely naked—hope you don't mind."

"Rats. If only I could see! Quick, explain said nakedness." She could always count on Cole to distract her. Smiling, she waited for his answer.

"Pretty much just golden skin and muscles… everywhere. Not to mention a huge cock. Wait, is that too much? Have I gone too far for your innocent ears?"

Nikki burst out laughing. "Not at all, I have a very vivid imagination. Do continue."

"Huge cock."

"You said that."

"It bore mentioning again, just in case you didn't hear me the first time."

"My hearing's amazing. You know, blindness does that."

"Ah, and here I thought you just liked staring at me."

"Well, that too. You're a really nice, colorful blur." She shrugged while he stopped them, probably to press the Walk signal button, then grabbed her arm again as the beeping sounded. "It's a nice blur. I promise."

"I've always wanted to be a blur."

With a giggle, she swatted him in the chest. Soon the scent of lemons and sugar filled the air.

They were at the hotel. It always smelled fresh without giving off that bleach- or Lysol-sanitized feel. It smelled clean, like a new leaf. Fresh starts.

Classical music assaulted her ears. She made a face.

"You hate sushi and classical music. Are you even human?"

"Stop. I have a very good reason for hating classical music."

"I'm waiting." They moved toward the music.

She swallowed the tightness in her throat. Classical music had been playing that day on the way to the hospital. Brant was humming along—he'd been so excited.

So excited that they were going to have a baby.

Her heart slammed against her chest violently. It hurt. It still hurt so much.

"Whoa, whoa." Cole held her by the shoulders. "Why does it look like you're about to cry?"

"I really"—she sucked in a breath—"*really* hate classical music."

"I'll fix it." He kissed her hand and released it. "Why don't you make your way over to the bar? Oh, and before I forget." He placed a mask over her face. "A mask made for a princess. You're welcome."

Nikki touched the mask as he finished tying it behind her head. "It covers my entire face."

"It's a masquerade party," he said simply, like it was a valid reason. They walked hand in hand toward a noisy blur of people and movement.

"Right, usually people just put masks over their eyes."

"Not you." He gave her a soft shove. "Order a drink while I go beg for some Jay Z."

"Twenty One Pilots works too!" she called out before fumbling around for a bar stool, only to have a warm hand graze her knuckles. Shivering, she jolted back.

"Your boyfriend pushed me in the pool today," a sexy-as-hell voice said from her right.

Heat rushed to her face. That voice had a way of wrapping around her, making her want. "He's not my boyfriend."

"Maybe tell him that—or better yet, tattoo it on his forehead, since he keeps forgetting."

Suddenly nervous, she didn't know what to do with her hands or her body or really anything. So she stood there. Like a loser. Totally out of her element. Gulping, she tugged at her white strapless dress. All she knew was that the silk felt amazing against her legs and that it had a train that danced around her ankles.

"I'm disappointed," Brant said in that raspy, familiar voice of his.

Hurt, she sucked in a breath, only to have him take a step closer and grab her hand.

"Disappointed I can't see your face."

"I could have boils under this mask and you'd never know."

"With a body like that, would any man in his right mind really care?" he stunned her by saying. Wait, didn't he know it was her? He had to, right? Unless he was already drunk?

"I can't decide if that's insulting or really sweet," she said with a shaky laugh, looking away at all the rest of the colorful blurs moving around her.

"I've been accused of both on multiple occasions." He chuckled, which added to her discomfort. "Now, what can I get you to drink?"

"White wine." *Idiot.* She tolerated wine. She loved fruity drinks, but she'd said the first thing that popped into her head.

"George," Brant called, "white wine for the lady and the usual for me."

"Lime, Mr. Wellington?" George asked.

"You know it."

Wellington.

Her entire body seized. Just hearing someone else saying his name did bad things to her.

She shivered. The years had made him into a very angry man, that she knew; what she hadn't counted on was the years molding his body into the perfect male specimen just begging to be licked from head to toe.

Great, now she was thinking about licking him?

Stupid massages. Stupid, stupid, kisses.

Time slowed as her fuzzy brain put together pieces that didn't fit, that shouldn't have fit. She should have known yesterday, when Cole was acting weird, when her body responded so erotically to Brant's.

"Excuse me." She barely managed to get the words out before Brant tugged her hand and pulled her flush against him.

"Are you all right?" He steadied her, grabbing her by the waist.

That damn touch. So familiar. It had been everything. Her anchor. Her life.

And suddenly she was transported to a time when his hands were always on her, when he couldn't get enough of her, when she thought she might die if he didn't kiss her.

So many things had changed.

"Yes, I'm..." Her hands were shaking so hard she couldn't think straight. Was it selfish? That the last thing she wanted to do was tell him who she really was, that the girl beneath the mask was in fact the girl he'd both kissed and yelled at earlier. It was only a matter of time before someone recognized her and said something.

Emotions warred against one another. Hatred that he was hitting on her. How many women had he been with since they were married? Maybe it was more jealousy than hatred, but they both stemmed from anger that he'd been with others when, for her, it had always been him.

And Cole.

Great, now she felt guilty about Cole. Damn it!

Why did Brant have to be the only man to ever make her feel anything? Why did he have to be her soul mate? Brant Wellington, no matter how arrogant and angry, was clearly not someone you just got over.

It burned that the only man who made her feel alive wanted nothing to do with her—would shove her away if she peeled back her mask.

"Maybe you should have water instead?" he joked, releasing her a bit and placing a glass in her hand.

"Dance with me!" Cole announced, jerking her away from Brant's attention. She wasn't sure if she was thankful or annoyed, as he pulled her toward the floor and whispered in her ear.

"Wasn't sure if I was playing the white knight that saves you from the evil king or the white knight that falls on his own sword so he can actually have a chance at you."

She smirked beneath her mask and then tears welled in her eyes.

"Shit." Cole sighed. "I was supposed to fall on my own sword, then? Is that how this date is going to end?"

"No." She brought a shaky hand to his shoulder as he twirled her around. "It's just... my body has a hard time reminding my brain that he's the evil king, that's all."

Get yourself together, Nik!

"You looked like you'd seen a ghost," Cole whispered.

She snorted and looked down. "It feels that way. Whenever Brant and I talk, it's like the past is exploding in front of my face."

The music shifted from classical to "Close" by Nick Jonas. *Great, Cole, good choice.*

She was dizzy, overwhelmed, hot.

"He's watching you," Cole whispered. "He's angry."

She snorted. "He's always angry. It's kind of his thing."

"Not the type of angry where he wants to fire me. If I didn't know any better I'd say he's jealous."

"Impossible." She ignored the little spring of hope that threatened to burst through her chest.

"Very possible." Cole sighed and spun her around. The heat from his chest pressed against her breasts, and it felt all wrong. Because it was Cole, and she was lying to herself when she thought it would be possible—especially after Brant's kisses—to feel anything for anyone but him, even if his horrible personality came right along with that body.

So did his past.

So did the memories.

And her treacherous brain kept trying to remind her why they'd been so perfect before, why they'd laughed so much, why it had been *everything*.

Until they lost all of it.

"I should go..." She pulled out of Cole's embrace.

Cole grabbed her by the arm. "Wait."

And then he left her.

CHAPTER FOURTEEN

Does the damsel need rescuing?" came Brant's rough voice.

She licked her lips, imagined his mouth, then mentally slapped herself for being so weak. He brought nothing but pain, and no matter how good it felt to touch him, he was still the same Brant who'd abandoned her, who'd refused to fight. He had no right trying to rescue anyone when he couldn't even rescue himself.

White-hot anger surged through her. Yes. That was what she needed, to remember how much he'd destroyed her.

She hated him. Right?

Right. She nodded, like an idiot.

"Was that a yes?"

"Why are you offering?" she countered. "I wasn't aware I looked like I needed saving."

"You looked"—his hands wrapped around her waist—"lost."

Too close to the truth, so close she almost tripped over her feet and slammed against his chest—which would have been bad, since his body had a way of forcing her to forget all the reasons why he was a horrible human being.

Hell, he was about to find out really soon who she was if he kept plowing her through people and objects that she couldn't see! Why? Why not just this once? Could she be that girl again, the innocent girl getting swept off her feet by one of the most attractive men she'd ever seen? If she closed her eyes she could still see the arrogant smile he'd worn right along with his stunned expression when his pick-up lines hadn't worked.

Brant stopped and twirled her once, then began dancing with her. "One dance."

One dance.

She knew it wouldn't be just one dance, not with Brant. Brant was never satisfied with one of anything.

"But—"

"You know," he interrupted, his lips caressing her ear as they moved back and forth. "My ego's taken a bit of a hit, since you seem to want to run in the opposite direction. The least you can do is dance to one song."

She swallowed past the swelling in her throat; the need to sob against his shoulder and ask him why he left warred with the desire to slap his perfect face and scream at him for abandoning her.

"One song," she finally said, surprising herself as she closed her eyes and allowed her body to sway to the music. Maybe if she closed her eyes tight enough, she could imagine this was a normal work party, she was still his wife, he was still her doting husband.

She could still see. She still had a baby. Maybe two by then.

Her stomach clenched as her heart flipped so painfully that she let out a rough exhale. And then the damn man started to hum.

Every cell in her body went on high alert as her skin prickled with awareness. Every inch of him was perfect, from his just-shaved chin as it brushed against her neck, to the way his hands embraced hers with such intensity that if she were any other woman she'd think he was swearing never to let go.

Tears filled her eyes.

Please don't let go. Not again.

Life was cruel—fine, take her sight, take her baby, take her soul mate, but don't tease her with what it felt like to have everything feel so right again, so perfect, only to have it ripped from her fingertips. The magic of the moment was going to shatter; she waited for the inevitable, for him to realize who he was dancing with. She braced herself for a fight when the smooth-talking guy would go from Jekyll to Hyde.

The last time she'd danced had been at her wedding. With her cheap store-bought dress and the simple white daisies that decorated each table. They served homemade cupcakes.

Brant had said it was the best dessert he'd ever had, and then he'd dipped his finger in the frosting and drawn it across her lips.

Don't let go.

"I won't," he whispered, his lips tickling the outer corner of her ear.

Had she said that out loud?

She must have. Because he clung tighter, his chest pressed against her breasts so hard that they moved like one person.

The song ended too soon. The dream faded right along with the music.

Nikki braced herself for the rejection, for Brant to find another woman that caught his eye—after all, he was notorious for sleeping around with celebrities, models, pretty girls.

And her time was up. The spell was broken.

And she found out a long time ago that he wasn't the kind of prince who ran after the princess, just like she'd discovered that she wasn't the type of princess who wanted him to chase her until it was too late. Until the moment was gone.

Sighing, she hung her head and stepped away from him. Sometimes, she thought it was actually a gift that she couldn't see just how perfect and drop-dead gorgeous his list of women were—at least it salvaged her pride to not have to stare at them in the newspaper and wonder.

"Want to go for a walk?"

"What?" She jerked her head so hard she nearly took out his chin. "Sorry!"

His smile was impossible to see, but his laugh… it was rich, sexy. If she had a choice of hearing his laugh or seeing his smile, she'd choose hearing every single time. There was something about the way his laugh wrapped around her body like a hot electrical charge.

"For a masseuse, you're kind of clumsy," he joked.

"Probably because I'm so used to touching giant men

with muscles all day long that it zaps the strength and coordination right out of me."

He froze. "Hmm. How does Cole feel about you massaging all those guys?"

"I'm sure he's used to it," she answered carefully, then froze. "By the way, how was the afternoon swim?" Her mind worked a mile a minute.

"Frigid," he said in a clipped tone. "I think Cole's way of making it up to me was allowing me to dance with the prettiest girl in the room."

Her heart clenched. So he did know who she was. So why was he acting nice? Kind, even, especially since after the massage he'd been such an ass.

"Fuck." Brant's voice had a sudden rough edge to it. "You know what?" It sounded like he was the one pacing now. "I have an idea."

She crossed her arms and smirked. Whenever Brant got irritated or wanted to change the subject, he would tug at his hair and say, *I have an idea*. It seemed some things never changed.

"No Cole." He was in front of her again, a blur of black. His tuxedo felt expensive on her fingertips, the silk of his jacket smooth. "No past, no future, just now."

Her lips parted. It was tempting. More than tempting.

"Just now, huh?" she repeated, her chest tight. "And what would be the end goal here?"

"Dancing." He twirled her, even though the music from the lobby was faint. Another twirl. "Maybe a bit of kissing."

His lips grazed hers.

With a moan, she returned the kiss, savoring his taste,

the taste that haunted her dreams. She was stupid to cling to him, stupid to hang on when she knew what would follow once this cease-fire was over. And yet, when he kissed her again, she met him halfway. Confusion warred with the need to be closer—with the sad fact that the only time she'd ever felt truly beautiful had been in Brant's arms.

"And if you're lucky..." he said in a low voice, "I may even get naked."

"Wow!" Still an arrogant bastard, wasn't he? "I'm honored."

"You should be. I don't get naked for just anyone."

"You sure about that?"

"Shit, does my reputation still precede me? Even now?"

"Does it matter? Since you said no pasts..." She shrugged. "If your past doesn't matter, then mine can't, either, right? Isn't that how these things work?"

He hesitated and then said, "Is that your way of saying I get to see you naked?"

"Does everything end with us naked?"

"God, I hope so." He crushed his mouth to hers again, sliding his tongue past the barrier of her lips as her body melted against him.

"Now what?" She reached for him again, trying to focus on his face, even though it was blurry. At least it was there, *he* was there in front of her, and he wanted her.

And maybe she was stupid for taking him up on his offer.

But it was Brant.

And she'd regret letting him walk away a second time—without experiencing him like this.

Just a girl. And a guy. Having a one-night stand.

What could possibly go wrong?

"Now..." He kissed her hand. "I take off your mask."

She sucked in a breath and pulled away. Taking off masks was a bad idea. It meant that the spell would break, and even though she knew it probably wouldn't end well, she didn't want him to see her face, the face that reminded him of everything they'd lost. "I have a better idea."

"Oh?"

"It involves blindfolds and duct tape."

He groaned. "I think I just fell in love."

Nikki laughed and rolled her eyes. "You do realize I could be envisioning something along the lines of *CSI* while you're all *Fifty Shades*, right?"

"Are you trying to ruin the moment?"

"Take me to your room." With a boldness that she'd never felt around anyone except Brant, she leaned up on her tiptoes and wrapped her arms around his neck so that she could feel where his mouth was. Then she licked his ear, blowing over where she'd just licked. "Please?"

"Hell, yes."

He grabbed her hand and took off in a near sprint. By the time they made it to the elevator, they were both out of breath.

"Fair warning—it's been a while since I've had sex sober," he admitted casually.

Fair warning—it's been four years since I've had sex at all. And the last time I did—I woke up to you gone. "Hopefully, you don't suck at it then, huh, Brant?"

"Trust me, that's one thing I don't suck at, but I may only last a few minutes before I take you. I've been wanting…" The elevator dinged.

"What?" she asked on a swallow. "What have you been wanting?"

"You."

CHAPTER FIFTEEN

Brant gulped.

He couldn't look away.

He licked his lips. He sucked in a breath as the dress slid down her legs. And just because life was that cruel, she was wearing white.

He loved her in white. Her wedding dress hadn't been as beautiful as the dress she was wearing now.

They hadn't been able to afford anything fancy, not with his grandfather telling him he was making a mistake by marrying so young—not with her parents basically disowning her for the same reason.

God, she was beautiful.

"No pasts." His voice had a hard edge to it. He was going to regret this, all of it, but he'd never had much self-control around her, and now? Now that he'd tasted her again?

"No pasts," she recited back, her eyes filling with tears.

"Come here." The words finally happened, and they were the wrong ones. They were seductive, calm, everything he didn't feel as his heart slammed against his chest with anticipation of touching her again, kissing her, claiming her.

She stepped out of her dress, heels still strapped around her ankles as she moved in a straight line toward him.

God, he needed a drink. A cold shower.

Hell, he was sure getting run over by a semi wouldn't be enough to stop him from kissing her—touching her.

She was his heaven. He was in hell.

"I'm the only one naked." Her mouth twisted into a shaky smile as she adjusted her mask.

"Not for long," was his hoarse answer as he reached for her perfect body and tugged it against his as he very slowly pulled her mask free, letting it fall to the ground by her feet.

Wrong. This was wrong. Maybe he really was the bastard everyone thought he was—because as wrong as it was—he couldn't stop himself.

He kissed her hard. He punished her with his mouth.

How dare she come back into his life and remind him of everything he'd had and lost?

She gasped with each kiss, exposing her neck, putting her soul into every movement.

This wasn't a one-night stand. This was the good-bye they'd never had. The one he fucking deserved after she'd put him through hell, after she'd pushed him away and nearly died in the choking flames.

Brant told himself he was doing it for selfish reasons. Because that was what good-byes were—selfish. It was one last touch, one last taste; it was a desperate, insane attempt to cling to something that was already gone.

Death had a way of breaking the living. And maybe that was why they didn't survive. Because they were both halves of a whole that didn't make it.

He'd thought he was almost over her. But her tongue slid against his, and he realized he was *wrong*.

Maybe that was their destiny, to always be in each other's lives but never get the happy ending.

It didn't matter, did it? No matter where she went, she was still a part of him, a beautiful reminder of his ugly past.

Her lips parted on the next kiss. He gripped her shoulders with his hands, then slid his hands down her back, again and again, his fingers dancing along her spine, memorizing the feel of her smooth skin and the way it reacted to his touch. Goose bumps rose and fell.

Brant breathed in the moment. One-night stand.

His grip on reality—on the situation—on the anger and the fear, and all of the ugly dragging him into the depths of hell—shattered in her arms.

Nikki's body shook as she deepened the kiss, slowly entwining her arms around his neck, holding on for dear life.

He ducked his head in her neck, inhaled, and shook with the need to do it again and again. Real. *She was real.* In his arms.

I'd find you anywhere, his heart beat.

No. Not anymore. This was the end. Not the beginning.

He kissed her harder. Rather than retreat, she met him with each thrust of his tongue, whimpering when his fingertips dug into her hips, dragging her underwear down her perfect legs and tossing them aside.

Brant drank her in.

One night. If he only had on more night with her, he would want it like this—with moonlight kissing her skin. No real barriers between them, and yet everything was standing in the way, wasn't it?

Even the air was charged with things left unsaid, baggage that refused to be dropped. Hurt that refused to be healed. Because healing was the most painful part of the process, wasn't it? And he was done with that sort of pain.

But pleasure? That he could do. Let it consume them both.

Nikki reached for his suit jacket, her hands shaking as she slowly undid button after button and pushed the jacket off his shoulders.

Every so often, her fingers would graze his chest. It was torture. He was strung so tight that by the time she finally tugged his shirt free, he picked her up and carried her to the massive bed. Then he turned down the lights until blackness covered the entire room.

Darkness covered her face. He was thankful for the dark.

Brant was a coward. An angry, lying coward.

He crushed his mouth to hers in a punishing kiss, a kiss that told her how much he still hated, which meant it also had to show how much he still loved.

He would always love. And that was the problem. Because the only way he could make it through his life was to let his hate and love coexist, and too often his hate won. Because hate at least didn't demand that same healing that love did.

Exposed. Bloody. Vulnerable.

Left it for dead—that was what she'd done to his heart. So yeah, he deserved this moment with her, the last night they never had. The last kiss she refused to give.

He stole it. Kept it. Coveted it.

His tongue skimmed her trembling lips over and over again. Her fingers dug into his shoulders as she clung to him, kissing him deeper, sucking his soul dry, marking him just as deeply as he was marking her.

A blast of heat surged between them as he slid his fingers down her thigh. When he found her core, she let out a little gasp.

He pulled his hand back and yanked off the remainder of his clothes. The silence crackled, sizzled, like the calm before the storm.

This would change everything. This would destroy her. Even the playing field.

And yet he couldn't stop.

The hate was winning. Even though his heart beat for her.

He kissed her again. His hands weighed her breasts, and with a groan he moved to her hips, positioning her body as she panted beneath him.

They were playing with fire.

And Brant—fucking burned.

With a sliding thrust, he invaded, he selfishly took his.

Nikki cried out, her nails digging into his skin, and then she matched his every movement, every rhythm.

"Hell..." He hissed out a breath. "You feel good."

She didn't say anything, just slid her hands slowly up the sides of his ribs. Then she hooked her hands around his neck and pulled him down for another series of possessive kisses that had him forgetting his own damn name.

She was his.

She'd been his since the minute he walked into that bar.

She would always be his.

He just hated that as much as he owned her—she owned him equally as much.

This wasn't about her. This wasn't even about them.

It was about Brant.

He shoved the guilt away, letting the pleasure take control, the same pleasure he told himself he deserved as his body said, *Good-bye*. And his heart said, *Not yet*.

Another thrust.

Nikki cried out.

His.

"You'll always be mine," he whispered in a hoarse voice. A sea of pleasure surged between them. Her body tightened around him, pulling him tight like it was promising never to let him go. Brant rose over her again. She was close—he could feel it in the way she tensed beneath him.

With a shudder, he kissed her back, his lips moving against her mouth. "Come on, sweetheart. Let go."

"I don't want to." She tugged his head down, kissing him again. "That will mean it's over."

She was destroying him, ruining the selfishness of the moment, making him feel everything. "It won't ever be over." The truth hung between them. "Let go."

He could feel the minute she gave him all she had. He would remember the feel of her climax for the rest of his lonely, miserable life.

An explosion of need followed by an uncontrollable surge of lust that slammed into him as he filled her to the hilt one last time and followed her release.

It was war.

Her surrender. His taking. Their death.

He rolled over onto his back, gasping for breath, as she slowly rose to a sitting position on the bed.

She was leaving? Like hell. With a grunt, he tugged her down against his chest, her cheek pressed against his skin.

"Stay." His voice cracked.

She hesitated and then released a soft sigh. "Okay."

Brant closed his eyes as his throat swelled with emotion. After all, the demons could be kept away for only so long. And he knew the minute he opened his eyes again—they would be back, reminding him of what he'd done, what he'd destroyed.

And this time—he would only have himself to blame.

Better that way. It would be better.

Her soft, even breathing filled the night.

Good-bye.

He was saying it to the old Brant. Just as much as he was saying it to her.

And they lived happily ever after. Except they didn't.

Wrong story. Wrong lives.

I've lost everything.

CHAPTER SIXTEEN

Nikki's eyes jerked open as a crack of sunlight pierced through the air.

No. She'd fallen asleep. In his bed.

And for a few minutes, it felt right. So she pretended. Pretended he wasn't an angry jackass. Pretended it wasn't a one-night stand. Pretended that she was able to take from him what he'd never given—a proper good-bye.

But she'd never given him a chance to say good-bye before, had she? She was complicit in this pain, this sorrow that was buried deep in her heart.

Ask me to stay, he'd begged with tears in his eyes. *Ask me!*

She'd ignored him. She was hurting too much. And he'd done everything in his power to make it better.

But when things got worse—so much worse—and she needed him the most, needed the rescue, he was gone. Just. Gone.

She breathed in the pillow; his scent lingered. This was a mistake, a huge mistake, because there was no coming back from this.

From the feel of him inside her. The feel of them together.

She had to get out. Before her heart cracked all the way open.

Clutching the cool sheets between her hands, she bit down on her lip and tried to think of what to do. First, she had to locate her clothes.

Right, and how was she supposed to do that? With a gulp she slowly sat up in bed and winced when Brant let out a groan. The weight of the bed shifted, and she froze as her entire body went on high alert.

Tears burned the backs of her eyes. She was an idiot. A complete idiot.

What? Did she really think it would be easy? Sleeping with the man who held her heart? Her soul? Things didn't look better in the morning, and she sure as hell didn't feel better, not for lack of trying on his part.

"Wake up." Brant's lips grazed her neck as he pressed into her from behind. "Spread your legs."

She woke up, all right. And came apart all over again, each orgasm shaking her body more intensely than before, until she had to fight to keep her tears at bay.

Not just tears of pleasure. Tears of absolute searing pain. Because it wasn't real. Maybe it never was.

Maybe they just had been too disillusioned, too young. The world had been theirs—until the world turned on them, and they turned on each other. It was so much easier blaming someone else than taking responsibility for your own pain.

She pressed a hand to her suddenly too-tight chest as his words washed over her.

"I'm not done yet," he growled hoarsely as he flipped her onto her back. "Hold on." He grabbed her feet and pulled her down the mattress. Her skin slid against the expensive sheets as she held on to his biceps for dear life, closing her eyes against the darkness that was suddenly not as dark.

He pulled her under. Sank into her deep.

"Me either," she whispered back, clawing at his body. "I'm not done yet."

He'd marked her. And she'd let him. And then she held on to him as he drifted back to sleep.

Be brave. No tears.

Clothes. She needed to get her clothes on, find some coffee, and try to escape without Brant or Cole finding out.

She gasped, slapping a hand over her mouth.

Not only had Cole completely abandoned her after one dance, but she hadn't even told him where she was going. He would be worried. Right?

Her purse had to be somewhere in that stupid hotel room, right? *Think, Nik, think.*

They'd walked in. She'd dropped her dress to the floor as well as her purse because, well, his hands had been all over her, and she'd been so desperate for him she hadn't thought past getting her clothes off.

His hands. His mouth.

Focus!

Okay, so the bedroom had been ten steps forward and four steps to the right. She focused on the blur of color on the wall. She could do this. She slowly got up and took a step, directly onto her dress. When she dropped to her knees, her shoes, purse, and mask were all lying right next to it in a neat little pile by the bed.

Frowning, she knelt down and grabbed for the dress.

Why had Brant arranged her things for her? Probably because he was trying to be nice, right?

He'd made promises with his body that he had no right to make, let alone keep. Then again, so had she.

One night. That was it.

With a shudder, she pulled on her dress and tried to quietly zip up the side. Naturally it was the loudest zipper on the planet, so with every tug she was convinced Brant was seconds away from jolting awake.

Oh, God, this is bad, very bad.

"Leaving so soon?" His sleepy voice had no right to sound like sex this early in the morning.

Her fingers froze on the zipper. "I, um..." Tears threatened.

"I think pancakes," he said in a bored tone. "Yesterday I tried the waffles."

What? Why was he talking about breakfast foods?

"You can finish getting ready." His gravelly voice was closer now, and then he was walking by her, smelling like sweat, sex, and really bad decisions.

"But—"

"It was fun, Nik."

It. Was. Fun?

She opened her mouth to scream or at least give him a piece of her mind when he silenced her with a finger, followed by his mouth.

The kiss was angry. He was livid.

She sucked in a breath. "I don't..." She shook her head in confusion.

"It was just sex, Nik. No need to get all tongue-tied, unless you want round four, and then I'm game."

Her eyes burned as hot as her skin, embarrassment, sadness. It meant something to her; *he* meant something to her.

Used to.

She was suddenly glad she couldn't see his face.

Hearing his voice, the anger, reminded her that the man who'd held her in his arms last night and made love to her early in the morning was gone the minute the sun rose.

Her Jekyll and Hyde.

She had nobody to blame but herself. It was easier to hate him. To hate herself. Than to allow herself to feel sad.

She clung to the hate, draped it around her shoulders like a blanket, and finally found her trembling voice. "I should get to work."

"Okay." He stepped away. His voice was emotionless. His stance casual.

She didn't recognize this lifeless man. Life had destroyed him and replaced him with someone safe. Someone numb. Someone she still, somehow, loved.

He placed her shoes in her hands and guided her by the elbow to the door.

As she walked out into the hall she heard the door shut quietly behind her. She turned and stared at the white blur. And then the sound of glass breaking ripped through the silence.

She made it as far as the elevator before she burst into tears. She wasn't even sure which buttons to hit, because she'd never been able to see the shiny one that said Lobby, meaning she had to run her hands along the buttons to feel the right one. In frustration, she just hit the bottom three and slunk to the floor in the corner of the lavish elevator, her shoes in one hand, her purse in the other.

The elevator dinged. Doors opened. She lost track of how many times.

And then footsteps sounded, and the familiar smell of peppermint and cologne filled the small elevator.

"Fuck." Cole kicked something, she wasn't sure what, and then he was on the floor with her, holding her while she sobbed in his arms.

* * *

Blood caked Brant's fingers as he scrubbed the soap over the cuts he'd gotten from punching the mirror and then slamming the expensive lamp into a million tiny pieces.

It looked like his life, that lamp. Broken.

With a roar, he shut off the water and stomped into the bedroom, stripping the bed of every sheet and shoving them into the corner followed by the pillows.

She was everywhere. Impossible to escape. Her scent, her body.

And suddenly he was transported back. To the loss of her. The painful realization that what they had was broken. And that every single thing in his life was infused with a part of her, a part of them.

He'd gone and done the unthinkable. He'd touched her. He'd kissed her. He'd fucking invited her back into his prison—except the joke was on him, because when she stepped out, everything about her remained right along with him.

The doors slammed against his face.

Trapped. He was trapped again. With all the memories of what they had.

And the feel of her beneath him, on top of him, there wasn't a place that existed on the planet where he wouldn't feel her—where his body wouldn't want yearn for hers.

Discarded sheets. Broken lamps. The bed.

He thought he should burn it all. But he knew it wouldn't help.

He'd survived it once. And he stupidly told himself he could do it again.

His hate boiled to the surface, only this time it was directed at the man staring back at him in that cracked mirror.

She might have pushed him away. He might have caused her both emotional and physical pain.

But this time? He went in with his eyes wide open. She went in blind. This was on him. All of it.

He clenched his fists and swore until his voice was hoarse. It was both too early and too late for whiskey.

His phone rang. With a curse, he surged to his feet and snatched it off the table. "What?"

Bentley sighed on the other end. "What happened?"

"Why did something have to happen?"

"Brant." Bentley sounded miserable. "We're twins... so I'm going to ask you again, what the fuck happened?"

Brant closed his eyes. It didn't work; he still saw her, still felt her. "I slept with Nikki."

"I'm on my way." The phone went dead.

Brant nodded even though his brother couldn't see him, and then got dressed, shoving all thoughts of Nikki away.

He had a job to do, right? Three days in, four days left.

Damn Nadine Titus. Damn her to hell.

CHAPTER SEVENTEEN

It took an hour of consoling, a hot shower, and three cups of coffee before Nikki felt like herself again. The minute she got into work later that morning, Cole met her and refused to let her out of his sight.

"Take the day off." Cole kissed her temple. "Seriously, you need it. Hell, take the rest of the week."

"Right." Nikki wiped at her puffy cheeks. "And who's going to take on the clients?"

Cole was silent.

"That's what I thought," she mumbled. "Plus, I'm not running away, I won't..." Because that was what Brant did. And she refused to be guilty of the same thing, of not facing her past.

Cole snorted. "Do you really think that asshat deserves you? He slept with you, and he treated you like a slut!"

"To be fair, I did the same thing," she countered.

"That's different," Cole grumbled.

"Why?" She jerked away from him. "I knew exactly

what I was doing. But I wanted"—her throat constricted—"I wanted him too much to walk away."

"People always think the heart is pure. Which is bullshit—hearts are greedy little bastards that promise to be strong. They promise they won't break, but they do. They always fucking do."

The hurt in his voice was tangible. And felt way too personal.

"Cole—"

"Serious talk, Nik." His voice deepened as he took a step in her direction and then pulled her in for a hug. "You're the best friend I've ever had, but you've never been mine."

"You're my best friend, too."

"Good." He sighed and kissed her on the forehead. "Don't worry. I'm sure I'll get over the rejection, though it may take a few years. Hey, maybe I can start a cat farm for the lonely? Cole's Cool Cat Farm."

She laughed through her tears as she wrapped her arms around his muscled body. "That's really creepy."

"Cole's Creepy Cat Farm? Nah, it doesn't have the same ring. Hey, I'm the one that's going to die alone, so the least you can do is support my dreams."

Another giggle escaped. "Ugh, why do you have to be so perfect?"

"Perfect for everyone but you." He sighed. "Let me know if you have any cancellations today, and I'll make sure asshole Brant isn't anywhere near you. Think of me as your personal restraining order."

"Sweetest thing you've ever said to me."

"I'm good with words. Imagine what I can do with my mouth."

She sighed and looked away.

Cole tilted her face back toward him. "I'll take care of him, all right?"

"Don't kill him."

"I'm too pretty for prison. I was thinking something less violent, like ripping his dick off and feeding it to the cats at my new farm, but that would make the cats suffer, and I'm all about love. Either way, his cock is mine."

Nikki winced.

"That came out wrong."

"You think?"

"Sorry, I blame lack of sleep since you disappeared on me last night only to end up in the boss's bed."

"He's not..." Her eyes widened. "Oh hell, he is technically our boss, isn't he?"

"Sleeping your way to the top. I've never been prouder to call you friend."

"Ugh."

"Go. Your client's waiting." Cole turned her around and sent her down the hall to her massage room.

With a defeated sigh, she opened the door then shut it quietly behind her. "Where would you like me to—"

Brant.

His scent was everywhere.

"You were saying?" His calm, detached voice made her blood run cold.

"You weren't on my schedule." Was that her voice? The weak, quivering one that was on the verge of tears?

"Nope, but Bill sends his regards. He's enjoying a poolside brunch with unlimited mimosas—his wife's a big fan."

"Yeah, I bet she is."

"I think I hurt my back." Did she seriously have no effect on him? "Crazy night last night."

He was cool. Aloof. Joking about something sacred.

She'd never hated him more.

"Funny, I'd think your back would be used to those types of nights," she snapped.

"Oh," he laughed, "it is."

Her heart twisted painfully as anger surged through every bone in her body. "So why would last night be any different?"

"I had to do all the work."

"Bullshit!" It was out before she could stop it, and then she was covering her mouth with her hand and praying for the floor to open up and swallow her whole. Great start to the day. Wake up in the boss's bed and then yell curse words at him.

His chuckle was dark, emotionless. "Hey, you're the one who asked."

She let out a shaky breath. *Just get through the next hour.*

"Oh, and I booked you for a ninety-minute."

She was in hell.

* * *

Hell.

He was in hell. But damn, the burn felt worth it.

The minute he'd stepped into the lobby, his eyes had searched for her. Maybe because he was a masochistic bastard and welcomed the pain—or maybe because deep down he knew he'd been a complete dick and wanted to apologize.

That had been his intention, at least. Until he'd seen

her talking to Cole in the hallway. Until he saw them hug right before he stepped into the room.

He wanted to beat the guy within an inch of his life.

What? So Brant was just a one-night stand and Cole was…her supporter? Her confidant?

Did Brant even have a right to be pissed?

You left. Your fault.

He shoved the guilt away and focused on her hands as they basically pulverized his skin hard enough to leave permanent damage.

"Is this too much pressure?" she asked in a sweet voice.

"Nope." He bit back a curse. "Tickles."

He didn't think it was possible, but she pushed harder, using both elbows to bring him to his knees. "How about now?"

"Is bruising part of the process?"

"Why are you here?"

"It's my job."

"Not here at the resort—here in my massage room."

He sighed. "I won't say anything."

She stopped massaging. "I don't understand."

His hand gripped hers, and his movement told her he'd flipped over onto his back. "Nadine Titus, the insane woman who got you to bet on me at the auction, and is technically my boss—which means your boss's boss. I won't tell her if you don't."

She jerked away as if he'd slapped her. "So you came in here because of your job? To threaten me?"

"I'll pay you."

She'd never felt more used in her entire life. "You should have just paid me for sex last night, would have saved yourself all the trouble of coming down here."

"Would have, but I was all out of cash."

Her body trembled. It was just sex to him. It had been more to her.

And now he was paying her off. The man she loved was gone.

"I don't take bribes."

"Funny," Brant sneered. "Since it seems that a few weeks ago you took one from my boss to bid on me. What was the plan, Nik? Did you think I'd take one look at you and forget the past? Move on? What the fuck did you think would happen?"

Nikki shook her head once, twice, then found her voice. "You're right, I don't know what I was thinking. Maybe I just wanted to keep my job. Did you ever consider that the auction was about me more than you?"

He didn't say anything.

"Maybe I just didn't see a way out where I wouldn't get fired."

"Bull...shit." Brant gripped her arm, then slid his hand down until their palms pressed against each other. "It was more than that and you know it."

Her throat all but closed up. And then she made a mistake. Rather than keeping her anger between them, she tried. She laid down the olive branch, because a part of her needed it, needed the closure, needed to fix what was broken even if she hated him, even if it left them both bleeding. She refused to become Brant Wellington. The ugliest, most beautiful man she'd ever known.

"Brant, don't you think we should talk? Don't you want—"

"No." He cut her off. "I don't want. Not anymore."

"Brant." She reached for him, only to have him step away from her. "It's been four years—"

His laugh was cold. "Four years, two months, one day." He paused. "Seven hours, three minutes, two seconds. I know exactly how long it's been. It's burned into my memory just like it nearly burned you alive and took your sight. I know, Nik. We both live with it in different ways. You may have lost your vision, but I *have* mine, which means when I look in the mirror all I see are reminders. Count yourself lucky."

The door slammed behind him as a tear slid down her cheek and then another.

She remembered a time when Brant was caring, when he wore his emotions on his sleeve, when seeing him angry would have been laughable. This Brant Wellington had his feelings on lockdown.

Nikki hated that day. The day things started to change, the day the light left his eyes, because it was the same day her vision left hers.

"We have to talk about this," he pleaded as Nik fought to get out of bed. How long had she been sleeping? Days? Hours? At least when she dreamed, she dreamed of their child.

But every time she woke up:

Emptiness.

Their baby was gone. Dead. Buried in the cold, hard ground.

"No." She put a pillow over her head. "I can't... it hurts too bad."

"Nik." Brant's voice was filled with pain. "I'm hurting, too."

"I gave birth to a dead baby!" she wailed. "You didn't even stay to hold my hand!"

Brant shook his head. "I couldn't. I—"

"All you had to do was stay, I begged you to stay, and you ran!"

"Because I was losing my mind!" he yelled back. "Afraid this was it, that I was going to lose you, too, lose everything! How many times do I have to say I'm sorry? I am, Nik! So damn sorry!"

"You broke us!" She threw a pillow at his face. "You did this!"

"I love you."

"Don't!" she sobbed. "You don't get to say that to me, not now."

"I do." He was on his knees by the bed. "I love you. So much. Please, just get out of bed. I have a surprise for you."

"No."

"Nik, please."

Maybe it was the pleading in his voice, or maybe it was the fact that she knew she couldn't stay in bed forever—stay angry forever, stay hurt forever.

Slowly, she pushed away from the mattress and grabbed his hand as he led her into the bathroom.

There were at least thirty candles lit, rose petals covered the floor, and the bath was filled with steaming, scented water.

An expensive bottle of champagne she knew they couldn't afford rested in ice near one single wine-glass filled halfway with orange juice.

"One meeting, and I'll be home, all right?" He

kissed her temple. "We can talk, maybe make dinner? Just... take a bath and relax."

"I don't know if I can make it past this," she admitted. "I don't know how."

"Together, Nik." He tugged her against his body. "We do it together."

He didn't kiss her again.

There was no yelling.

They simply stared at each other, so many words left unsaid, so much hurt between them, because that was what you did, you lashed out at those closest to you, and they'd done their fair share of lashing out ever since they'd lost their little boy.

He'd yelled.

She'd yelled.

And now, the silence.

With a nod she turned around and started stripping.

It was the last time she would ever see his face.

CHAPTER EIGHTEEN

Brant stormed out of the spa, yelled at Annie, even though she wasn't doing anything except her job, and headed for the bar.

George took one look at him and poured him a shot of whiskey. Once Brant took it, George handed him soda water.

"Whiskey. Not water," Brant barked.

"Ah." George refilled the shot glass. "Finally drinking to remember, are we?"

"It's all the same." Brant lifted the shot glass to his lips and tossed it back.

"Nah, people who drink to forget, they're calmer about it, happy drunks that turn into blubbering messes once you get alcohol in their system. You're angry before you've even touched the stuff, which means you're remembering, and by the look on your face, you want the memories, you punish yourself with them."

Brant scowled and slammed the shot glass back down on the bar. "I didn't ask for your advice."

"Oh, don't worry, it's always free."

Brant let out a rough exhale just as Cole made a beeline in his direction. "Oh, hell."

He braced himself for a punch.

Words. Fighting. Broken chairs, glass, possible drowning.

But when Cole stopped in front of him he didn't throw a punch, he didn't as much as blink. Which was slightly more terrifying.

"Your better half just checked in with *his* better half and the entire Wellington and Titus families."

"I don't know what to do with any of the information you just gave me."

"Miraculously, we have a big enough suite for all of them."

"I'm not going to like the direction of this conversation, am I?"

"But we had to connect it to the presidential suite to make sure there was a bathroom for everyone, because according to Nadine, she doesn't share."

"There it is," Brant muttered.

Cole's mouth twitched into a pleased smile. "I also took the liberty of cleaning up the broken glass, the lamp."

Brant winced.

"The torn sheets, the shattered mini bar."

Behind them, George whistled.

"And the blood in the sink."

Brant sighed. "Don't ask."

"Wasn't gonna," Cole snapped.

"So as far as they're concerned..." Brant shoved his hands into his pockets, trying to find the thank-you that was getting caught in his throat. "No nervous breakdown this morning?"

"Nope."

"Why would you do that for me?"

Cole shook his head sadly. "It's because I love a girl who's in love with a complete dick. A man who sure as hell doesn't deserve to see her naked and yet did, for the last twelve hours, and then had the fucking nerve to send her blindly away as if she knew how to work the damn elevator without running her hands along every single button in order to find the lobby!"

With every word, Brant felt sicker and sicker.

Cole's features softened. "Just...do everyone a favor and stay away from her, all right? Finish off the rest of the week. And leave."

"Fine," Brant snapped. "You know..." He lifted the glass of soda water off the bar. "If you weren't in love with Nik, I could probably respect you a little more."

"Should we come back at a better time?" Nadine strutted into the bar area in the tallest red heels Brant had ever seen.

Bentley chased after her and made a strangling motion with his hands while his wife followed behind with Jane.

"She needs a bell," Bentley said tightly.

"Read my mind," Brant added with a glare. "Was it completely necessary to bring every last family member with you?"

Bentley pointed at his wife, Margot, who pointed to Brock, who pointed to Jane, who rolled her eyes and pointed at both Grandfather and Nadine as they ordered drinks.

"Right." Brant nodded. "So nobody's taking responsibility for any of this?"

Bentley held up his hands. "I tell Margot everything."

"And I was texting Jane," Margot admitted sheepishly.

"And I was in the longest board meeting of my life listening to Grandfather and Nadine argue over toilet paper—they picked the two-ply, by the way."

"Wait, then how did they end up knowing about this little mini vacation if they were in the meeting?"

Brock snorted. "How do you think? I was tracked. I think they like us to believe they don't know how to use technology, but I could have sworn my phone made a beeping noise the entire drive to the resort only to have them honk their horn behind me and yell out 'Surprise!' "

Brant shuddered.

"Thanks for squeezing us in, Cole." Bentley held out his hand to Cole.

"Yeah," Brant said tightly. "Thanks."

"Just doing my job." A self-satisfied smirk settled over Cole's face. "I'm needed elsewhere." He eyed Brant and added, "Remember what I said."

"Like I could forget," Brant muttered under his breath, as Cole gave him one final look of disgust and walked away.

"Making friends, I see." Bentley slapped Brant on the shoulder. "Is that the guy who pushed you into the pool?"

The whiskey went sour in Brant's stomach. Hell, he was a complete jackass. A complete and total dick. He'd just wanted her to hurt, but in trying to hurt her, he'd hurt himself. He hadn't been able to get her out of that hotel room fast enough; he couldn't let her see him break.

And then he'd screwed up again by lashing out.

That seemed to be what they were known for now. Arguing. Fighting.

And then she'd done something unexpected—rather than beat him, slap him, yell at him more like he deserved, like he wanted her to—she offered help.

And he'd wanted to take it.

Except she'd see it all. She'd see how much he still buried the pain.

And Nikki, being Nikki, would have stayed. She'd want to fix what was broken. She'd want to talk.

And dealing with it meant remembering it—all of it. It meant living through it again, and he wasn't sure he could handle it. He had barely survived last time.

Hell, he'd barely survived sleeping with her.

Talking with her? It would mutilate him.

He needed to at least let her know that he was going to stay out of her way as much as possible—and that she'd get her wish.

It was just that the thought of walking out the door made the anger lessen and the sadness sink its hooks into his gut.

He inhaled. God, he could still smell her on his skin.

With a shudder, he closed his eyes and tried to calm himself.

"What's he doing?" Nadine's irritating voice pierced his concentration. "I had no idea our Brant was a man of faith!"

Or he could just be needing a minute so he wouldn't strangle someone.

"Bet he is now, if what Bentley said about a certain

someone working here has any truth to it," Brock commented.

"Helpful," Brant said through clenched teeth. "Look, why don't you guys get settled in and we can meet for lunch?" Basically, give him five freaking minutes to regroup.

Nadine fluffed up her hair and grabbed Grandfather's hand. "Well, it's been at least two years since my first visit, and when I was here last it was all business because of the acquisition. Perhaps your grandfather and I will—"

Bentley made a choking sound and clapped. "All right, then!"

Nadine glared. "I was merely going to say we would—"

Brock coughed wildly into his hand. Jane patted his back. Margot smirked behind her hand.

Nadine crossed her arms and grinned smugly. "—get naked."

Brant let out a groan. "You." He shoved Bentley toward them. "You deal with this. I have somewhere to be."

Bentley grabbed Brant's arm. "Are you"—his eyes darted from left to right, likely searching Brant's face for any hint of crazy—"are you okay?"

"No." Brant jerked away from his twin. "Would you be?"

"I have no clue," Bentley whispered. "Since you never told me what happened, since you left me and the rest of the family in the fucking dark."

Fresh guilt slammed into him wave by wave: the woman he ran away from, the family he didn't rely on, the brother he refused to lean on.

"Later." Brant choked out the word. "Can we talk about it later?"

"Yeah." Brant didn't miss the disappointment in his brother's voice. "We can." His eyes said that he doubted they ever would, because nothing had changed.

Yet Brant knew, as he clenched his fists and made his way toward the spa lobby—again: Everything had changed.

Because that was how life worked.

"Annie!" Thank God, she was at her desk without Cole lingering. "I need a favor."

"Nope." She tapped the computer keys and squinted at the screen. "Fresh out."

"Annie." *Think, Brant. Think! Charm. Use your charm.* "Can I call you Ann?"

"Call me Ann and I'm going to impale you with this pencil." She snapped it between her fingers and then dropped the pieces onto the glass countertop. "Will that be all, Mr. Wellington?"

He glared. "Threatening your superior?"

"Sleeping with the employees?" she countered sweetly.

"Bullshit," he lied. "Wait..."

"I see those wheels turning." She still wasn't looking at him. "I'm the receptionist. I know everything."

"It's not what you think."

Tap, tap, tap. "Uh-huh. Look, I'm kinda busy, so why don't you go ruin someone else's life like you did Nikki's, mm-kay?"

"Fuck." He ran his hands through his hair. "Everyone knows?"

"Not everyone." Annie grinned just as one of the maids walked by with her cart. "Hey, Julie, did you know Mr. Wellington broke poor Nikki's heart and left her in the elevator to die?"

Julie's eyes widened and then narrowed before she marched off.

"Now everyone knows." Annie smirked. "Doesn't it say in the company manual—you know, right next to 'No sleeping with the employees'—that communication within the company is encouraged?"

"Not that kind," he snapped.

Tap, tap, tap.

"Stop! Typing!" Yeah, he was losing his mind. "What the hell are you even doing? Typing in appointments? Playing solitaire?"

"Oh no." Annie grinned widely, and her voice dripped with sarcasm. "I'm writing a novel about a prick who falls on his own sword and bleeds to death. It's alarming how much you look like him."

"You realize I could fire you, right?"

Annie hid her laugh behind her hand.

"Hell." Brant needed a drink. Ten drinks. All the drinks. "Nadine Titus just checked in."

Annie stopped laughing.

"And I need to find Nik." So he could what? Yell at her again? Apologize for sleeping with her? Using her? Bribing her? The list was getting way too long. He didn't know what the hell he would say. Maybe because he'd been trying to get revenge, to punish her for ruining them.

He'd discovered that as angry as he was, he didn't want to let her go. He didn't want to do the right thing.

The right thing would be walking out of that resort and never speaking to her again, expect possibly to give her an apology. He groaned.

"She's with a client," Annie said quickly. "She's booked all afternoon, and if you interrupt her—"

"Yeah, yeah, it makes the resort look bad." He grabbed one of the pens from the reception desk and scribbled down his number on a piece of paper. "Text me the minute she's free so we can talk. Until then, I'm off to find Nadine Titus."

"Going to confess to Nadine Titus? I'm impressed," Annie said.

"Not a chance in hell." Brant shook his head. "I know this might come as a shock, since clearly all you do is gossip—but I'm here to do a job, and she just happens to be my boss. Now, is there any other employee gossip you think I should know about before I give her a report?"

"Report," Annie repeated. "As in a report on the employees..."

Brant smirked. "On all the employees. Yes."

"N-no." Annie hung her head, and he felt like a jackass all over again. Making her feel threatened, making her wonder about her job when she was just protecting a friend.

The woman he slept with. The one he couldn't get out of his mind. The one whose scent refused to go away.

It had to be her. It had to be this resort.

Damn it, Nadine.

He really should have kept the auction money, done his pity date, and been done.

And yet, he had to wonder if it would have left him in the same predicament. Wanting what wasn't his to want, not anymore. And finding ways to get it—even if it cost him everything.

He shoved the thought away.

Just like he shoved the emotions that came right along with it—sadness, anger, and most of all, guilt.

"Just text me when she's done." He felt the need to say it again, this time more gently.

Annie stared at him, like she could see right through him.

He turned around and walked off before she saw too much—before she saw the hole in his chest he'd been desperately trying to fill with everything but the one person who made it in the first place.

CHAPTER NINETEEN

Everyone was staring at him.

Grandfather's eye twitched. Nadine hid a smug smile behind her third glass of wine. And his brothers shared confused expressions with their significant others while Brant still waited on his drink.

The one he'd ordered forty minutes ago along with everyone else's. They brought him the wrong one twice, adding enough lemon to kill a man in the first one, dumping salt in the second.

"Really, how hard is it to make a martini?" Nadine asked the room while Bentley eyed Brant with interest. "Has this been happening the whole time you've been here?"

Brant's eye twitched. "Actually no, the bar service has been exceptional." At least up until he slept with Nikki. Then everything went to hell. He left that part out, though.

The waiter returned to their table with fresh drinks for

everyone but Brant. He placed the bread basket on the far end and then very casually removed every last piece of silverware in front of Brant's chair and left.

Well, that was expected. Apparently if he wanted to have a good meal he was going to have to go to the bar across the street.

Nadine frowned. "Do you not...use silverware?"

Brant bit his tongue.

Jane, Brock's wife, narrowed her eyes at him, then slid over her silverware and whispered, "What did you do?"

"Nothing," he hissed under his breath.

The waiter returned and handed Brant a sippy cup. Humiliation complete.

Nadine's eyes bugged, "My, my, do you get to order from the kids menu, too? I've heard the nuggets are wonderful."

The kids menu sure enough followed. Along with a bib. And plastic silverware.

"Thank you," Brant said through clenched teeth when the waiter nodded innocently.

"Just following your orders, Mr. Wellington." His orders. Right. More like Cole's orders.

Jane kicked him and quietly said, "Seriously, what did you do?"

Brant stared down at the Sesame Street bib. "Nothing good, I can tell you that."

"Brant." Jane let out a frustrated sigh. "You know if you want to talk—"

"—I don't talk," Brant snapped. "Sorry, I didn't mean to say it like that."

"Yeah, you did," Bentley piped up.

Nadine whispered something to Grandfather then pointed at Brant's plastic fork. "Is this normal behavior?" she asked Brant.

What was normal?

"Well, you did say to make sure to assess every part of the menu. Tonight, it seems I'm eating fries, a Go-Gurt, and a smiley cheeseburger."

And maybe if he was good he'd get a chocolate sundae.

His body jerked to attention. Over a fucking chocolate sundae. Nikki loved chocolate.

Why? Why did everything come back to her?

He checked his phone again. Two hours. Didn't she get breaks?

"So." Nadine folded her hands on the table. "What do you think so far? About the hotel?"

Brant set down his phone and sighed. "The staff is"—he paused as the waiter returned with salads for everyone else and placed an order of carrot sticks in front of Brant—"stellar. Their attention to detail is impressive, right down to the guest-specific itineraries."

Nadine frowned. "Is there anything else I can do to serve you?"

Brant cleared his throat.

The waiter finally glanced at him. "Yes, Mr. Wellington?"

"Food?"

"Oh." His eyes widened with fake innocence, the bastard. "I was under the impression you were fasting from fried foods."

"Fasting," Bentley piped in. "From food?"

The waiter nodded seriously. "Cole has notified the

entire staff that you mean to take on the Zen retreat as part of your experience here."

"Oh, how lovely!" Nadine clapped her hands. "I've heard it really helps a person embrace their inner child!"

"My...inner child." Brant nearly choked on his tongue as a vague recollection of the program entered his fuzzy memory. "So you...don't eat normal food on this fast?"

"On day one, you are allowed one alcoholic drink at night, but other than that, water and juices it is!" He rubbed his hands together. "The chef was just putting together your Zen for the afternoon."

"My Zen." *Unbelievable.*

"Oh, here it is!" He quickly pulled it from the approaching tray. It was a chunky, green-looking thing that had him gagging before he even smelled it.

"Bottoms up!" Nadine cheered. "Oh, Brant, truly, this is wonderful. I knew you would do a good job, but this is above and beyond. Most people are too afraid of the meditation practices with the Zen program to even embark on this journey! And now I'll have your expert opinion on all the facilities here!"

He looked between her and the green drink. Cole Masters was going to burn in hell.

With a grimace, he picked up the drink and held it to his lips. It smelled like sour milk and cherries.

"The rotten goat's milk smells worse than it tastes, I promise." The waiter winked.

Bentley made a gagging noise and scooted away from Brant while Brock paled.

Brant was only able to choke down one sip before he bolted to his feet and made a beeline for the bathroom, emptying every last ounce of breakfast and green poison into the white porcelain.

Two sets of footsteps sounded. A knock on the stall door.

He jerked it open. Brant and Brock stood on the other side, expressions grim.

Bentley spoke first. "I don't suppose this is a good time to fill us in on why the staff's trying to kill you?"

"I slept with her." Brant shoved past them to the sink. "Abandoned her." His hands shook as he splashed his face with water. "Killed our child." Oh, God, he was going to be sick again. "And I'm the reason she's blind." He glanced up at his brothers' horrified expressions. "Take your freaking pick."

CHAPTER TWENTY

Hey, you got a minute?" Cole's voice interrupted Nikki's trip down memory lane as she sat in the dark.

Remembering Brant's hands. His words. His lips as they trailed across her skin.

Clearing her throat, she forced out a cheerful and hoarse-sounding. "What's up?"

"Any reason you're sitting in the staff room?" His voice dipped. "In the dark?"

"The colors give me a headache," she admitted. "And I'm miserable enough without having to deal with a jackhammer inside my head."

"Nik, you really need to see a doctor if you're getting headaches."

"Everyone gets headaches." She shrugged. "So, what's going on?"

"I think I broke Brant."

"Are you going to break out in song and dance? Because you sound downright thrilled."

"I enrolled him in the Zen program."

Nikki gasped. "Cole!"

"What?"

She covered her face with her hands and groaned. "You know that program is only exclusively for people going into meditation training, yoga—hell we had two *monks* cry last week in the hot yoga tent!"

"Jackasses always survive things like that. He'll be fine, plus it will teach him a lesson."

She groaned. "That's not your job."

"The hell it isn't!"

"Cole!"

"What?"

She sunk back in her chair. "I don't want to fight."

"I thought you'd be happy?"

"I should be," she admitted. Happy that Brant was going to spend the next three days getting tortured, but instead the whole revenge plot Cole was spinning left her empty.

She just wanted Brant.

To talk to him.

Punch him in the face.

Touch him.

Then punch him again.

Her feelings weren't any clearer now than they were earlier. How could he touch her the way he did last night? And then act the way he did this morning? And why was it bothering her so much?

He'd used her!

And she'd let him. Then used him right back.

She let out a sigh as the realization sunk in that maybe she had something to say to him too, something like *Sorry*, even if she didn't fully mean it.

Sorry meant she'd made a mistake.

And as much as she wanted to prove that it was, the memory of his touch reminded her that it wasn't.

"There you are!" Annie's voice sounded perkier than usual. "I've been looking everywhere for you! Brant needs to see you."

She could feel Cole tense next to her.

"He's in the lobby restaurant having lunch with two of the hottest guys I've ever seen—no offense, Cole—and by the looks of it Nadine Titus has discovered the fountain of youth. I'm totally going to ask her about it once she's done groping the old man."

"Annie?" Cole interrupted.

"Yeah?"

"Less detail next time."

"Sorry." She laughed "So, you want me to take you over there?"

No. In fact she wanted to run in the opposite direction.

"Oh, and Cole, Brant said something about needing to interview staff members to see if they're best at home within the company."

That was it, she thought. Either get fired or meet with Brant. At least that was what it felt like.

Better get it over with now. Even though facing his family sounded about as fun as swimming with sharks. His grandfather hadn't approved of their relationship, their early marriage. That was why they had initially kept the pregnancy a secret.

Everyone said they would fail. And it killed her that they had turned out to be right.

Maybe they'd been too young, but they were madly in love—and after all, didn't love conquer everything?

It was a lie. A fantasy.

With a groan she stood. "Sure, take me over."

"Wait." Cole grabbed her hand.

"Cole, not now—"

"Shh." He ran his fingers through her hair and then pulled a rubber band away from her wrist. He collected her hair in a low ponytail and then very slowly ran his hands down her shoulders. "Make him painfully aware of what he lost the minute he sent you into that elevator alone, then you give him hell."

Tears filled her eyes. She gave a jerky nod and was met with a soft hand. Annie's perfume was always spicy with a hint of lemon; it reminded her of fresh starts.

And how she wished it wasn't just a fantasy. But reality. Fresh starts, just like love, didn't really exist anymore, at least not in her world.

They walked down the long corridor, only to come to a sudden stop.

"Where's your lipstick?" Annie whispered.

"In my purse, but it's back in the staff lockers."

"Hold still."

A berry-tasting gloss was spread across Nikki's mouth before she could protest.

"Now blot."

She rolled her eyes and followed Annie's instructions.

"You look pale." Annie pinched her cheeks—hard.

"Ouch!"

"Better." She exhaled. "All right, let's do this. I so deserve a promotion."

"Yes, that's exactly what I was thinking when you just twisted my cheeks and bruised my face. 'Gee, give that girl a raise!' "

Annie slapped her on the butt and laughed. "Tell your boyfriend all about it."

"Cole's not my boyfriend."

They turned a corner. Annie stopped walking and let out a little sigh before pointing Nikki in the right direction.

"Yeah, I wasn't talking about him—I was talking about the sexy-as-sin guy who's staring you down like you're the last woman on earth—like you're his sunshine after years of living in a thundercloud. Cole does not look at you the way Brant Wellington does, and I'm not sure anyone ever will."

"Oh." She didn't know what else to say and really didn't trust her voice not to crack with emotion. Well, that was depressing.

"Well, my work here is done." Annie dropped her hand. "Nice to see you, Brant. How's that fast coming along?"

"Probably about as good as that novel you're writing during work hours. Tell me, does the prick ever redeem himself?"

"I never spoil an ending." She laughed and walked off.

"So it's true. All employees hate you, even the female ones," said a man's voice from somewhere to Nikki's left. It was close in tone to Brant's but without the trademark huskiness Brant's voice had developed over the last four years. "And what about you, Nik? How do you feel about my evil twin?"

Bentley.

Nice setup.

Palpable tension swirled around the room as someone sucked in a sharp breath.

"Nikki!" Nadine yelled, saving the day. Within minutes, Nikki was surrounded by a stifling amount of Ralph Lauren perfume and getting hugged within an inch of her life. "Brave," Nadine whispered in her ear. "Shoulders back. Told you things would work out for the best."

The best? All they'd done was have sex and fight!

"Shhh," Nadine whispered. "He's headed over here, and by the looks of him he hasn't given up the fight. Why else would I force you to go to that damn auction?"

Nikki shrugged. "So he'd see what he's missing and come crawling back?"

"No," Nadine whispered. "So you'd realize that with or without him, you're strong enough on your own. You're fine alone but better together—and both of you needed that push in order to see it."

Nikki flashed her a watery smile. "We fight more than anything."

Nadine patted her back. "Good."

A masculine hand grabbed hers, their fingers sliding past each other, sending a shiver of desire racing through her body. "Are you hungry?"

She wanted to pull away from the man who was putting on a show for his family, the one who hid his anger and asked if she was hungry, offering to feed her before yelling at her or firing her.

"No." She forced a smile. "But I bet you're starving. How's day one going?"

"After lunch, or the lack of it, I'm killing Cole, just thought you should know."

"He has good intentions."

"Bullshit," Brant snapped. Apparently angry Brant

wasn't just simmering below the surface anymore. "He wants me to suffer, and he's probably right. I deserve all of it—but he's trying to kill me so he can have you all to himself."

"He's had me all to himself for four years," she said honestly, irritated that she couldn't see Brant's expression, but if the complete silence that suddenly fell was any indicator, she'd just said the wrong thing. Again.

She was lashing out. Just like he'd lashed out earlier.

Ugh, she wasn't that person. She didn't want to be that person, miserable like Brant because she was still living in the past, unable to move beyond the bitterness, the pain.

"So..." Bentley cleared his throat. How had she not originally recognized his voice? After all, it was the voice of the man who'd hit on her relentlessly, always trying to convince her that she'd chosen the wrong twin—at least before she lost contact with the family.

But from the moment she'd met Brant, seen his perfectly sculpted lips, the strong lines of his jaw, the twinkling green bedroom eyes that always seemed to be at half mast, as if he was thinking of her naked, she'd been his. All his.

She shivered.

"Are you cold?" Amusement danced through Bentley's silky tones.

"No. Sorry. Brant." She turned toward him, and slipped her hand away. "You needed me?"

"Well." That gravelly voice interrupting them could only be Charles Wellington. And then the smell of cigars floated in the air, cementing her suspicion. "It's been a while, Nikki. I wasn't aware you worked here."

"Ever since the accident," Nadine broke in. "Isn't that right, Nikki?"

What did the woman do? Look through her employee files?

"Right." Could it get any more awkward? She half-expected Brant to throw a chair or just start yelling again. The last thing they needed between them was yet another reason to feed the anger, and the accident had been his tipping point more than hers. In fact, it was almost more terrifying that he wasn't reacting.

"Accident." Charles's voice developed a rough edge. "You mean the fire?"

Nikki stiffened.

"Grandfather." Brant's voice was tight. "Don't."

"What?" Charles let out a sigh. "From what I've heard, Nikki is lucky to be alive. That must have been terrifying, being caught beneath the supporting beams."

Memories flashed through her mind, a blur of color and pain. "Yes, it was horrible." She didn't want this. The trip down memory lane in front of Brant and his entire family. Not being able to see his face, to know what he was thinking.

For the first time in her life, she truly *felt* blind. Unable to read the emotional temperature of the room.

"I, um..." She didn't have her walking stick; she had nothing but hope that she'd somehow be able to make a run for it and not ram headfirst into a table. "I need to go."

As fast as she could, she turned on her heel and put her hands out in front of her to keep from stumbling. A chair came out of nowhere—or so it felt—and hit her in the shin. She stumbled to the right and slammed against a table, only to bounce back and run right into a passing waiter.

The sound of glass hitting glass was almost as bad as the searing pain she felt when hot coffee came into contact with her arm, followed by something sharp. She fell to the floor with a thud, her hair covered in whatever other liquid had been on the tray.

Maybe if she just closed her eyes?

And hid under the table?

Tears threatened.

Helpless.

She was helpless in front of the only man she'd ever loved—and the family who'd never truly wanted her.

Swallowing past the giant lump in her throat, she tried to stand, teeth chattering from the shock of the burn and what was starting to feel like a really nasty cut on her arm.

"Nik!" Brant's scent was everywhere. "You're hurt."

"I'm fine."

"You're not fine."

"Brant!" She didn't mean to yell his name. "Just... leave me alone. Please. I can't do this right now. I can't do this..."

He ignored her pleas as he scooped her up in his arms and started walking. She tucked her head in his neck, wanting to scream at the unfairness of the situation. He wasn't supposed to be a hero. It was hard to hate a hero. It was hard to forget one, too.

And it suddenly occurred to her like a light going on in her head.

He'd always been her hero. Always.

So much so, that even when he had failed her, she'd

still imagined he'd come back, he'd save the day. And when he hadn't...

It was like she lost a part of her innocence, her faith in humanity, and her love for the man who had promised he would never leave her. And when he did, when he finally did do exactly what she asked, he didn't turn back.

She choked down a sob as Brant kept walking.

Elevator doors closed. A ding sounded.

She hated that elevator and the ding that went with it—because it made her remember this morning, after they'd used each other. The morning after she'd felt his body beneath her. The morning after she was reminded why his leaving nearly destroyed her.

Doors opened, warm air kissed her skin, and then a lock sounded, the door closed.

His masculine scent was everywhere.

She was back in his room.

Shivering, she clenched her teeth to keep from saying something she'd regret, like, *It feels like home in your arms. In your bed.*

Because the last thing she needed was to be in his arms or his bed and start an all-out war again.

If she thought about it hard enough she was going to cry all over again.

He gently set her down on the couch and left.

Where had he gone?

The spray of water hitting porcelain reached her ears, and then she was scooped up again—and stripped.

CHAPTER TWENTY-ONE

Brant's blood was boiling, his rage barely in check. His grandfather had no fucking right to bring up the past in front of the entire family—in front of the hotel staff. What the hell had he been thinking?

The pain in Nik's eyes was like a punch to the gut. And then she ran.

He knew how desperate she had to be to run when she couldn't really see. The doctors had always said it was possible she'd get her vision back, but the chance of it ever happening was grim at best. Obviously that ship had sailed. Guilt attacked full force, ugly and painful.

His stomach dropped as his shaking hands lifted her shirt over her head; his fingers unhooked her bra then skimmed down her hips, tugging her black pants down to the white tiled floor.

Teeth chattering, she wrapped her arms around herself and stared blankly ahead, her face pale. Beautiful. So striking. Her full lips parted as her body shook, her olive skin just begged to be touched.

But the look on her face sobered his thoughts. She looked afraid.

Your fault.

The skin on her right forearm was turning a bright pink.

"Keep your right arm away from the water," he said gruffly.

"'Kay." She breathed out a sigh and then held out her hands to reach for him.

He pulled her into his arms, and she let out a little gasp.

"What?"

"You're naked."

"Not all the way." He smiled down at her even though she couldn't see him. "I figured the best way for you to clean up was with a shower partner."

"And let me guess—you're volunteering?"

"Yeah, well, it's my hotel room, my rules. Besides, I don't see anyone else jumping at the chance."

"Probably because nobody else is here."

"Lucky you," he whispered.

She sucked in a breath and jerked her head away. He'd almost kissed her. He'd wanted to touch those lips, to kiss them into submission, to press her against the shower wall and worship her body.

And then what?

Leave them both more fucked than they already were?

No, the last thing he needed was to kiss her; hell, even touching her was doing a number on his self-control. Because he wanted to run, just like she'd just done. He wanted to run until his legs burned, until his chest ached, until his bloody feet brought him to the end of the world, where memories of what they shared and the reminder that it was that good would be gone.

An apology hung between them.

He knew he should go first. But how do you apologize for something you're still not sure you're sorry for?

And if he did actually apologize, that meant he'd been wrong, and being wrong meant acknowledging how much he'd fucked up.

It would force them to deal with the present. And the past. And grieve.

He shuddered beneath the hot spray as it massaged his back. After a few minutes, she relaxed against his chest, the tips of her breasts sliding against his skin, making it impossible not to react.

Brant clenched his teeth. "How's the arm?"

"Hurts."

"I'm sorry." His eyes burned; he squeezed them shut and kept talking. "I'm so damn sorry he brought that up, he had no right."

She sighed. "Normally I'm okay with answering questions about...about the fire." Her voice weakened. "But in front of you, your family...and your grandfather sounded concerned and then everyone else was quiet, like they had no idea how serious it really was."

"They didn't," Brant admitted. "Only Grandfather knew. He helped me cover up the truth of how bad it was from my brothers."

She pulled away, her eyes glancing up at him. He could almost believe she could see him. "What do you mean?"

"I never told them."

"About the fire?"

"I—" He took a step away.

"Brant!" She reached for him.

He was a complete ass. Because he wanted to leave her there, in his shower, in his hotel room, he wanted to run and never look back.

"I can't." God, he didn't recognize his own voice. "Don't make me talk about this." About how he failed his child—and then her.

"So that's it?" She threw her hands in the air. "You just ignore everything that makes you sad? To what end?"

"Sad?" he yelled. "You think I'm sad?" He moved closer, pressing her body against the tile, pinning her arms above her head. "I'm fucking devastated!"

She sucked in a breath.

"I'm destroyed!"

Tears mixed with the water streaming down her face, trickling in her mouth.

"I'm empty!" he roared, releasing her hand and slamming his against the tile over and over again. "I almost killed you! You lost your sight weeks after losing our ch—" He couldn't even say it. He backed away.

Nikki grabbed his arm. "Say it."

"Sometimes..." His voice trembled. "Sometimes I think I would have been a horrible father."

Nikki didn't say anything.

He kept talking. "I still get nightmares. I can't even make it through a baby food commercial without losing my shit."

She hiccupped out a sob and released his hand.

"I think, how the hell would I have been able to take care of one tiny life, when I couldn't even take care of my own wife? When firemen had to break her out of our shitty apartment because I couldn't afford something nicer with a working fire alarm? A miracle." Brant snorted in disgust. "They said it was a miracle you were even alive. And when I saw you at the hospital you weren't yourself—you were in shock."

Nikki shook her head. "No. Stop."

The words wouldn't stop coming. "You said, 'My baby died, and now I have nothing. I have nothing.'" Brant shuddered. "You still had me, or at least I thought you did, and then when I found out that you couldn't see all I kept thinking was 'I did this, I ruined her life.' I should have never married you."

She jerked back as though he'd slapped her.

"I ruined your life. And then I was too hurt to live it with you. Too angry at you for saying those things even though you were in shock. Too angry at myself for not being enough. And too fucking devastated to deal with the pain." Brant leaned back against the tile wall, then sunk to the floor, putting his head in his hands.

"Brant?" Nikki held out both hands, feeling around the shower. "Brant?"

He wanted to ignore her. To let her believe he'd left. But the look on her face, the real fear that it could possibly be true, wrecked him. "Here, I'm right here."

She slowly lowered herself to her knees and felt around, her small hands tapping the floor until she found his foot, and then she slowly slid both hands up his body. "Are you looking at me?"

"What do you think?"

She hung her head, her wet hair sticking to her cheeks.

"All I ever do when I'm with you is look at you" he said gruffly. "It's a kindness that you can't see."

"Why?"

"The eyes are the windows to the soul," he whispered. "And you've always owned mine."

"Even now?"

He was quiet and then shuddered out an exhale, leaning back against the tile. "Even now."

Awareness sizzled between them like an electrical current, and then she was laying her head against his chest. "Sometimes I have dreams I'm still pregnant. I wake up empty."

He clutched his eyes shut and tried to swallow. "I'm so damn sorry."

"You couldn't fix it, Brant. You can't fix everything."

"Trust me, I know."

"And you have to trust me on this." She pressed an open-mouth kiss to his wet chest, her lips searing his skin. "You would have been the best father in the world."

He stiffened. "You're wrong." He didn't trust himself to say any more, so he held her in his arms, until the water turned cold, until she shivered in his embrace.

And just like that, the moment was gone. So many things still left unsaid. So many things that needed to be said.

He'd opened his mouth a million times to apologize, to tell her he still loved her—to beg her to love him back. To say what he should have said four years ago, to do something beyond allowing the words to fade away.

But he missed the moment, too afraid that he wasn't worth the risk. Too afraid that the cruelty of the universe would catch up to them again and ruin everything good between them.

So rather than seize the moment, he let it pass and held on to the brief seconds when she was in his arms.

The anger was still there boiling beneath the surface, but it was being pacified by the feel of her in his arms, by the words she said.

He wanted to believe her.

That he would have been a good father, that it wasn't his fault, but the thing about truth is it doesn't change your opinion of yourself when all you ever see when you look in the mirror is the lie.

Her fingers slid against his wet arms, and then her palms pressed against his cheeks. Water slid down her lips.

And those empty eyes locked on his in a way that he didn't deserve.

He'd always felt more with her. The faith she'd always put in him was staggering.

Whole. Things felt whole in her arms.

CHAPTER TWENTY-TWO

The last thing Nikki wanted was another walk of shame through Brant's hotel room and onto the elevator. She hadn't thought of anything except Brant.

And the fact that neither of them were yelling.

Talking. He talked to her. Opened up.

Cracked his shell and let her see inside as if she wasn't blind. It wasn't enough. And at the same time, it was too much, because in that moment, he was Brant, *her* Brant.

The Brant she'd fallen in love with.

The Brant she'd hoped to see again at the auction.

The Brant she'd slept with.

The Brant she still wanted.

With a shiver, she held her head high and moved to open the bedroom door, only to have it jerked open before she could get the chance.

She stumbled against a warm, rock-hard chest. Her hands pressed against the skin, and a slow throb started pulsing through her body.

"I got you a robe, and clothes are getting sent up." Brant's low timbre always had a way of causing shivers to wrack her body, as if she'd never heard a man's voice before. Were things different between them now? Better? Did she even want to go there?

Who was she kidding?

Brant wasn't the type to just blurt out his feelings and then take another leap toward the very person who pushed him out of his life.

The truth was, she didn't remember saying any of those things to him. For four years she'd thought he'd just given up on them because he couldn't take it anymore, because she'd finally pushed him away. And when she'd gotten hurt she just assumed he couldn't deal with one more thing.

It had hurt her deeply.

They lost a child. And then she lost him.

Instead, he was suffering with his own silent pain over her words, words that she didn't even remember saying about how he took everything from her.

Would he have stayed?

Had she not deliriously blamed him for everything?

She'd unintentionally wrecked him, and at the same time she was so angry that he would hold something like that against her when she was in so much pain.

It was jarring to come to the realization that she'd been just as guilty. The last thing she'd wanted was for the love of her life to leave her.

She gulped and touched the clothing. "Thank you."

Brant backed her up into the bathroom, and the door clicked shut. "We have company."

"Here?"

"Drop the towel, Nik."

"I'm cold."

"That's why I got you the robe. Besides, the last thing you need is to walk out there almost naked in front of my entire family."

She groaned. "They're all here?"

He nodded. "The towel?"

She sighed. Her hands clutched the towel so tightly her knuckles were probably turning white.

"Would it help if I closed my eyes?"

A nervous laugh escaped. "We had sex last night, you just showered with me, saw everything, and even though most of my dignity is gone, I'm pretty sure my honor is still intact."

"Not for lack of me wanting to strip it away." His voice was close, his hands on her shoulders as the heat from his body surrounded her.

She let out a little gasp, her lips parting, opening, waiting for a kiss.

"I want to try."

Her heart nearly stopped as it bounced in her chest with excitement. "Really?"

"I'm saying this wrong." She felt him pull away, physically, emotionally. "I want to try to be...friends."

Friends.

After everything they'd been through. After sleeping together. After rescuing her, saying all of those things in the shower? After admitting that she still owned him? He wanted to be *friends*?

"Yeah," she found herself saying, like an idiot. "That's a good..." She nodded a few times. "Let's do that."

Don't cry. Do. Not. Cry.

He exhaled and touched his forehead to hers. "Thank you."

Sure, no problem. Just rip my heart out and stomp on it.

"Well." She pulled away; she had no choice. It wasn't even the sting of rejection, it was the feel of hope dying. She'd *hoped*—it was a dangerous thing, especially where Brant was concerned.

Stupid. She was *so* stupid.

With a sigh, she dropped the towel and quickly reached for Brant. A terry cloth–type material met her fingers, and was slid over her body and tied so tight she sucked in a breath.

He knotted it at least four times.

"Is that necessary?"

"The last thing I want"—he jerked the material tighter (*Another knot? Really?*)—"is this robe opening up and showing anyone what isn't theirs to see."

"You included?" She just had to say that, didn't she?

He was close again, she could feel the heat from his lips as he whispered, "Me included."

"Brant!" Nadine's voice was shrill, loud, and completely welcome. Nik needed to get away from him, away from his heat, his so-called friendship, and the freaking way her body still yearned for him. "Get out here!"

Brant swore. "I've learned it's best to just do as she asks and then figure out an escape plan."

"Noted." She tried smiling, she really did, but leaving that bathroom, with all its confessions, with all its feelings—it felt like the minute she closed the door all would be lost. It was ridiculous, but that bathroom represented the first time in four years that Nikki had actually had some closure or at least had heard Brant explain why he'd left, why he'd done what he did.

The door opened, then closed again. Brant cupped her face. "What's wrong? You look like you've seen a ghost."

She shook her head, willing the tears to stay in. "Nothing, I'm fine. I just...I'm tired."

"Nik—"

She forced a smile and reached around him to push the door open.

"There you are!" Nadine announced, and suddenly Nikki was in a choking plume of flowery perfume, and getting tugged down a hall and gently pushed onto a nice, plush chair. Colors of blue and brown blurred in front of her; movement caught her eye.

She probably looked exactly how she felt—like hell.

"Now..." Nadine patted her hand. "Since Brant's here on the Titus dime, *working*..." She made sure to accentuate the word *working*, even adding in a pregnant pause after it. "...why don't we leave him to it? The men can join Brant, and we women can enjoy a spa day!"

Lovely. "Relaxing" at a spa she worked at, with her boss. Ugh.

"Actually." Nikki stood. She couldn't just take time off like that, especially with how busy it was. "I have to get back to work—once the clothes arrive."

"Oh." Nadine sounded upset. "How unfortunate. I was really hoping to try the Zen room."

"No," Brant interrupted. His voice had Nikki jumping in her seat.

"What do you mean, *no*?" Nadine's voice rose.

"I mean no, Nikki shouldn't go back to work. She's

injured, and the injury took place on the clock. She should relax."

"My thoughts exactly," Nadine said in a *Well, that's all there is to it* voice. "So, shall we try the Zen room while the men go to the meditation tent?"

"Meditation? Tent?" Brant repeated. "Why the hell would we go to a tent?"

"You're in the Zen program." Nadine laughed. "Oh dear, did nobody tell you about the meditation practices? It's for meditation."

"No," Brant said through clenched teeth. "Because some jackass who hates me is the one who signed me up for it." On cue, his stomach growled.

Nikki hid a smile behind her hand.

"No chance in hell," came Brock's voice, "that any of us are going into a sweat tent to meditate."

"Actually"—Bentley drew the word out—"I think it's a great idea."

"The hell you do!" Brant yelled. "Wait... why do you have that smile on your face..."

Nikki loved this. The way they interacted with each other. The way that even when they fought you could tell it was out of love.

And suddenly, it was too much. Her heart sank.

When she worked hard, when her feet were exhausted after a long day's work, it was easy to lie down on her giant bed and convince herself she was happy, that she didn't need anything else in her life. She had a great job and great friends, and she was good at what she did.

Suddenly the room fell quiet.

Her cheeks heated. "I'm sorry, I—did I miss something?"

"I said your name four times," Brant announced. "Are you sure you're okay?"

"Yup." *Friend.* "Are the clothes here yet? Like I said, I really need to get back to work."

Nobody said anything, and then suddenly she heard Brant's voice.

"Yes, hi Annie, it's Brant." He cursed. "Yes, the prick who's dying a slow death in your romance novel...oh, poisoning? How wonderful, thank you...No, no, I'm not being sarcastic." Another sigh. "Well, as long as there's hope he doesn't completely lose all sexual function."

Nikki smiled and then the smile was gone. Friends. Great, already she was getting comfortable with a man who wasn't in her life anymore.

"Yes, how many clients does Nikki have this afternoon? Cancel them. Immediately...No, you only get raises when you perform well outside your normal duties. Yes." He paused. "You've never seen your employee handbook?" He groaned. "That's clearly a problem. Do me a favor and get Cole to meet me in the lobby. Yes, I'm aware I'm expected in the meditation tent, but my brothers cheerfully volunteered to take my place."

"Bastard," Brock grunted.

"Bye."

Brant thought he was doing her a favor, but what did he expect her to do? Sit with Nadine and the other two women whose voices she still hadn't heard yet, and, what? Gossip? Talk about shopping? Pretend that this week wasn't going to end in a few days? That as nice as they were, she didn't belong in their world anymore?

In Brant's world?

The more she thought about it, the angrier she

became—yes, maybe irrationally so, but still! That was her job! And her job was all she had, especially since he'd made it clear that there was no future between them, that this was just them healing, trying to move past everything. He had no right to just run around and make demands. Besides, what if Nadine didn't think Nikki could do her job? What if she fired her? What if she got replaced? Okay, now she was really making leaps with her assumptions, but after such an emotional and confusing morning, she was having a hard time being rational.

A knock sounded at the door. "Clothes are here."

She quickly jumped to her feet, then immediately felt stupid. How was she going to navigate the room? She didn't even know how many people were in it with her. Watching her.

Warm hands, Brant's hands, met hers, as he gently walked her down a hall and placed a garment bag in her hands. He opened a door. He walked in with her.

"I can change by myself," she said in a terse voice.

"I'm here to supervise." He sounded bored. "That's all."

She was too tired to argue. And she was confused. One minute he wanted to be friends, the next he was supervising her undressing? Really?

"Fine." She found the zipper to the bag and pulled it down. "Then at least turn around... friend." She heard his sharp intake of breath, ignored it, and felt around for the clothes. "A dress?" She rolled her eyes. "You had the staff bring me a dress?"

"It was either a nice wrap dress from the gift shop or an I HEART AZUL T-shirt with board shorts."

She quickly pulled the soft cotton dress from the bag and felt around for any clue on how to put it on.

"Pull the sash." Brant's voice interrupted her search. "Put your arms through the holes—"

"I know how to put on a dress, Brant. Trust me, I've been doing this by myself for years." She was lashing out. Again.

And suddenly she wanted to go back to the bathroom. Or even better, back to the angry Brant who yelled and threatened. Because at least that she knew how to deal with; it was a mess, but this? This she didn't understand how to navigate without getting hurt.

After five minutes of struggling, she finally got the dress on and they walked back down the hall.

"You look beautiful!" Nadine clapped her hands, and suddenly she was being suffocated with a hug and a cloud of sweet-smelling perfume. "Doesn't she look beautiful, Brant?"

"She always does." His words came out gravelly, tense.

"And those curves." Nadine pulled away. "Such gorgeous curves. And those plump lips, don't they look plump, Brant?"

Brant said nothing.

Nikki kept her head high.

Why would he? They were friends.

"I think you look beautiful." Bentley's silky voice said from her right. Was Brock still there? Charles? Sometimes she just wished people would announce themselves so she'd know.

"We should get going." Brant's hand touched her elbow, and then he was tugging her away, his fingertips barely grazing her arm, like he was afraid to touch her.

She said a quick good-bye to everyone. He released his hold on her elbow and pressed the small of her back, urging her forward. The minute she was in the elevator his hand dropped.

The silence was awkward. Tense. Painful. Tears stung the backs of her eyes.

"You do look beautiful," he whispered as the elevator descended. "Any man would be lucky to have you."

Any man. Not him.

Somehow she found her voice. "Thank you."

And suddenly the elevator was too small. The memories too big. She felt like she was suffocating.

When the elevator doors opened she lunged into the lobby in an effort to escape—everything.

But especially him.

CHAPTER TWENTY-THREE

Nik—" Brant chased after her. The last thing he wanted was for her to hurt herself again.

Or end up with her naked in the shower when he was trying like hell to keep his distance. It was difficult enough with the way the dress hugged her curves.

Nadine had taken one look at him, smirked, and decided to give him a rundown of exactly what she saw him appreciating. By the time she was done, he was as hard as nails and ready to lose his mind, just praying for the elevator to keep going so he wouldn't be trapped in a small space with Nikki. Instead it stopped, they both got in, and he was suffering in silence, trying to decide between slamming her against the nearest wall or punching through it with his face.

She was so beautiful. And now she was running away from him or at least trying to.

What the hell happened between his confession and

him getting her clothes? He was *helping*. She needed the day off—damn it, she deserved it.

She beat him to the spa lobby. "Annie, call my clients back. I'm feeling fine."

Annie eyed Brant and then Nikki. "I, um, he's my boss. I'm sorry, Nikki."

"Please." Nikki's voice was pleading. "I need the distraction. Please."

"Nikki." Brant gave Annie a confused look. "Your hand's injured—your job is to massage people, how the hell are you going to manage that with a burn?"

She stared down at the ground, hands on hips. Damn, she was pretty. "You can't just come in here and order me around."

"Actually, he can. Boss." Annie gave me a weary look. "But if it makes you feel better, the two clients you had were more than happy to reschedule."

"Fine." Nikki nodded and then made her way down the hall. "I'll be in the staff room."

"Nikki, wait." What the hell was up her ass, and why did he suddenly feel so guilty for trying to make things easier on her?

"What?" She turned around, her expression blank. "Did you need anything else from me, or am I free to go relax in silence?"

"What the hell's your problem?" That came out wrong.

"My *problem*?" Nikki let out a breath and hung her head. "Nothing. I'm fine, Brant. Everything's fine." She marched off, leaving him completely clueless as to what he had done that was so wrong.

A slow clap sounded behind his back. He turned to see Cole grinning like an idiot. "Well done." He frowned at Annie. "Is Brant the emergency you called me about?"

"I can't deal with you right now," Brant muttered.

"You sort of have to," Annie piped up. "Employee handbook? I'm not trying to be a pain, but I've seriously never seen one before. Ever."

Brant glared at Cole. "How the hell have you been training them?"

Cole rolled his eyes. "Annie, the employee handbook, that blue thing that's under your desk with the words *Employee Handbook* on the spine? The one that your nephew used his crayons on when he visited last year?"

She grinned innocently. "Oh, *that* employee handbook."

"The very one," Cole said with pretend shock in his voice. "Annie, what's going on?"

Annie leaned back in her chair. "What? Sue me for wanting to win the pool. I had to find some way to get you two together."

"Pool?" they said in unison.

"Yeah, the employees are taking bets to see which one of you guys is going to get a black eye first…bonus points if you both take off your shirts." She sighed. "Can't blame a girl for trying."

Another employee, Carol, walked across the salon and into the lobby, took one look at them, and her smile deflated. "Nothing?"

"Eh, I should have come up with a better plan." Annie sighed. "Plus Nikki was already storming out of here by the time Cole showed up."

"Oh?" Carol leaned against the desk. All eyes fell on Brant. "Stormed out, huh?"

"This isn't sharing time," Brant muttered, running his hands through his hair. "And I was doing her a favor."

Cole pulled out a chair and sat, his expression amused.

Brant pinched the bridge of his nose. "I canceled her afternoon clients."

"Idiot," said Cole.

"Why would you do that?" asked Carol.

"You know she needs to stay busy," added Annie.

"She's injured," Brant pointed out. "I'm not sorry for being concerned for her!"

"Concerned?" Cole stood.

Carol sucked in a breath while Annie pulled out her phone and held it high.

"You have to angle it!" Carol barked at her.

"Concerned," Cole repeated. "You abandon her for four years, suddenly come waltzing back into her life, and you think you have the right to be concerned?"

"I was her *husband*."

"Yeah, well, I'm her best friend!" Cole yelled.

Carol elbowed Annie, whose eyes were wide with excitement. "Don't stop recording."

"You think you know everything?" Brant shook his head in disgust. "You know nothing."

"Oh, yeah?" Cole crossed his arms. "Try me. You may have been there for her when you were married, but I was the one who picked up the pieces when she started working here. And when you leave, again, I'm going to have to do the same damn thing!"

"The hell you will!" Brant shoved his chest. "That's not your job!"

"And it's yours?" Cole sneered. "Four years and she still has nightmares. Four years and she still cries over you. Four years, Brant. You're going to destroy her—again. And the worst part? This time, you'll know exactly what you're doing, but because you're a selfish bastard you're going to take every part of her with you and leave me the pieces, the pieces that I would take if she let me—but she won't. Because I'm not you."

"That was beautiful," Annie said, wiping her cheeks.

Brant stared straight ahead, his heart pounding so hard his chest hurt. "You don't think I'm hurting? That I don't know why she cries? Do you think for one second that I don't hate myself for leaving her? Hate myself for allowing her to push me away when she needed me the most?"

Cole swore. "Then do the right thing."

"I'm trying!"

"By micromanaging her life? *Sleeping* with her?"

"I told her I wanted to be friends!" Brant yelled.

The room fell completely silent.

Cole's jaw fell slack.

And both women shook their heads like he was the absolute biggest idiot in the known universe.

"Please tell me you got that on camera," Cole said aloud.

"All of it." Annie gave him a thumbs-up. "I'm thinking of slowing down the last part and then adding an idiot meme over his forehead."

Brant glared at Annie then jutted out a finger at Cole. "I'm trying a different tactic. I'm going to be her friend, just like you are. I'm going to be there for her. I'm trying to do better. She deserves at least that."

"She has enough *friends*." Cole kicked the tile floor, paced in a semicircle, then kicked the ground again. "And it's never been enough. Because none of us are you."

Hope flared in Brant's chest only to die back down again when he realized that if she never saw him as a friend, as someone she could trust, how could they ever move past everything?

And why did he suddenly want to? What changed?

Everything. Everything had changed in that bathroom.

Hope flared in his chest. Because she hadn't known the real reason why he left. Amazing what a few words strung together in a sentence can do.

She didn't mean to say the words back then. He was just too angry and hurt, too done to stay and let her apologize. He was too afraid. Fear had turned into anger.

Brant gulped and looked down.

"I was afraid," he admitted out loud to himself, to Cole, to Annie, and to Carol. "I was afraid."

Annie sighed.

Cole clenched his teeth and then exhaled. "Afraid?"

"Have you ever loved someone so much that it hurts to breathe, only to realize after they leave that it hurts because somewhere along the way you stopped living for yourself and instead you were living for them? Only them." Brant swore. "I was so fucking afraid that I'd lost her, and a part of me wanted to be punished for adding one more thing to the list of fuck-ups, so when she was delirious with pain and blamed me? I took it. I took it because my worst fear came true. And because I blamed myself for everything. I deserved it. And then I lashed out because I was afraid it was true. Better that she hate me just as much as I hate myself—sometimes hate is easier than sadness."

"Why are you telling me this?" Cole asked. Annie and Carol had quietly gone back to work.

"Not everyone gets second chances."

"No," Cole agreed, his eyes narrowing. "Do you really think you have a shot in hell now?"

"Not really." Brant bit down on his lip until he tasted blood. "But what if...I earn that trust again?"

What if he could win her back? What if he lost? What if the past was still too much for them to overcome?

God, he hated what-ifs.

And again, the temptation to just walk away was so strong he felt paralyzed. It would be easier.

Anger and pain always were. There wasn't any fighting it; you just succumbed to the darkness and the stark realization that you'd never come out of it.

But peace? Love? They demanded to be fought for.

He just wasn't sure if he was too battle-scarred to win that sort of fight, at least without help. He wanted to win her—but he had to deserve her in the first place. After seeing the look on her face in the bathroom when she assumed he'd left her, it was going to take a hell of a lot more than friendship to get her to forgive him for walking out on her—for walking out on them.

"I'm saying I'm going to regret the next few days," Cole finally said.

"Meaning?"

"I'm going to help stop the stupid."

"You're the stupid in this scenario," Annie piped up, "just in case you weren't already aware."

"Got that, thanks." Brant clenched his teeth as a merciless pounding pushed to the front of his head.

"I can't believe I'm saying this..." Cole swore, popping his knuckles. "But I'm going to help you win her back."

"What if I don't want her back?" *Oh look, the stupid just came out.* Of course he wanted her back, he was just terrified that once he had her, she would get ripped away again—or worse, that he was the bad luck in this scenario, and he would hurt her more. God, he'd never forgive himself if anything else happened to her.

Cole marched toward him and shoved Brant's chest. "Then leave. Now. Save me the time, save her the pain. Or go after what you want. What *she* wants. Choose."

Brant's head didn't have time to make the calculations. His heart reminded him it would hurt, that it would mean more conversations like the ones in the shower, that it would mean pain. It would mean remembering.

It would mean grieving.

I have everything.

I've lost everything.

Such a small baby.

Such a big fire.

So many painful moments wrapped themselves around his head like a vise.

He sucked in a sharp breath. "I'll always choose her." Even when it hurt. Even when he knew it could destroy them all over again. If they couldn't face their demons four years ago, then what the hell made him think they could face them now?

Hope.

And the fact that he wasn't going to give up again.

"Great." Cole's demeanor shifted, all traces of tension left his face. "Then we need to go to the meditation tent."

Brant grit his teeth. "I'm not going to the meditation tent."

"Yes." Cole grabbed him by the shirt. "You are."

"Cole, do a woman a solid and let me know if you guys start fighting again," Annie called out.

Carol nodded while Cole opened the door for Brant. "I overheard part of what your grandfather said at lunch."

"That's not creepy at all. You spying on me, Cole?"

"I make it my business to know everything, and the waitstaff has been very...helpful in that area. The way I hear it, outside your grandfather your family doesn't know shit about what happened the night of the fire, and you're going to need their support when you screw up again."

"*When* I screw up again?" Brant nearly tripped over his own feet. "For someone who claims to want to help me, you aren't very optimistic."

"Because I don't like you."

"It's not like you shit rainbows, either. You were friend-zoned from the start," Brant grumbled.

"Ouch. Good one," Cole mocked with a sarcastic edge to his voice. "If you want to win her over—and get out of that zone you're about to join me in—you won't be able to do it on your own."

Brant stopped walking. "You want me to talk to my family?"

Cole shrugged. "Your family saw the worst and still somehow didn't kill you in your sleep. They're willing to put you in the best light possible, whereas someone like myself may want to remind her that you abandoned her in her time of need." The bastard smiled, and Brant could have sworn there was an extra pep in his step. "Come on, I don't have all day."

CHAPTER TWENTY-FOUR

Rule number one: We need her to remember you for the man you were, not"—Cole gave Brant an antagonizing look and shoved him toward the meditation tent—"the jackass you are."

"I'm not a jackass."

"Denial won't help you."

Brant clenched his teeth. "I'm only an ass to you."

"You slept with her and abandoned her, and that was yesterday," Cole pointed out. "You wrote her up, threatened to fire her, have been—"

"Fine, I get it, I'm an ass." Brant held up his hand to get Cole to stop talking.

They walked toward the tent near the back of the resort. Outside of the tent, Brock, Bentley, and his grandfather all sat around a campfire with nothing on but shorts. Sweat poured down their backs, and Brock had just spit out an insane amount of water only to take another swig and glare at Bentley.

Cole rolled his eyes as both men approached the group sitting out by the fire. "So, how's the Zen program?"

Brock shot daggers in Cole's direction. "Bentley saw a bright light, then asked Jesus to take the wheel, all the while shoving Grandfather, aka the wheel in this scenario, toward the flames. All in all, it's been a great start to our afternoon. Sad you missed it."

Bentley dumped water over his head and cursed. "It was hot as hell in there."

"Behold!" Grandfather held out his arms to Brant. "Your future, should you choose not to take your head out of your ass. Hell." He pointed to the tent. "But I think the real thing is a lot hotter."

"Yeah, I'm going to have to pass." Brant tried turning around but Cole blocked his every move. "Seriously, man?"

"You need all the help you can get, and you need people who actually put up with you on your side. I don't count since I'm still on her team."

"I like him," Bentley piped up.

Brock patted the wooden seat next to him.

"You may enter the circle." Grandfather spread his arms wide. "How's the resort business? Nadine says you've managed this place quite well."

"Let's talk business later." Cole eyed Brant.

With a grimace, Brant sat next to his grandfather and waited. The flames licked higher and higher, and with the intensity of the heat, Brant wanted nothing more than to back away.

He hated fires. Nothing good ever came from fires. They burned. They destroyed.

"So what brings you out here, then?" Grandfather

interrupted Brant's dark thoughts. Already Brant wanted to bolt; each flame licked higher and higher, reminding him of things he'd rather forget. "So far, the Zen program has been quite enlightening. We spent the last half hour in meditation sweating our asses off and came out here for a quick break before going back in."

"You go right ahead," Brock grumbled.

"Actually," Cole said, glowered in Brant's direction, "I need your help, all of you."

Brant wasn't entirely sure he liked where this conversation was going or the way his grandfather's eyes twinkled at the request.

"Oh?" Grandfather rubbed his hands together. "Anything. Name it."

"Brant"—Cole said his name with a hiss—"is trying to learn how to properly woo a lady."

"Oh, dear God."

"Whoosh." Bentley swiped his hand in the air. "Oh look, the floodgates of hell just opened. Run along, Grandfather—"

"Shut up and let an old man speak, Bentley." Grandfather hesitated a minute then started smiling. Brant wasn't sure if he should plug his ears or make a run for it. Judging by Brock's and Bentley's matching nervous expressions, he'd be smart to do both. "You live by example—and use words if you must."

Brock spit out his water.

Bentley's jaw dropped.

And Brant couldn't look away from his grandfather if he tried. "What did you just say?"

"Actions always speak louder than words." Grandfather chugged out of his water bottle and placed it back on the wooden stump. "Words have the power to hurt, people remember words first, you can't take them back. But actions, well, actions can be excused, justified, that's why they call it a knee-jerk reaction. So, my advice, if you really want to stop being yourself"—there the snide remark was—"you need to prove to her that your actions mean something. Words are easy, actions are hard."

"Like his head," Bentley just had to add.

"And if actions aren't enough?" Brant asked. "Then what?"

Grandfather frowned. "Then you're doing it wrong."

Brock chuckled and shrugged in Brant's direction. "The man has a point."

Cole's smug grin wasn't helping, either.

A flame hissed in Brant's direction. He jerked backward and nearly fell off the log.

"Son..." Grandfather stared into the orange flames. "Why didn't you tell me?"

There it was, the pain, burning through his chest, demanding to be dealt with. "You knew there was a fire."

"Yes. I knew there was a fire. I also had no idea that your wife was nearly killed in it or that she lost her sight because of it. The minute you separated, you told me that I finally got my way. That the universe was against you just like your own family."

Brant sucked in a painful breath of air. Those words. He'd said those words. To his own grandfather. They had been spoken out of pain, regret, hatred for the cards he'd been dealt. "And you turned into a different man. A man, I don't even think *you* recognized anymore."

"Because it was easier," Brant found himself saying. "Ignoring the past, walking away, doing the easy thing that I wrongly assumed she wanted me to do. She said things"—he quickly glanced at Cole and then back at the ground—"things that at the time made me so angry, so sick to my stomach, so...broken, that I didn't think I had any other choice. I thought if I stopped hurting her, it would stop hurting me. We'd already lost so much, I was holding on by a thread and then the thread snapped. I walked away. I did the easy thing, the thing that hurt less, or at least I thought it would hurt less. When you get cut you stop the bleeding. That was my way of stopping the bleeding. I just didn't know at the time that every single day was a new cut, a new reminder of the past, and you can't run from it. It's exhausting, and eventually it catches up to you even when you're as careful as I've been."

Brant looked around. "Now look at me. I'm sitting outside a meditation tent with my half-naked grandfather, a stranger who wants to sleep with Nikki, and my brothers who keep looking at me like I have two heads. And Nikki, it brought me back to Nikki. Full circle." Brant tossed a stick into the fire. "Running just got me back to my original state, only now I'm exhausted, confused, still angry, and"—his voice cracked—"it was a setup. All of this." Brant sighed. "Working for Nadine, seeing Nikki again."

"Noooo," Brock said in a *no shit* voice.

Grandfather eyed him sadly. "The question is: What action will you take because of it?"

"That's not an easy answer."

"Then I guess you better decide if you want easy or hard." Cole stood. "And I'd make my decision pretty damn fast, because I'll be only too happy to sweep her off her feet once you're done destroying the stability beneath them."

Brock pointed back at Cole. "Seriously. I really like this guy."

"Speaks jackass fluently. It's incredible," Bentley agreed.

Brant stood on shaky legs and scowled at Cole. "Any other advice?"

"Baby steps."

"Huh?"

"Up until a few hours ago you've been a complete jackass, so now you need to do something nice—and when I say nice, I mean something that doesn't make her yell at you or cry or run away."

"Easy."

"Hah!" Cole shook his head. "If it was easy, you would have already done it. Let's go."

"God, you're like the Ghost of Christmas Past."

Cole shuddered. "Hate that movie, especially the Disney version."

"I couldn't knock on doors for months. I was always afraid they would come alive and swallow me," Brant agreed.

Cole smiled and then his stern expression was back. "All right, you've got a girl to win back."

"And you're still doing this out of the goodness of your heart?"

"Hell, no. I just want to be there to watch you fail," he said in a serious voice. "Also, I may have told Annie to add in an extra five hundred dollars to the bet if you get the black eye next."

"You're going to punch me?"

"Not me." Shaking his head, Cole grinned. "But I wouldn't put it past Nik. And let's be honest—they never specified who had to punch you."

"Some friend you are."

"More like enemy with a vested interest in the next black eye you get."

CHAPTER TWENTY-FIVE

It was official. She was a zombie. It had been two hours since she'd walked away from Brant.

Two hours of sitting in silence while trying to eat her feelings. The only problem with the staff room? It had about a billion types of sugary treats that promised happiness only to suck it away the minute the last taste left your lips and attached its fattiness to your body.

She'd been moping. Feeling sorry for herself.

The fact that Brant was a complete idiot wasn't helping. They'd shared something in that shower this morning, and now, now it was like he wanted to just suddenly ignore the fact that they'd both been that vulnerable. He wanted to be *friends*.

Twenty minutes later, she found herself sitting at the bar while George took her order.

"IPA, please," she said, and regretted it the moment the

words left her mouth. She used to drink IPA when she was with Brant, before actually, but not since. She'd been drinking one the night they'd met.

The night her world had changed.

He'd approached her. He'd chased her. He'd been relentless. And then he'd announced he was going to marry her, like a complete lunatic.

And like a hopeless romantic—she'd actually believed him.

Because it was Brant, who could convince anyone of anything. He oozed sex appeal, and you felt confident around him just because *he* was so damn confident.

She smiled to herself as George placed a cold bottle in her hands. "You okay there, Nik?"

"Yeah." The condensation from the bottle spread across her fingertips. "I'm good." Not really. But the last thing she wanted to do was get drunk and then blurt out all her feelings.

"All I'm saying"—Brant's voice sounded to her left; did he see her?—"is that your ideas suck."

"Wow, let me down easy," Cole responded.

Brant? With Cole? On purpose?

"Look, I know you're her best friend, but...she's different." Her heart sank. "You can't use typical ways to get her to like you. Hell, I had to trick her to fall in love with me and even then I'm pretty sure the minute she realized what a complete asshole I was—"

"Am," Cole corrected.

Brant groaned. "Fine, what an asshole I *am*, better?"

"Much."

"Let's just say she probably regrets the day she gave me her phone number."

"Wait..." Cole's voice grew closer, and she braced herself for discovery. "She actually willingly gave you her number?"

"Believe it or not, I can be charming."

Cole burst out laughing, then quickly sobered. "Sorry, man, I thought that was a joke."

"Do I look like I'm joking?"

"No, you still look pissed about the tent incident."

"It was twenty minutes of self-inflicted torture. My grandfather stripped down naked, and I think the rest of the people in the Zen program were officially traumatized for life."

"Eh, that's the program: letting go, finding yourself. The hotel guests expect it to get a little crazy. That's why we're the best." Cole laughed.

Brant didn't respond.

Did they see her now?

"You know?" Cole cleared his throat. "I just remembered I have something to do."

Suddenly a warm hand touched Nikki's back, and she leaned into it. She couldn't help it.

"Hi." She tried to keep the tremble out of her voice, but it was impossible not to react to his touch, probably as impossible as it was for him not to touch her. They'd always been that way. It had driven their friends crazy.

Can't you guys keep your hands off each other for one damn second?

And Brant would answer, *If she was your wife, you wouldn't let her go either.*

But he had. He so had.

She sucked in a breath when she felt the air move around her, and his familiar cologne floated into her nose as the sound of a bar stool being pulled closer to hers invaded her senses.

"IPA, huh?"

She smiled, shoving all the painful memories back inside, back where they were safe from being discussed.

Maybe he was right. Maybe friendship was all they had to look forward to after breaking each other. Maybe it was what each of them deserved.

"I haven't had one in a...long time." She was just about to lift the bottle to her lips when Brant's warm hand pressed against hers before taking the bottle away. She imagined his lips touching the glass, his tongue lapping up the bitter liquid, catching any drops before placing it back in her hands. "That's good."

"Yeah," she croaked. Damn her memory. Damn his mouth. "Just like old times, huh?"

She wanted to slap herself. Really? What happened to keeping the memories on lockdown?

Instead of jerking away, lashing out, or tensing, Brant leaned in and whispered, "Admit it, you fell hook, line, and sinker."

She bit down on her bottom lip. "You said you were from the future. How could I resist?"

"Okay, maybe not that part. That part was cheesy."

"All of it was cheesy." She laughed. "But you know me. I like cheesy."

So now he was going to tense? She waited for him to say something.

"Holy shit." He stood. "I have to go. I have to— Do me a favor."

Her heart sank. "Sure."

"Um..." He sounded frustrated but a bit excited, too.

"I need you to meet me in my room at, say..." He hesitated again. "Ten tonight. Can you do that?"

"Brant, I don't really think, that, um..." God, how could she even say this? "I don't know if that's a good idea."

"Just as friends." His voice dropped, it went all low and sexy, damn him. "Please?"

"Okay." Yup, she was an idiot, just begging to get her heart broken again by the only man capable of doing it twice. But something about his tone was different from this morning, from what it had been the past few days. Something that gave her that stupid hope again. Hope mixed with the idea that maybe they deserved friendship and the emotional closure that came with it. "Ten."

He left in a blur of color. She stayed glued to her seat, playing with the paper label on her bottle.

"Haven't seen that boy that excited since he arrived a few days ago," George pointed out. "Could have sworn he was ready to break out in song and dance. He nearly skipped out of here."

"Brant?" She made a face. "Are you sure?"

"Honey, whatever you said to him lit a fire, that's for sure."

"That's ridiculous. All I said was that I loved cheesy."

"Cheesy?" George repeated. "As in cheesy foods?"

"No." She laughed. "As in cheesy pick-up lines and dates. We were talking about the first time we met. Long story short, he was hilarious but totally lame, and I loved it." She'd loved *him*.

"I see." George chuckled. "Well, then."

"What? What do you mean you see?"

George said nothing.

"George, I know you're still there!"

"Right, I'm just choosing to ignore you. Don't want to ruin the surprise, now that man is finally drinking to remember."

"You're not making any sense."

He chuckled. "I'm old. I rarely make sense to anyone. Now, why don't you finish off that beer before you tear that label to shreds?"

She did as George suggested and then, because she couldn't get him to spill any more information about Brant, she wandered back into the hotel to find Cole.

And when she finally found him—in his office of all places, something that never occurred to her, since he was usually always on the move checking on the staff—he was laughing. "You bastard!"

"Cole?"

"Gotta go," he shouted.

"Are you with someone?"

"Phone, er, there was a person on . . . the other end."

"Typically how that specific technology works, Cole."

"Did you need something?" He sounded like he was hiding something, and he was one of the worst liars in the world. "I have to go check on . . . Carol."

"Carol?" she repeated. "What's wrong with Carol?"

"Hair dye . . . emergency." He coughed. "Apparently someone wanted green, they got red, didn't ask how, but you know it's my job to problem-solve."

"Great." She took a seat. "Exactly why I came looking for you."

"Nik—"

"Cole."

"Fine." He sighed loudly. "What problem am I solving?"

"Brant invited me to his room tonight."

Cole said nothing.

"Do I need to repeat myself?"

"I heard you."

"And yet you aren't throwing chairs and cursing. What gives?"

Cole shifted against his desk. The movement was slight, but it was enough for her to notice that he had moved. "He told me."

"What, he called and asked permission or something?" She burst out laughing. "You can't be serious!"

"Not permission, he just...had an idea that, shock of all shocks, wasn't stupid, that's all."

"Why?"

"Why what?"

"Why discuss me with the enemy?"

"My enemy, not yours."

"Still. You're not making sense. Why are you even talking to each other? Aren't you supposed to just fight with each other?"

Cole grabbed her hands, holding them between his. "Have you ever thought that maybe the universe is giving you a second chance?"

"And after everything that's happened between me and Brant, you're suddenly on the universe's side?"

"You look at him differently," Cole admitted, dropping her hands to her lap. "You look at me like a friend, you look at him like—" The air crackled with tension. "You look at him like you can actually see."

Her mouth dropped open. She wanted to deny it, to tell him it was because he was familiar, because she'd never had closure, because he owned a part of her she'd never gotten back.

But she couldn't deny it.

Her eyes, blind as they were, searched for him with an intensity she'd fought for the last four years—because even when he wasn't physically there, she still searched.

That was all she'd been doing.

Searching. Waiting. Hoping. Praying he'd come back.

Did that make her pathetic? Or just hopelessly in love?

"Look, I'm not saying you can trust him, I'm not even saying this is going to end well. I saw what happened the day you came to work for me; you were a complete wreck. I never want you going back to that place, but the thing is..." Cole cursed. "I can't believe I'm telling you this, but—he looks at you the same way. A man doesn't stare at you the way Brant Wellington does without having his reasons. It's something I've never experienced or even seen until now, which makes me think that even though I want to punch him in the face ninety percent of the time—he's the better man for you. Because he looks at you like you're the reason he's alive. And you look at him like you'd rather die than live without him."

She didn't realize she was crying until Cole handed her a tissue and then pulled her into a tight hug. "Go tonight. Okay?"

Nikki didn't trust herself to speak, just nodded her head and got her tears all over Cole's perfect shirt. "Sorry for crying."

"I'm used to it."

"You are not!" She smacked him on the shoulder. "Jerk."

"There we go..." He laughed and tilted her chin toward him. "Nik?"

"What?"

"Make him grovel."

She grinned.

CHAPTER TWENTY-SIX

You came!" Brant blurted loudly, stupidly.

"Yes." Nikki laughed. "Why are you shouting?"

"I just—" *Great start, Brant. Awesome.* "Sorry, I was just..." *She likes cheesy, so* own *the cheesy.* "...excited." And it occurred to him that he really was. It wasn't anger that was pressing against his chest, making him feel like he couldn't breathe.

It was excitement. Joy.

Huh. Imagine that.

"So? Can I come in?" She smiled brightly at him, and he wondered what she must think of everything.

"Yes." He clicked the door shut behind her. "I sent Nadine and Grandfather out to a late dinner and bribed the staff to get them drunk. I locked my side of the suite, so if they wander in...I blame God."

She barked out a laugh. "Noted."

"Second." Hell, he was having trouble concentrating as she wet her lips and blinked up at him. "My brothers are off with their wives enjoying the poolside bar—I told both of them if they stepped foot inside this room I'd kill them. The wives gave me their word that they'd distract them, going as far as to take off their clothes so that the guys don't get any ideas to interrupt us."

"And what exactly would they be interrupting?"

Here goes. "Date number one. Well, technically it was date four."

"I'm confused."

"I'm re-creating your favorite dates. With you."

Her mouth dropped open. "I don't know what to say."

"'Yes' would be good."

She was quiet. Too quiet. His heart sank.

And then she gave a weak nod. "Yes."

Thank God. "Just so you know, by saying yes you're agreeing to spending the night with me."

She tensed.

"Fully clothed."

She smiled. "We didn't sleep together on our fourth date?"

"Hell no. I believe I told you when we first met, I don't just let anyone in my pants." Wrong thing to say, since lately that was all he'd been doing. But she didn't miss a beat, simply rolled her eyes. "What? What's that look?"

"You're . . . different."

"Bad different?"

She shook her head. "Good different." A deep frown marred her pretty features. "Why are you doing this?"

"I thought that was completely obvious."

"I'm blind, so . . ." She lifted her shoulder in a half shrug. "I can't really read your expression. All I know is you sound lighter, happier."

"I am."

"Good." She almost looked upset about it.

"Because of you." Because he was with her. Because she said yes. Because suddenly things felt hopeful.

"How so?"

Brant spread his hands across her bare shoulders and ran them up her neck. "You deserve the chance we never had. I want to give that to you. A chance to go on after the b-baby." He swallowed the thickness in his throat. "After the fire."

"And...and how are you going to do that?"

"By reminding you why we were so damn good together. Why we fell in love. Why we stayed that way despite everyone telling us we would never make it." He pressed a kiss to her lips. "I'm seducing you—and giving us closure at the same time."

"I don't understand." She gripped his wrists, her fingers digging painfully into his skin. "You're seducing me and giving me closure?"

"I define our relationship as *before* the accident. Because after? After, we were nothing, we were too broken, too damaged. There was never an after. Only a before. I'm giving us the after. And I'm giving you the choice you never had."

A tear slid down her cheek, colliding with his hand. "And if I walk away in the end?"

His heart twisted inside his chest. "Then that's your choice. But now, at least you have one."

She nodded. "This is pretty heavy for a first date, you know." Her smile was back, but it was forced.

"Well, you're the one who asked." He leaned in to kiss her again, only to have her pull away at the last moment.

He knew it wouldn't be easy, but he just wanted to taste her, to make her understand that he wasn't going anywhere, not unless she wanted him to.

Brant sighed, then pulled away and reached for her hand. "Follow me."

"Where am I following you to?"

"On our fourth date, we went stargazing. I wanted you so damn bad—wanted to slam you against the nearest wall, and, well"—he grinned—"you can probably fill the rest of that vivid image in. The point is, you wanted to freaking star-gaze. And I couldn't say no, even though my body hated me. So, I came up with an idea. If we stargazed, then I could at least feel you up, and if I felt you up, then you'd most likely kiss me, and if you kissed me, maybe I would get some action."

"Your mind's a terrifying place."

He laughed, then took her arm again and led her outside to the large patio overlooking the resort. The hum of the outdoor hot tub filled the air along with the strong smell of chemicals. He'd purposefully turned off all the lights in an effort to make it romantic and to see the stars, and he was momentarily pissed when he looked up and it was cloudy.

Maybe it would clear up?

Not that it mattered. He knew she couldn't see them, but that was part of his plan.

He let go of her hand long enough to grab the nearby blanket and laid it on the ground next to the cheap champagne and plastic Solo cups.

"All right, just lay back here." He helped her sit down and then very carefully sat down behind her, straddling her.

She tensed.

"Is this okay?"

"Is this how our date went?"

"You don't remember?"

She shook her head. "I remember loving the stars and telling you it was one of my favorite dates." She sucked on her bottom lip. "And I remember that you smelled really good back then."

"And I don't now?"

She laughed and tensed a bit in his arms like she was afraid to relax. "You always smell good. It's really irritating, believe me."

"Are you saying I irritate you?"

"Not right now." She breathed out a sigh and scooted back against him. "Okay, Brant, tell me about the stars."

He glanced up and almost told her the truth. No stars. Nothing but heavy clouds that threatened to burst open at any minute.

But God, her face.

She was smiling—it was everything.

His throat burned as he watched her expectant face. "They look like glitter in the sky, like thousands of diamonds twinkling just for us. I see"—his hands moved to her face as he gazed into her eyes—"I see fire and passion. I see joy, beauty...I see you."

"In the stars?"

"Yeah." He didn't take his gaze away from her face. "In the stars."

He kissed her.

She pulled away and stared ahead. "Is this the part where I get felt up?"

"God, I hope so."

She laughed. A real laugh.

He didn't kiss her.

Knew that it wasn't time yet, that she didn't trust him enough not to do something stupid, and since his track record had pointed toward stupid he sat there, content with just holding her.

Until a raindrop slapped his cheek. And then another. He ignored them and kept kissing her. Until a crack of thunder sounded.

"I don't remember this happening on our date," she joked, crawling out of his lap. He wrapped the blanket around her to protect her from the storm and guided her back inside the hotel room.

"Shit." He almost forgot the champagne. Brant ran back outside, getting his clothes completely soaked as he picked up the champagne and the cups. When he got back inside, she was laying the blanket on a nearby table.

"Everything okay?" she asked. Her eyes searched the room, darting from left to right in an effort to either focus on him or whatever direction he was coming from. His throat burned. His heart ached. He'd done that to her. He'd broken her and then broken them.

"Yeah." He licked his lips and slowly moved toward Nikki. "Everything's great."

"It was a good date." She put a hand out and placed it on his chest then moved it to his shoulder.

He took her fingertips in his hand and then kissed her cheek. "Date's not over yet."

"Because you never felt me up?" she joked.

"Well, that, and because we never drank our cheap champagne."

Her eyes lit up. "Please tell me it's the grocery store Brut that only costs four dollars and ninety-four cents."

"The one and only." He laughed. "You remember?"

"Only important things like the fact that you bought it for me every year on my birthday. To go along with the homemade pasta."

"And when you say homemade, you mean—"

"You bought the box mac and cheese and put a candle in it, yes. That kind of homemade."

"I'm a wizard with mac and cheese, admit it."

"You're…something." She grinned and then held open her right hand. "Okay, champagne."

"Ah, so now she's excited."

"Aw, was I not excited enough when we were talking about you feeling me up?"

"I'd prefer you throw a parade next time or at least jump into the air, but I'll take whatever I can get."

She laughed and then laughed harder before sobering. "I miss this."

"Nope." He cupped her face. "We aren't going to do that, okay? Let's just focus on the good, maybe if we do that…" God, he hoped he was right. "Maybe the bad won't seem as bad if we remember the good."

"Brant." Her voice was sad. "Friends talk. We need to have that talk otherwise none of this is going to work."

"I know," he admitted. "Just…not yet."

Tears filled her eyes. "Okay."

Thank God. He wasn't ready for it yet, ready for the talk that could send her out of his life for good. Because once they traveled that road, Pandora's box would be ripped wide open—and what if she couldn't move past it?

What if he couldn't? What if all they had was now?

"Hey, Brant?"

Damn thing was impenetrable. He twisted the wire off and covered the cork with a towel. "Kinda busy saving the day here, Nik."

"By opening a bottle?"

"I'm a man, it's what we do. Well, it's what I do. Son of a bitch, this thing won't come off!"

"Brant." She warned.

"Fine. Sorry." The cork finally came loose. "You were saying?"

"It rained."

He glanced behind him, more like a torrential downpour. "Yeah?"

"How can you tell me about the stars if you can't see them?"

"The same way you recognize things without seeing them, I guess." He wanted to touch her again, to kiss her. "I did it from memory, and when that failed, I just looked into your eyes."

CHAPTER TWENTY-SEVEN

She was overwhelmed.

So overwhelmed.

He'd kissed her good night on the cheek and then walked her all the way across the street to her apartment, only to kiss her again, ask if she needed anything, and walk away.

Or she assumed he walked away. He could still be standing out in the front of her apartment building, and she'd have no idea.

Sometimes not seeing sucked.

She bit her lip, then smiled. But tonight? Tonight it didn't suck, because Brant had told her about the stars, because his voice had been like coming home. They'd teased. They'd laughed.

No yelling. No breaking things. Just the Brant she remembered.

Moisture burned in her eyes before she wiped the angry tears away. In theory, she understood what he was doing, but it was still confusing as hell. Did he really want her? Or was he doing this out of guilt? And what happened when, at the end of everything, she fell for him all over again only to have him walk away again—or worse, decide that she wasn't worth it.

She shook the thought away. She wanted to trust him. But trust had to be earned.

Look at her—one date in and she was already falling for him all over again. Who was she kidding? Even when he was angry she never really stopped wanting him, at least the old him, the one she knew was trapped in an angry prison of their own making.

Brant Wellington, player, millionaire, sex god—ex-husband—was wooing her. She'd have to be an idiot to turn him down—even though she had a sinking feeling it wasn't going to end well. How could it? With so much damage still done? So many things left unsaid between them, and then tonight when she'd mentioned talking he'd said, *Later*.

Putting it off wasn't going to make it any less painful. So she'd agreed. What other choice did she have? When faced with the one man she still ached for?

Nikki went through the motions of getting ready for bed only to blink up at the swirls of grays and blacks above her. Thinking of his hands. And the way they felt against her skin.

She shivered and then imagined she was in his bed; he was holding her and promising to never let go. Focus on the good, he'd said. The before, the after, not the in between that had destroyed them.

* * *

Nikki was woken up by what sounded like knocking. What time was it? Where the hell was she?

The pounding came again, only this time it sounded like urgent knocking. Softness surrounded her.

Bed…she was in bed. Oh God, she hadn't set her alarm last night.

More knocking. She shot out of bed.

"Crap!" Her knee hit her nightstand as she bolted away from the mattress and made a mad dash to the door. "I'm late. I'm sorry!"

Cole's blurry figure stood before her. "Don't be." Was he laughing? "I wrongly assumed you slept with Brant last night and woke him up at the ass crack of dawn. He was not pleased. And I couldn't hold back the shit-eating grin on my face."

"What? Why?" Nikki bumped into a chair and scooted it away as she went to the fridge.

"Because he didn't get laid and I know it. Happiest day of my life."

She groaned. "I thought you wanted me to try with him."

"Oh, I do. I just find great satisfaction from you making him work for it. Hey, how about tonight you put on something sexy, rub all over him, and then walk away? Only take a picture of his expression right before you do. I want it as a screensaver."

"Very funny."

"Or, wait." The sound of him snapping his fingers echoed through the small one-bedroom unit. "Tell him to wait for you naked, blindfold him, then leave him with an ungodly amount of roses around his body for the maids to find."

Nikki tipped back some orange juice and wiped her mouth. "You done?"

"I'll think of more later, I'm sure," Cole said cheerfully. "Also, lucky you, the very first appointment of the day is in less than an hour and it's Nadine Titus."

Nikki froze. "Do you think she'll... be picky?"

"Last night the woman was tossing shots back with George and Mr. Wellington like they were water. My guess, she's going to be snoring through the whole thing or nursing a hangover."

"Good." Nikki nodded as her palms started to sweat. She knew Nadine was going to pry; she couldn't help herself. She was like a shark when it came to matchmaking—relentless.

And part of Nikki just wanted to keep what was happening between her and Brant—at least, the details.

Cole interrupted her thoughts. "You need help with anything?"

"Nah, I'll be ready in fifteen."

True to her word, Nikki was knocking on the door to her massage room about twenty minutes later.

"Mrs. Titus?"

"I think by now you can just call me Nadine or Grandma." Her soft voice piped up. "Sounds weird being a missus when you've spent half your life being a mistress."

Nikki smirked and made her way around the table, placing her hands on the sheet. "Sounds good, Grandma." Her own grandma was dead; her parents had rejected her marriage to Brant right off the bat, and they had been estranged ever since. Which meant she really didn't have much of a family outside of Cole and the staff.

"I have to ask." Nadine stretched her arms above her head then tucked them back under the sheet. "What's best? The angry kiss or the makeup kiss?"

Nikki froze. "I'm sorry?"

"Well, he's such an angry one, that Brant. Does he kiss that way? Or does he kiss you tenderly? Or maybe he does both?"

"Um..." How the hell did she answer that?

"Oh, how nice, he does both." The woman wouldn't stop talking. "You know, back in my day we never labeled kisses. Kissing was kissing. These days there's tongue, there's... well, I won't go there, but there's this thing you do to a man that can—"

"All right!" Nikki found herself shouting. "How about we try a deep-tissue relaxation massage. You can even fall asleep." *Please, God, make her fall asleep.*

Nadine yawned. "Oh, okay, dear. Thank you for giving him a chance again."

"You sound so positive that I am."

"Well, you are standing straighter. Your smile's brighter. Last night when you were under the stars—"

"Wait, weren't you at dinner?"

"Never mind that. You looked like you were home. It was a good feeling. Just give him a chance. That man has a lot of love to give."

Nikki shivered as memories she'd kept locked down seemed to break free. His hands. His body. Their kisses. Shower sex. Elevator sex. So really, just sex everywhere all the time—which was probably what led to getting pregnant.

Not that they hadn't been trying. Because Brant really had wanted a big family. And so had she.

Tears welled in her eyes when she thought of all of

their moments, their love, the way he always made her feel like the most beautiful woman in the world, the way he'd tried so damn hard to be perfect.

Only to fail. When she'd needed him the most. Because she had pushed him away. Because she had said hurtful things.

"Nikki?" Nadine interrupted her. "Are you okay? You've been rubbing my bunion for a good two minutes."

Nikki jerked back. Bunion? "Really?"

"No, no bunion, I just don't want to be rubbed raw. If you need me to reschedule..."

"Sorry. I was thinking."

"Of Brant?"

It was hopeless, the woman was going to be a talker. "Yeah."

"I love a good story. Tell me about Brant's hands."

Nikki froze. "What? What do you mean, his hands?"

"Or better yet, his body. Explain him through your eyes."

"But I can't really see."

"Exactly. What do you feel?"

Nikki spent the next hour telling Nadine everything: The way his cheeks were rough at night because his beard always grew in too fast. The smell of his skin after a shower. The feel of his chest under the palm of her hand. The way he held her in his arms, gentle, firm, all the ways he held her hand.

And slowly, it was as if she were falling in love with him all over again.

"All right." Nadine yawned. "I think our time is up. Thank you for the lovely story."

Nikki blinked and then whispered, "Thank you for helping me remember."

"Sometimes, we repress the things that hurt most. I know there's more in there, more hurt, but that's for you two to work through."

Nikki wasn't sure she was going to be able to work the rest of the day; she was emotionally spent.

"Oh!" Nadine clapped her hands together. "Brant told me to give you this."

"Brant? Brant sent you here?"

"For a massage, yes, but mainly to give you this."

It was in Braille. Nikki's fingers trembled as they ran over the card stock. "It's an invitation."

"To an early Thanksgiving dinner."

"Right, but it's . . . summer."

"Brant has it in his head to re-create Thanksgiving dinner, so we're going to re-create it."

And suddenly, Nikki realized she wouldn't survive this seduction, not at all. Because the only Thanksgiving they had ever spent with his family was the day they had told them they were pregnant.

There had been a food fight. Yelling. It had been horrible. She'd left in tears. Brant had sworn to never talk to his grandfather again. And Bentley, his own twin, had taken his grandfather's side.

Thanksgiving dinner was a reminder of all she'd lost—and it was hard not to struggle with the choking fear that history was about to repeat itself.

"Be brave," Grandma Nadine whispered.

"Brave," she repeated.

"You have it in you. All women do. Especially those of us who have lost."

CHAPTER TWENTY-EIGHT

Brant paced in front of the large table. Where was she? Nadine swore up and down she had given Nikki the invitation.

"Stop." Bentley took a long draw from his drink. "You're going to wear a hole in the carpet."

"Bullshit, its hardwood!" Brant fired back, irritated that he was irritated.

Bentley held up his hands, a stupid grin on his face. "My, my, how the mighty have fallen. What was it you said to me a month ago? You'd burn in hell before you let Nadine get her claws into you?"

Brant's eyes narrowed in on his brother's arrogant smirk.

Brock joined them, tilting his glass to his mouth. "I could have sworn he told me the same thing."

"Ganging up on the weak, really?" Cole said as he approached.

"Dickhead," Brant muttered. "Glad you could make it."

"I always make time for friends." He said it to both

brothers before looking at Brant and adding, "And assholes, though since our talk it seems like you've turned over a new leaf. Even opened a bottle of champagne all by yourself!"

"High five, man, that shit's hard," Bentley teased while Brock choked on his drink.

The women were already seated at the table next to Grandfather. They gave him so much attention it was as if they'd adopted him.

Brant checked his watch again. "She's late."

Cole rolled his eyes. "She's blind. It takes a while to get a dress on when your best friend isn't there to help you fasten it."

"That's it." Brant moved toward him but was held back by a laughing Bentley. "Come on, just one punch."

Brock glanced between them. "I thought you guys were allies now."

"Allies. Enemies." Cole shrugged. "Basically the same thing, right, Brant?"

"Right." Brant counted to ten. "Besides, you may be the one helping her put the dress on—but I will *always* be the lucky bastard helping her take it off."

"I think Brant just won fake Thanksgiving," Bentley announced, as Nikki made her way into the large banquet room.

"Mine." He hadn't meant to say it out loud. But by the way Cole was looking at her—he didn't give a shit if he announced it to the world and then forced her to wear a T-shirt that said PROPERTY OF BRANT WELLINGTON.

Right, because *that* wouldn't piss her off.

It wasn't as though he owned her.

God, he wanted to, though.

Hell, he'd do anything to be owned by *her*.

She was wearing a simple black cocktail dress that fell just above her knees. It had capped sleeves and hugged every curve of her body. He nearly groaned when he saw a sliver of skin through the cutouts on the side of the dress. What he wouldn't do to be able to put his tongue in that spot right above her hip.

"You came." He reached for her hands and lifted them to his lips, kissing the backs of each of them and then squeezing, his body refusing to let go.

"Why do you keep sounding so surprised when I show up?"

He pulled her in for a hug and whispered, "Because every time you walk away, it feels like the last." He kissed the side of her neck. "And then I spend the night in agony until I see you again, only for the process to repeat itself."

"You're getting too good at this seduction thing." She moaned low in her throat when his mouth met hers in a too-brief kiss. "It's a bit terrifying."

"My ability to romance you?"

"Or maybe just my ability to fall for it."

"Touché."

He looped her arm through his and led her to her seat at the table. He'd planned everything.

Thanksgiving dinner. A redo from the past.

The only thing he didn't repeat was the candles. He hated them—and the last thing she needed was to be near fire, not after what had happened. Maybe it was just Brant who was irrationally angry at anything fire related, but he didn't want to take any chances that he'd ruin her night.

Again.

"Date number?" She asked once he gently showed her where her water glass and wineglass were.

"Thirty-seven." He placed a napkin in her lap. "But remember, still only date two for us."

"For the after."

"Yeah. The after."

"And how many of these are we going to get?"

"Two more." He watched her face fall. "But I promise they may just change your life."

"Let me guess: One of us gets naked?"

He barked out a laugh. "For that, you get extra dessert and wine."

"Wow. I get rewards for good behavior?"

"Always," he teased, his voice rough.

She giggled behind the wineglass she'd just picked up and nodded. "So you want me to be good....not *bad*?"

He groaned. "Shit, that backfired."

"Totally."

"I'm rusty."

"Wow, that's romantic. Tell me more."

"I'm from the future?"

"Nice try. It only works once, Casanova."

"Damn it." He pounded the table with his fist in a playful gesture, gaining the attention from all of his shocked family members. Margot watched him a minute longer than everyone else, tears in her eyes.

That woman, with her penetrating green eyes, saw way too much. She nodded toward Brant and then continued talking to Bentley.

Was it only a few weeks ago that in a drunken stupor he'd confessed some of his secrets to Margot? Pushed her into the arms of his brother?

Brant was just about to speak when Grandfather clinked his glass and stood.

Oh hell. Speeches were definitely not part of the plan.

He shot Nadine a worried look, but she was too busy staring up at Grandfather with doe eyes, clasping her jeweled hands together like he hung the freaking moon.

"I have something to say."

"Whiskey," Bentley coughed. "Quick, more whiskey."

Brant gripped Nikki's hand and waited for the inevitable. Well, at least his grandfather really was repeating history. Only at the original Thanksgiving dinner, he'd stormed out of the house after telling Brant they were too young and were ruining their lives.

Fun times.

Maybe Bentley was right about the whiskey. If this was going to be anything close to what happened last time, he'd need to bathe in it in order to forget the hurtful words, the things said.

Everyone was tense. Even Brock's smile was frozen on his face as he looked between Brant and Grandfather.

"I was wrong," Grandfather announced. And then sat right back down and continued talking to Nadine, his ruddy cheeks going darker, like the conversation they were having shouldn't take place anywhere near the kids' table, or any table for that matter.

Brock smirked while Bentley rolled his eyes and gave Brant a knowing look: *See? I told you he wasn't out to ruin all of our lives!*

"Did he just"—Nikki cleared her throat—"apologize?"

"Yeah, or as close to an apology as we're going to get." Brant said, dumbfounded.

"For what?"

He turned to face her. "If I was guessing, I'd say everything."

A smile spread across her face as she carefully reached for her wineglass and lifted it in the air. "Well, I guess the only thing we can do is a toast."

The minute she lifted her glass everyone else quieted and followed suit.

"To Thanksgiving." Brant didn't look away from her gorgeous red lips. They matched the wine in her glass, and he wanted to lick them just once that night.

"To Thanksgiving." As they toasted, the first course was brought in.

"So..." Nikki took another sip of wine. "Why did you pick date thirty-seven? I remember crying a lot, but I was highly emotional at the time."

"You're a woman, so it's forgiven."

"Insulting, but thank you." Her eyebrows arched. "You got in a huge fight with your entire family. Bentley yelled, you yelled, Brock glared, and I vaguely remember your grandfather threatening to disown you—again. So, why do you think this would be one of my favorite dates?"

Brant knew this question was coming. He just hadn't prepared for it. He wanted to lie, to crack a joke, to ignore the burn inside him.

"The truth?"

"Always the truth, Brant."

"It was the first night I felt like a real family. Because in that moment, we truly only had each other." His hand moved to her stomach. "And a tiny life that was completely dependent on us."

Her eyes welled with tears as her lower lip quivered.

"I'm sorry," he rasped. "Would you rather I lie?"

"Sometimes the lie doesn't hurt as much, does it?"

"Nik, I've spent the last four years numbing the pain. Seeing you again makes me believe that maybe the best way to live isn't to ignore it but to learn how to survive it with the ones you love by your side."

"Are you saying you love me?"

"Are you imagining I ever stopped?"

She kissed him. Hard.

Over a course of some sort of fruit salad that Brant couldn't give a shit about. And when she pulled back, they had the attention of the whole table.

"Is everyone staring?"

"Absolutely not," he lied.

"Lying to a blind woman, Brant?" Her smile was magnetic, captivating. "That's not very gentlemanly of you."

"When have I ever been a gentleman?"

She grinned wider. "You have your moments."

"Shh. I'm supposed to be the evil twin."

"Oh, believe me." Her voice lowered. "I'm well aware."

The sound of silverware scraping plates filled the room as he leaned in and whispered, "Please tell me that was a sexual innuendo and not my imagination."

"Must everything be sexual?"

"With you? Yes. Every single time."

Her lips parted.

And that was when Brant noticed the silence.

He jerked back to see everyone watching and Nadine holding up her leopard-print phone in the air.

"Put that down," Grandfather scolded her. But Nadine simply grinned harder.

"Good salad?" Nikki's voice cut through the silence.

"Amazing," Grandfather choked.

"Best salad ever," said Jane.

"Oh, please, honey, like you're thinking about salad." Nadine snorted, "But yes, it's very lovely, crisp, just the right amount of flavor as it hits your tongue. And those little balls"—Grandfather choked again, earning him a slap on the back—"they simply burst with flavor all over." She spread her arms wide.

"I think we stopped talking about salad." Bentley gave Brant a shake of his head and stabbed a mozzarella ball with his fork. "But I will admit that burst of—"

Brant cut him off. "Bent. How's the zoo?"

"Ah, strategic subject change from Brant's balls." Bentley leaned forward. "I see what you did there."

"She's never seen my balls," Brant said defensively, pointing at Nadine.

Nadine simply shrugged and took a long gulp of wine. "Not my fault you don't have them."

Cole burst out laughing. "Can you adopt me?"

"Oh, honey." Nadine nodded with an excessive smile while she eyed him up and down. "What a splendid idea. Do you have any women in your life?"

"Abort." Bentley coughed. "Abort."

"Other than one that's taken, that is," Brant just had to say. Nikki squeezed his thigh under the table, giving him a little jolt.

Eyes turned. He shrugged them away. But beneath his calm façade, he was burning.

Her hands inched higher.

What the hell was she doing? She'd always been flirty when they were married, but the woman he knew now was cautious. And yet her hand kept moving up, which just made him all the more aroused.

Because in all his calculations he'd never thought she might actually seduce him. Especially since she'd rejected every kiss. He tried to stay still and took a long drink of water.

"I really don't remember this version of Thanksgiving, Nik," he said out of the corner of his mouth, as Cole and Nadine started bickering at the other end of the table.

"Well." She scooted her chair closer then slid her hand beneath his napkin, grabbing him fully, giving enough of a squeeze that he hissed out a curse. "You've been trying so hard to give a new version, I thought I'd help."

"God, I love helpful people."

"I thought so."

"Volunteering is really..."

She moved her hand.

"...so...selfless."

"Well, I was short some hours this week."

"I'd be more than happy to sign off on—" He reached for his wine to keep himself from kissing her, from flipping her over the table next to the turkey and asking her to spread her legs. Yeah, that would go over well.

"Sign off on...?"

"I'm sorry, what were we talking about?" He kept his voice low as he rolled his hips against her hand. "So close."

"Yeah, it's nice sitting this close," she said in a completely innocent voice. Another gentle squeeze.

"I love your hands," he blurted. "I think I'm obsessed with them."

"What was that, dear?" Nadine called across the table.

Brant froze.

Nikki tensed.

"Ham!" he said quickly—and a little too loudly. "I'm obsessed with hams."

Nadine narrowed her eyes. "How... interesting."

He was saved from embarrassment by the arrival of the next course, and attention was once again diverted away from them. And once dessert was served, he began counting down the minutes until he could excuse them and finish what they'd started.

Bentley stood. "A toast."

Brant glared. Bentley grinned at him over his glass and took a long swig, then yawned. "To a very happy early Thanksgiving."

"Hear, hear!" Brant tossed his glass back, stood, offered his hand, and mentally calculated how long it would take to get Nikki back to his room. At least six minutes. Give or take one minute if they had to wait for the elevator. Then again, he could strip her naked once they were safely inside the elevator.

Everyone stood.

"You forgot part of the date," Nikki whispered in his ear.

He turned to her, frowning. "I did?"

"Walk me home and find out."

CHAPTER TWENTY-NINE

What she wouldn't give to be able to read minds. To be able to figure out what Brant was thinking right that moment. He'd been silent all the way to her apartment, and the silence felt somehow darker, tenser, the minute he stepped foot inside her living room and closed the door quietly behind him.

"Home sweet home." She spread her arms wide. "Also, you should probably make a noise, Brant. I can't see you, so when you don't speak I can only assume you've either left to dig through all of my things or you're staring, and both are creepy."

Brant was still quiet.

She reached out then jerked back. He was a muscled blur standing right in front of her; the darkness of his suit blended with the darkened room.

"Brant?"

"This," he said, his voice hoarse, angry-sounding, "is where you live?"

Shame hit her so violently that she stumbled backward a bit as tears stung her eyes. Stupid! She hadn't even thought to clean up. She knew there were at least four dishes piled up inside the sink from earlier that week, and she knew firsthand from Cole that nothing in her apartment matched.

It was tidy. Probably smaller than Brant's closet, and most likely reminded him of a first-grader's classroom more than a grown woman's apartment. The red blur of throw pillows caught her attention right next to the bright purple throw blanket that she knew was placed between the two of them.

What was she supposed to say? Or do?

"Don't give me that look," he whispered. "Just answer the question. This—this place is where you've been living for four fucking years?"

She swallowed the giant watermelon lump in her throat and gave him a jerky nod. Why was he so angry? She suddenly felt sick to her stomach. Things had been going so well! What happened? Where did they go wrong?

This was her life now.

She lifted her head, refusing to be ashamed of what she had to do to survive.

He didn't really know the new Nikki, the one who was so poor when they separated that the only job she could find was working as a greeter at a car dealership before the massage therapist job finally opened at the resort.

"It's my home," she said proudly, crossing her arms. "Besides, where else was I supposed to live? On the street?"

"Your walls are pink and red," he said in a harsh voice. "Your couch is yellow. It has holes in it."

Each word hit like a physical slap, and she flinched.

"Your kitchen counter is orange with white flowers. You have exactly two mismatched green chairs and a table I've only ever seen on *Brady Bunch* reruns." He breezed past her, and the *smuck*ing sound of the refrigerator being opened preceded a bright light spilling into the room. "You have no eggs, no cheese, nothing but milk." She heard a cupboard open. "Oatmeal and cereal."

Tears slid down her face. So this was how her fairy tale would end? This was how they would gain closure? With her rich and beautiful ex-husband taking stock of all the things she didn't have? Was he really that hateful? That the deal breaker would be a list of things about her apartment that bothered him?

"I like oatmeal and cereal, and I like my home," she said in a shaky voice. "Now, please leave."

"No."

"No?" she repeated, wishing like hell she could see him so she could slap his arrogant face off. "Fine, then I'm calling the cops!"

"I'll just hide the phone."

"Leave!" she screamed.

"No." His hands braced her body. "I'm not leaving you. Not now. Not ever fucking again."

"I did fine without you!" she screamed in what she hoped was his face. "I survived! I'm happy!"

"Well, I'm not!" he roared back at her, stunning her into silence. "You were supposed to get money, Nik!"

She frowned. "What do you mean?"

"From me. You were supposed to get money so you didn't have to work. So you could do whatever the hell you wanted."

"I seriously have no idea what you're talking about."

"My lawyers—"

"Lawyers?" She suddenly couldn't breathe. Yes, she'd talked to one of his lawyers years ago when they'd divorced, but the lawyer had never mentioned anything about money. "You mean the guy who called me and said I needed to sign papers?"

"Nik—you were supposed to sign papers so you could get money and so our divorce would be—" He suddenly stopped talking. "Tell me I'm not losing my mind here. Tell me you know what I'm talking about."

She shook her head over and over again. "Don't you think I would be living in at least a bigger place if I did? But does it matter anyway? I wanted to start over. And I have."

"Sweetheart..." Brant cupped her face. "That's not the point."

She sniffed. "Then what is?"

"That you were never supposed to have to struggle. You never had to. Do you really think after all these years that I would walk away without making sure you were okay? Do you really think that's the kind of man you married?"

"But—" She blinked at the blur of a face in front of her. "You just, you left, you said we were too broken, you said good-bye, you didn't even—" *Don't do it—shove the memory back.* "You didn't even kiss me good-bye."

"Because I never would have fucking left if I did." Brant crushed his mouth to hers, his lips punishing as he spread his hands around her back and lifted her onto the kitchen table. His fingers slid up her thighs and squeezed. "I wouldn't have been strong enough to walk away."

"So it took strength to walk away?"

"That and a heavy dose of anger, shame, and hostility, and a hell of a lot of guilt."

"And now?"

"Now, you'll have to murder me to get rid of me. Just make sure we're still married before you do it, though, or you won't get the twenty million."

She broke the kiss. "'Still married'?"

"I say twenty million and you fixate on the marriage part?" He nuzzled her neck as he continued attacking her with his mouth.

"But"—ah, it was hard to think straight when he kissed her like that—"why would we still be married?"

His lips found hers again before he pulled back. "Because you only got the money once you signed the divorce papers. If you didn't get the money, then my only assumption is something happened with the paperwork." Her heart thudded so wildly in her chest she thought she was going to have a heart attack. "Meaning you're still my wife."

He silenced her protests with another kiss. And another.

"And if that's the case"—his grip tightened on her ass as he slowly moved one hand up to unzip her dress—"then it seems like I'm finally home."

Home. He was home. *She* was his home.

She arched beneath him as he tugged the dress down to her waist and then lifted her up only long enough to take off the rest of her clothes and lay her across the table.

"Home," she repeated, reaching blindly for him as she heard the sound of another zipper, more clothes flying everywhere, and then warmth, so much warmth.

Heat.

His chest against hers.

His breath fanning her neck as his tongue slid across her lips, teasing her tongue. Brant's teeth nibbled her ears as he poised at her entrance. She felt his throbbing heat.

And she wanted every inch of him.

With an all-consuming kiss that left her gasping for air, he rose over her and slid into her—stripping away any restraint she thought she had, and making her insane for him.

Only him.

It had only ever been Brant.

CHAPTER THIRTY

He moved inside her, he took his time kissing her, and when the sensations of her heat surrounding him, clinging to him, nearly pushed him over the edge, he stopped and focused on her all over again.

Nikki gasped as a sea of pleasure built between them. He plucked kiss after kiss from her mouth like he was picking berries, then sucked her juice between his lips, addicted to the way she tasted more than any alcohol, any drug.

Her body tightened around him, her legs wrapped up in his, their bodies as close as physically possible. She flew apart seconds later, and when he followed, he watched her face, the wonder, the love, the sheer perfection of her lips as her head fell back in surrender.

"You're perfect," he whispered.

"We're still married."

"God, I hope so," he whispered. "Now, focus on us, this, here, right now." He kissed her again. "Promise?"

"Promise."

He breathed out a sigh of relief, then pulled away from her and helped her to her feet. "I'm pretty sure the last Thanksgiving we spent together included shower sex. In fact, I'm positive."

"Are you?" She grinned. "I'm pretty sure table sex trumps shower sex."

"How would you really know if you can't compare the two? That sounds pretty unfair."

"And you're all about being fair."

"I would hate to hurt the shower's feelings."

"Oh, so now you're worried about the shower."

"Nik, I'm just trying to be selfless here."

She laughed and grabbed his hand. "Eight steps past the kitchen, three steps into the bedroom, and two steps to your right."

Guilt damn near crushed him as he followed her through the small apartment. She should be living in the penthouse; she should at the very least have a roommate, someone to help her.

Four years. Four years she'd lived like this. And for what? His pain? His pride? His inability to forgive himself? To forgive her for the hurtful and justified words she had thrown at him?

He flicked on the light to the bathroom and froze as she started feeling around to turn the shower on.

A picture of her and Cole sat on the counter. He was hugging her, looking directly into the camera, and she was looking away.

It haunted him long after they showered and went for round two. It haunted him when he tucked Nikki into his body and told her to have good dreams. It haunted him hours later when he went in search of food while Nikki got ready for work.

And when he was sitting at the hotel an hour later in the lobby, he was still haunted.

"What?" Cole waved a hand in front of his face. "You know, for someone who just got laid, you don't look very happy."

"I left her money," Brant admitted. "She never got it."

"No shit. I've seen her apartment, helped her paint the walls and everything."

Suddenly it was too much. He'd left her. And Cole had been there the entire time.

He felt sick, so sick he wasn't sure he could even have the business meeting he'd planned while Nikki took care of her next two clients.

"Brant?" Something in Cole's voice changed. "Are you okay?"

Brant nodded.

Cole waved over one of the waiters and ordered lunch while Brant stared into his coffee cup.

"This isn't about the money, is it?"

"We lost our child," Brant blurted. "To go through that at any point in your life is unimaginable. To follow it up with a fire that nearly kills your wife—only to find out you're the reason it started. To take someone's sight a day after you held her while she cried herself to sleep." He shook his head. "I can't explain that type of pain, or how desperate it makes a person to want to make it all go away."

Cole muttered out a few curses and leaned on the table. "Nikki told me, she had her reasons for telling me... what I don't understand is why you feel like *you* need to."

"You were there for her when I wasn't."

Cole locked eyes with him. "Yeah. I was."

Leave it to Cole to make it harder on him than it already was.

"What if I can't make her happy? What if I just hurt her—what if the hurt between us is so big, so great, that we can't start fresh?"

"You have brothers."

"Huh?"

"Brothers," Cole said again. "And yet you're sitting here, asking me for advice?"

"Family sees the best in you no matter the cost," Brant said honestly.

"And me?" Cole grinned.

"I'm pretty sure every time you see my face it takes an insane amount of self-control not to punch me or run me over with a car."

"You'd be right," Cole grunted. "On both fronts. Lying to you doesn't help me out, neither does kissing your ass."

At least they agreed on that.

"So?" Brant spread out his arms and sighed. "What do I do?"

Cole stared at him long and hard. The silence wasn't uncomfortable.

Finally, Cole frowned and leaned back against the chair. "I think you have to talk about it. All of it. I think you need to lay yourself open, vulnerable, bloody, beaten, and ask her the question you've been avoiding since you came here."

"What's that?"

"Are you worth it?"

* * *

"You ready for our next date?" Brant asked, opening up the door to the limo and helping Nikki inside. She slid across the plush leather seat. He tried to keep his tone happy, light, but if she could see his face, she'd see it was pale. If she traced her fingers around his mouth, she'd feel the strain lines; if she could see his eyes, she'd see nothing but pain.

"You sound different," she pointed out. "We can do the date another time, if you aren't feeling up to it tonight." She reached out to touch his thigh.

The door closed behind them. The limo moved. His heart slowed to a painful rhythm in his chest as a piercing silence filled the car.

"Brant?"

"This date..." He cleared his clogged, betraying throat and squeezed her hand. "It isn't one of my favorite memories. It's one that never happened. But one that needs to happen, all right?"

"Should I be scared you're kidnapping me?" she joked, her eyes a bit watery. Could she sense his sadness? The swirling cloud of doom hanging over them, the chasm still separating them, that would be separating them until he did this?

"Can't kidnap something you already have, right?" he answered in a sad voice.

"No." She blinked down at their joined hands. "You can't."

Too soon, the limo pulled to a stop. Too soon, rain started pounding on the roof of the car.

"We're here," he announced, pulling out an umbrella before the door opened.

With a smile on her face, Nikki put her hand in his. He pulled her under the cover of the umbrella. His body was tense, his face tight, his eyes already filled with tears.

"Where are we?" She sniffed the air. "I know it's raining, we're outside, and I'm standing on grass, but that's about it." She ducked her head against his chest. "Brant?"

He didn't trust himself to answer. But he knew he could at least hold her close, keep her safe from the rain even if that meant that he couldn't keep her safe from the tumultuous emotions building up inside—ready to explode and destroy anything in their path.

Brant Wellington was a dangerous man when he lost control, and he knew, in his heart, all hell was about to break lose.

They might not survive it. But in order to make it to the end, they had to go through it.

No more numbing. No more ignoring.

He stopped walking and pressed the single, thornless rose into Nikki's trembling hands.

"Here lies Noah Arnold Wellington." His voice cracked. "May you fly on the wings of eagles and into your Savior's arms." Nikki fell to her knees, grass staining her jeans as she pressed her palms against the cement headstone. Tears poured down her face. Brant continued. "Born on August 1, 2014, died—" He couldn't stop the choking sob that escaped.

I have everything.

I've lost everything.

Run.

Nikki reached up and grabbed his hand. He joined her on the cold, wet grass, the umbrella long forgotten as rain mixed with his tears and hers, running from their cheeks onto the ground they had been forced to bury their child in.

"Died," Nikki finished, "August 1, 2014." She buried her head in Brant's chest. "Seconds after he changed our lives forever."

They sat in silence.

They cried in silence.

He was fucking done with silence.

"I'm sorry." Two words. So simple. So full of meaning. "I'm so damn sorry." He squeezed her harder. "I'm sorry we lost him. I'm sorry." The floodgates opened.

And the dam broke, causing the chasm between them to collapse as she grabbed his face with both hands and said the words he'd been needing to hear for the past four years: "It's not your fault."

It was. Everything was his fault.

"He died because he wasn't healthy. There was no heartbeat, Brant. It's not your fault."

"Maybe if the apartment wouldn't have been so old, so—"

She kissed him. She tasted like salt and regret. So much regret.

"Brant, it was not your fault. It wasn't mine. It was life. Life happens. Just like the fire happened. You were trying to do a good thing. You were trying to help me."

"I was terrified," Brant admitted. "Terrified that I'd lose you just like I lost him—and then, rather than deal with the fact that you were pushing me away—wanted me gone, the guilt..." He shook his head. "On top of the risk that I almost lost you, too, that you blamed me, it was too much to handle. I felt it. All of it. I was sick with it. Sick with feeling. I just wanted it to stop."

"Ignoring it doesn't make it stop."

"No."

"I came here, you know," she admitted. "I never got this close—it hurt too much—but there's a maple tree over on the far side of the property. I used to imagine I was here playing with him in the leaves, rather than visiting his grave and dusting those same leaves off of it." Her voice broke. "I used to dream he was still alive. You were with us, in every dream. I'd close my eyes and I'd see you laughing with me, chasing him, hugging him, and I'd tell myself, *My life is perfect*." She sighed. "And the best part was, when I opened my eyes, I saw nothing but shapes, so I really could imagine you were one of them."

Brant couldn't stop the pain as it sliced him from head to toe, and when he didn't think he could take it anymore, he collapsed against Nikki.

And let go.

He grieved.

For their son.

For them.

For lost time.

For all of it.

CHAPTER THIRTY-ONE

The silence was good.

It was finally good.

Not filled with things left unsaid, things that needed to be discussed. A giant wall of emotions was always built in those silences.

But this silence was different.

She embraced it as Brant clung to her like she was his lifeline. For four years she'd thought she needed him. Never once did it occur to her that he needed her more.

Or that maybe it wasn't the man's job to chase; maybe the woman needed to choose to fight, too. Choose to fight for them when tragedy hits the man in the knees and keeps him down.

"I shouldn't have pushed you away. I shouldn't have said those things." She ran her hands over his perfect face. "I shouldn't have made it easy on you to leave. I was too hurt. Too rejected. Too angry. And I think a part of me felt like maybe I deserved to lose you too."

His mouth fused with hers over and over again.

She pulled away. "Forgive me?"

"There's nothing to forgive, Nik."

They stayed in each other's arms for another few minutes before they made their way back to the car.

Brant was quiet the whole way back to the resort, but a part of her wondered if he wasn't just emotionally exhausted and needed to process what had just happened.

The driver opened the door, and Brant once again helped her out. "You're free the rest of the night, right?"

She nodded.

"Good." His voice was gruff. "I have one more date planned for us tonight."

"And then what?"

He didn't answer her, not right away. Insecurity threatened. She shoved it back.

"I have to check on something important." His voice wasn't the same. Again he sounded angry. Like the old Brant.

It fanned the already growing insecurity to life.

They had finally broken down all their walls, or so it seemed. They grieved. They had closure.

And now he was walking away?

She jerked her hand away from him just as the smell of mint and cologne permeated the air. Cole? What was Cole doing in front of the hotel?

"Thanks, Cole, I'll be back in a few hours." Brant said.

The sound of a car door slamming jolted Nikki's

thoughts into action. She analyzed every little thing about that day and tried to match it with Brant's actions, with him getting in a car, with him leaving.

She touched her tearstained cheek for a few seconds before turning in Cole's direction. "Do you know what's going on?"

"Maybe."

"And you're not going to tell me?"

"Nope."

"Four years of friendship, and you pick his side?" She wiped her tearstained cheeks and waited. What if that was it? What if all he needed was to be free?

"He plays dirtier." Cole laughed. "Now, I'm under strict instructions to give you the best few hours of your life, and since sex is clearly out of the picture, that left me with only one option."

"Nikki!" Nadine's high-pitched voice had her nearly jumping out of her skin.

"Really?" she hissed. "That was really the only other option? Sex or Nadine?"

He laughed. "It's not just her. The rest of the family thought it would be fun to have dinner together and drinks, and who am I to say no to free food?"

"You work here. The food is always free, Cole."

"And drinks."

"Oh, like George would ever charge you!"

"I hate to say this, but you look like hell. Why don't I have Nadine take you back to Brant's room first so you can at least freshen up real quick?"

Her clothes were wet. She'd most likely cried all her makeup off. And her hair was pulled back into a tiny low bun that felt like a rat's nest on her head.

"I live across the street." She sighed, suddenly feeling exhausted. "I think I can manage."

"Want me to take you?"

"I'm fine." Plus some time to herself would be helpful. In fact, a nice shower would do wonders for her right about now. "Besides, when you say drinks and dinner I'm assuming it's going to be a long night. They won't miss me for thirty minutes."

Cole kissed her temple. "Go. Just be careful crossing that road."

"I'm blind, not deaf. You can hear cars, Cole, just like you can hear the little Walk signal."

"Smart-ass."

"You love me."

"Apparently it's not enough to love you—you have to love me back." He squeezed her hand. "Oh, and did you hear the good news?"

"What?" Something about his tone made her leery, or maybe it was just the fact that now that there was nothing keeping her and Brant from being together—she was afraid the universe would create another reason. She shook the feeling away and focused on Cole. "What good news?"

"Titus Enterprises is giving us money to hire more staff and increasing everyone's salary. It seems that their new VP of acquisitions loves this place. Or maybe he just loves someone who works there."

She elbowed him in the side. "You know it's not me. It really is an incredible resort. You've done a great job, Cole."

"Yeah—that's why I'm getting promoted."

"What?" Her stomach dropped. "Promoted? Are you

serious?" She hugged him tight and then had a minor freak-out. "But you'll still be my boss, right?"

"No, but I'll always be your best friend."

"Cole."

"Nik, don't do this, not now. It's not like I'm leaving yet."

"You're leaving?"

"Do you really need me that bad?" he joked. "Nik, you have him. You have Brant."

"Do I?"

"Let me be your eyes." Cole sighed. "See what I see. A man in love. A man willing to lay down his life for you. A man willing to fight wars. A man willing to die a thousand deaths. A man who will stop at nothing to have you."

"You see all of that?"

"I see it." He tapped her chest. "But I know you feel it."

"I'm still scared," she admitted. "So scared I'm going to wake up and it's going to be gone. He's going to change his mind. Or freak out, or default to bad habits I just—"

"Trust him."

"Says the guy who hates him?"

"Says the guy who finally found out a way to respect him despite our differences. Now, go shower—you smell."

"Love you, too." She smiled at him, then turned toward the direction of her apartment, her heart heavy, her mind confused, but completely hopeful that she could trust Brant, that he had a plan. Even though she was worried that he didn't.

He'd held on to his hate for so long. She'd held on to

her anger at him for abandoning her. And it was something they shared.

Now…that familiarity was gone.

And what did that leave them with?

She frowned the entire way to her door.

CHAPTER THIRTY-TWO

Brant hurried his ass off and was still late for dinner, arriving back at the resort in time for the dessert and champagne to be served.

His eyes searched for Nik, only to see an empty space next to Cole. Panic flared in his chest. Where was she? Was she okay?

"Brant." Grandfather stood, interrupting Brant's racing thoughts. "I take it things went well?"

"Yeah." Brant nodded, hoping his one-word answer would keep the old man from further questions. He had more important things to talk about—like where the hell Nikki was. "Cole," he barked.

Cole rolled his eyes. "What's up?"

"Where's Nik?"

"She called and said she was too tired to join us." He shrugged.

"So you just let her go back to her shitty apartment and sleep?"

"No." Cole's lips pressed into a thin line. "Because I knew you'd get your dick in a twist if she wasn't waiting in your hotel room as planned. I walked my ass over there like the best friend I am, packed her a bag, made sure she had room service sent to your bedroom, and tucked her in bed."

Brant clenched his fists while Cole gave him a smug grin. "You tucked her... in bed?"

"He took off her shoes," Bentley interjected. "Damn, she's got you wound tight." He stood and slapped a hundred-dollar bill into Cole's waiting hand. "Next time just count to five before you react. It may save me some money and I'll stop lining this schmuck's pockets. That's the second bet I've lost tonight!"

Brant glared at them. "What was the first?"

Grandfather motioned Brant over. "Sit down, have a drink with us."

"She packed lingerie." Cole crossed his arms.

"Brant, come on," Grandfather said again.

"Loyalty to Grandfather..." Bentley held out one hand and then lifted the other "...or potential sex?"

"Decisions, decisions." Cole sighed and shook his head. "However will you choose?"

"Son, you've been gone all night, so sit down and talk business. You're here to work, not socialize, right?" Grandfather called again, and this time Nadine patted the seat between them.

"Who bet against me?" Brant asked.

Cole pointed to Bentley.

"Dude." Bentley looked offended. "Blood is thicker than water, trust me, but I also know every man in this family has a sick, twisted loyalty to that insane grandfather of ours, so I predicted you'd stay and talk shop before heading upstairs. And by the look on your face I'm wrong, so..." He cursed and pulled out another hundred-dollar bill and gave it to Cole.

"Amazing. It's like I just got a bonus." Cole shoved both bills into his pocket and grinned. "Well?"

"Jackasses," Brant mumbled as he turned on his heel and sprinted toward the elevator, hitting the button at least five times before it would light up. The hell!

He stepped in and pressed the penthouse only to have a mom and her child both yell, "Hold the elevator!"

Moral dilemma.

With a curse, he put his hand between the doors just in time for them to step in.

"Thanks, mister." The boy saluted him like he was a soldier and then proceeded to press every damn button only to say, "Look, Mama, a Christmas tree!"

"I'm so sorry!" The mom's face reddened. "*Elf* is his favorite move!"

"Guessed that," Brant said in a dry tone. The elevator stopped at the next floor, the doors opened and closed, and the process was repeated for each floor thereafter.

Luckily, there were only six floors.

By the third floor, the small boy was dancing in circles despite the mom's best effort to keep him from colliding with the walls.

A smile played at Brant's lips when the boy suddenly wondered aloud, "Mama, where do babies come from?"

Brant choked back a laugh.

The mom gave him a panicked look and laughed nervously. "Um, you know, that's a fantastic question for Grandpa."

"He said to ask you."

"Rat bastard," she murmured under her breath.

"Rats?" The little boy said, "They come from rats?"

One more floor.

"Actually"—Brant knelt down to the boy's level and pointed up at his mom—"they come from love."

"Love?" He made a face. "How does love make babies?"

Brant shrugged. "That is for you to find out, once you're in love, I guess...but here's a secret: Your mommy and daddy's love is just so powerful that they made a little boy who has both his daddy and his mommy inside."

"Wow!" the boy exclaimed.

Tears filled the mom's eyes as the door opened for the fifth floor, and the boy bolted out. She stayed behind for just a moment.

"Th-thank you." She raised her hand to Brant's arm. "His dad was in the army. He died a few months ago. That was"—a tear fell—"That was probably something he needed to hear."

She walked off, leaving Brant in stunned silence.

How often had he ignored life these past four years? How many days did he numb himself to the pain, thinking he was the only one in the entire universe suffering? How was his pain any greater, any more justifiable than that little boy's?

He still smiled. He lived.

Damn it.

His son might have died. But Brant had died right along with him, hadn't he?

The elevator doors closed.

When they opened again Brant felt...different.

Imagine that, a conversation with a five-year-old was all it had taken.

Forget shrinks. He just needed someone innocent to remind him why life needed to be lived. Nadine had led him there, despite his best efforts to stay away, and all it took was for a little boy to give him the final push.

Life. Living. Definitely not for the weak of heart. But worth it, so worth it.

He tapped his card against the door to his suite and entered. The lights were lowered. He grinned as he stepped over a pair of black Ugg boots and then made his way into the bedroom.

"I thought you'd be sleeping," he said.

Nikki shook her head and changed the channel on the TV. "I was exhausted, fell asleep for an hour, and then woke up with more nervous energy than I know what to do with. Did you know that houseflies hum in the key of F?"

Brant frowned. "What the hell are you watching?"

"Not watching, listening." She grinned. "Also, sharks can smell even the tiniest amount of blood in the water—up to three miles away. I'm never getting in the ocean again."

"You're still obsessed with shark attacks?" Brant groaned. "Nik, how many times do I have to tell you—shark attacks are really rare."

Her face broke out into a breathtaking smile as she tossed the remote on the bed and hugged her knees, resting her cheek against them. "See, it was a good thing we never had a honeymoon, because knowing you we'd end up somewhere tropical, and I'd be the person in that one percent."

"It's higher than that."

She paled. "See!" Throwing up her hands, she leaned back against the headboard. "Never happening. You know a fun place to visit? The Arctic."

"Oh, so you'd rather get mauled by a polar bear?"

Her frown was adorable. "Brant, they're bears."

"Are you serious right now? Bears are insanely dangerous!"

"But *polar* bears are white and cuddly!"

"Right! And almost always covered in blood! There are a shit-ton of polar bear attacks every year. I promise you."

"Why are you ruining polar bears for me?" she moaned. "Thanks, dream killer. You gonna tell me that hippos aren't friendly, too?"

"Aw, babe."

"Brant! They're always smiling!"

"They are literally the second most violent animal on the planet. Believe me, you don't want to be near a hippo."

"Even though their ears move and, okay, I'm going to stop talking now because you're quiet and it's a mocking quiet. Stupid Animal Planet channel!"

"Turtles," he blurted, pulling off his shirt and sliding his pants down to the floor, kicking his shoes off then joining her in bed. "They're friendly."

She was quiet for a bit and then let out a loud sigh. "Okay, I can like turtles."

"I feel like I just ruined all animals for you in one single conversation."

"You did."

"Come here." He chuckled and tugged her against his near-naked body. "Are you ready for our last date?"

She froze in his arms. Was it apprehension or fear? Maybe both?

"Come on." He pulled her to a sitting position in bed and then moved so he was straddling her, stacking pillows behind him so he was sitting up straight with her leaning back against him. "There."

"This is our last date? Sitting in bed?"

"The night before our wedding," Brant whispered, his fingertips drawing slow circles on the inside of her wrist. "One of my favorite memories."

Nikki laughed; it was so pretty to hear her joy. "Brant, we stayed up all night and watched *The Godfather* Parts One, Two, and Three!"

"Because you were nervous."

"Because I was nervous," she repeated in a sad voice.

"Because your parents basically disowned you. My grandfather didn't approve. I was starting a new job, you were trying to get a job, and we were only twenty-one."

"The world was against us," Nik whispered. "And yet—" She twisted in his arms so they were face-to-face. "I knew they were wrong. I just..." Tears filled her eyes. "Every girl dreams of her wedding day, and those dreams always include family, laughter, cake." A tear slid down. "We still had fun, you and me, and it was nice of your brothers to show up with some close friends. At the time, I didn't care. I just wanted you."

"And now?" He almost didn't want to ask. "Do you need all of that?"

Nikki cupped his face with both hands and whispered, "I have everything I need."

I have everything.

I have everything.

I've lost everything—only to find it again.

Laughter, it was the first thing he thought of. They used to laugh all the time. They'd rarely argued, and when they did, they almost always ended up having sex afterward—amazing sex—earth-shattering sex.

"Are we really going to watch *The Godfather*?"

"I figured I could watch and give you a play-by-play. You hated all the blood and gore the first time, so we can skip to the good parts. Last time you gagged."

She smacked him in the chest. "I did not gag!"

"You gagged."

"Someone's argumentative tonight."

"I'm always argumentative."

"That's true."

They sat in silence, the glare of the TV the only light in the room. He could sit like this, with Nik in his arms, forever.

"Nik, I know this is our last date but—"

"I can't," she interrupted. "Let's just focus on tonight."

His heart sank.

Because what if she walked away after everything was said and done, after his surprise? Just like he had walked away. It would be her right. And the honorable thing would be to let her go since he promised he would give her the choice.

But this time it wouldn't be without a fight, one he intended to win.

"Tonight." He kissed the top of her head just as she slid her hand down his naked chest and followed it with an open-mouth kiss to his shoulder. "That feels good."

"I want that. To make you feel good." Her hands reached for the front of his shirt.

"I won't argue with that," he whispered against her neck.

"Wow, all I had to do was kiss you?" She pressed another kiss to his shoulder, then nibbled.

His voice lowered. "Well, you know what usually follows after kissing?"

"Ah, you mean cuddling?"

"Nik."

"Spooning?" she teased. "Battleship!"

"Watch me"—he pulled her fully onto his lap—"sink your ship."

"Silly man, I've already surrendered." God, he wished that were true, that her walls weren't still fully erected around her heart—but he would have no idea until he asked the question that had been burning since he started this plan of seduction and favorite dates: Would she choose him? For life? Not just for now, but forever?

"Good." He kissed her, and her tongue slid against his with light feathery strokes.

He was out of dates.

One plan remained.

Tonight. Tonight he would love her—and hope that tomorrow it would be enough.

CHAPTER THIRTY-THREE

Nikki tried to focus on his kiss, on the way his hands moved across her skin. She closed her eyes, feeling his hot breath on her neck as his kisses turned more aggressive, only to soften when he changed angles.

Brant had this magical way of always knowing exactly what type of kisses she needed, how to set her body on fire and make her breathless for him.

And tomorrow meant the dates were done.

Where would they go from here? How would they proceed?

But what if this really was good-bye?

Brant's lean muscles flexed beneath her touch as his firm lips pressed against her stomach, lower, and lower, until he slid down the remainder of her clothes and mapped her body with the trail of his tongue. Her head twisted frantically as his tongue explored her center, only to retreat and then return again, as if he were trying to memorize every single, private inch of her. His lips pressed and sucked her fevered skin until she was ready to lose her mind. Longing surged through her as she gripped his head and moaned.

"Have to be inside you. Have to feel you." He rumbled against her thigh before she tugged his head toward hers. Their lips met with a slam, a lick, another aggressive kiss that had her body coming off the bed in an effort to get closer.

She moved her hips against him as pleasure ricocheted down her body. Reckless. She felt reckless in his arms. Beautiful. Wanted.

She didn't need her eyes to see his beauty—she felt it in the way he loved her, in the way he touched her. His hands ran down her body with reverence, and his mouth slowly drank her in like he wanted to take his time. His tongue dipped into her mouth as he thrust inside her, filling her all the way and making her body tremble as he throbbed inside her. His tongue skimmed her lips as he withdrew and slid home again.

Home.

Home.

He was her home.

Longing for him, for what they'd had, hit her so hard it stole her breath away. Him, she just wanted him. He moved his mouth across her breasts, sucking, kissing, moving against her, destroying her for any other man, any other future.

When he surged forward again, her hips bucked beneath the pressure as a sharp cry escaped her lips. "I love you."

"I never stopped"—his lips dipped to hers again—"loving you, Nik."

"Is it enough?" She didn't mean to ask it aloud, didn't mean to shatter the moment, but he kept moving, kept kissing, kept loving her.

When she felt him tense, when her body couldn't take any more, he whispered, "It has to be, now let go."

"I can't." Tears filled her eyes. "That means our last date is over. It means facing an unknown. I can't."

Brant cupped her cheeks, kissing her tears, slowing his movements, deepening his thrusts. "You can. You will."

"Stay with me," she begged.

"I might have walked away, Nik." He pressed a hand to her heart. "But I never left."

She cried out as the tension built and then exploded around them. Tremors wracked her body as he kept kissing her cheeks, her tears, and then, finally her mouth.

Please, God, don't let this be the end.

CHAPTER THIRTY-FOUR

Brant woke up to his cell vibrating near his ear. With a grunt, he grabbed for it five, six times before finally swiping the right way and answering. "What?"

"You forgot to set your alarm."

He bolted out of bed. "Shit!"

"Relax." Bentley yawned loudly on the other end. "Brock and I took care of the details, the girls helped, and I think we're all on track. Damn, you're lucky to have us."

Brant sighed in relief and glanced down at a sleeping Nik. "Thanks, man. I'll be down as fast as I can. Will you do me a favor and grab my suitcase?"

"Sure thing."

"See you in a few."

"Yup."

Brant threw on his clothes, barely remembered to brush his teeth, grabbed his wallet and everything else he needed, and then went over to the bed and brushed a kiss across Nikki's forehead. "I'll always love you. Never forget that."

He left as quietly as he could. The minute the elevator doors closed, he grinned and then felt like throwing up.

It was time.

Yeah, throwing up was probably on the to-do list for the day.

* * *

He left.

She heard the tail end of his conversation. Get his suitcase? Was he in that much of a hurry that he couldn't even grab his own stuff? Rejection made her so numb she wasn't sure if she should laugh or just have a good cry and then rip the pillows to shreds.

He left. Again.

She could probably manage to get dressed on her own—there was a reason she liked wearing black; it always matched—but the point was, she thought he'd wake up slowly, offer her breakfast, and then they'd have the talk, decide how they were going to move forward, *if* they were going to move forward. Not this.

Emptiness.

A knock sounded at the door.

She nearly fell out of the bed.

The knock got louder.

It was followed by a series of hushed voices, two more knocks, and then finally, "Open the hell up!"

She jumped out of bed and wrapped the sheet around her body, feeling the walls as she made her way to the door and pulled it open.

"Bastard refused to give us the keys to this part of the suite!" Nadine said in her loud shrill. "I mean, doesn't he trust us at all?"

"No?" Sarcasm dripped from Jane's voice. "I wonder why."

"Aw, just look at you." Nadine sighed. "All rosy cheeked and exhausted from last night's sexual encounter. Oh, honey, you sit down and tell me *all* about it. Those Wellington men can be quite the stallions in the bedroom."

Nikki's smile felt hollow, sad. She didn't want to talk about Brant. About the sex. About the sorrow of waking up this morning and finding him gone.

"Are you here for his suitcase?" She tried to keep her voice even, her body from slumping, her hopes from shattering on the ground in front of them.

"Nope." Margot snapped the word. "Actually, we're here to kidnap you."

"Huh?" *Kidnap*? What were they talking about?

"Oh yes!" Nadine shouted unnecessarily. She was right in front of Nikki's face, making her dizzy with constant hand movements and a little nauseated from the strong perfume that was her trademark scent. "Jane, grab the dark jeans, oh, the shirt will look just lovely with that!" Shirt? What shirt? Her black shirt?

Before she could protest, the sheet was getting wrangled from her hand.

"Just—" Nadine jerked harder. "Let us help you get dressed!"

"I'm completely naked!"

"You can't see your own nakedness. Therefore, you can't be embarrassed!" Nadine said with one final heave; was she on steroids or something?

Cold air slammed into her body, and with a shiver, Nikki covered up as best she could.

"Ladies, we need the set."

"The set?" Nikki repeated. "What set?"

"Here you go!" The sound of tags ripping hit the air, and then she was getting a lacy strapless bra fastened around her body while simultaneously getting ordered to step into soft panties that fit her like a glove.

"Her ass looks amazing." Margot sighed.

"It better," Nadine said. "They're from France."

"My ass is from France?" Nikki wondered aloud.

"No dear, the lingerie set." She snapped her fingers. "Jane, grab the shirt, there we go now. Nikki, just lift your arms up over your head like a good girl."

What the heck was happening?

Why were they dressing her?

Furthermore, why was she letting them?

A soft cotton shirt was pulled over her head. She felt the front of it, pressing her hands down her breasts. It felt plain like most of her clothes, except for some weird writing that felt a lot like Braille.

She started to trace only to get her hands slapped away. "Feel yourself up on your own time," Nadine ordered. "Now, the shoes. Jane do you have the shoes, dear?"

"Yup!" Jane must have hoisted the shoes in the air, because another colored blur danced in front of Nikki's eyes, and then she was getting ushered into the bathroom to brush her teeth and wash her face.

Her arm nearly came out of its socket when Nadine pulled her into her embrace and very aggressively walked her out the door and onto the elevator.

Cheerful music greeted them.

A nervous energy buzzed among the three of them, and Nikki still had no idea what was happening.

Before she could protest, the elevator doors opened and she was taken through the lobby and into the spa.

Were they escorting her to work? What a complete and total letdown.

She didn't know what time it was, but by the smell of breakfast in the air as they passed the lobby it had to be before ten, since Azul stopped serving breakfast then.

"Yay!" Annie's voice sounded, and then clapping. Lots of clapping. "You're here!"

"At work," Nikki added. "What, I'm guessing an hour and a half early?"

"Work." Annie snorted. "The only person working today is Carol!"

"Here!" Carol shouted. "Oh, that shirt is just perfect!"

"What does it say?"

"Nice try." Nadine elbowed her. "We're here for our appointments."

Ugh. They really were going to torture her and make her do a spa day at her own workplace. Not that she wasn't thankful, but why couldn't they just let her suffer in silence? Cry in the shower so nobody could see the tears or her swollen face?

"Ladies!" Carol cleared her throat. "We have to stick to the schedule. Nikki will get her makeup done last just in case."

"Just in case what?" Nikki blurted.

"And then," Carol continued, ignoring her, "everything should be ready to go! If you have questions, Annie has extra copies of the itinerary, or you can always grab Cole."

"Cole? What does Cole have to do with getting my makeup done?"

Carol went on, "And do not let *anyone* in, got that, Annie? Nobody!"

Nikki could almost hear Annie rolling her eyes. "Carol, I'm a pro," Annie said. "I got this, plus Cole promised he would take off his shirt for thirty seconds if I don't mess up. I went and bought pepper spray, tear gas, and a pair of nunchucks just in case a fight breaks out. Those thirty seconds are mine."

"Oh, honey." Nadine sighed. "We need to find you a man."

"Eh, thirty seconds with Cole should last me at least a year's worth of fantasies. One time I had a dream he got attacked by wild dogs and came to work with shredded clothes." She sighed. "It was the best Monday ever."

"Annie!" Carol clapped her hands. "Focus, woman! Operation—" Silence. "Never mind, get it done!"

What the heck was going on?

Blurs moved in front of Nikki and then she was getting tugged into the familiar feel of the salon.

"If you cry," Carol said in a way-too-cheerful voice, "I'm going to slap you, okay?"

"Okay."

"I can't make everything waterproof, though God knows I try."

"Right." Nikki was pushed into a seat.

"Now. Let me work my magic."

CHAPTER THIRTY-FIVE

Brant stared at himself in the mirror, hands shaking as he tried to do his tie one more time, only to fail and nearly ram his fist into the mirror. Only he wasn't angry—he was about to lay all his cards out on the table, and he was terrified that Nikki would walk away because she didn't trust him.

With a deep breath, he grabbed his tie again.

"You're going to mess it up more than you already have" came Cole's voice, followed by his reflection in the mirror behind Brant. "Let me do it."

Brant smirked. "Admit it, you just want to strangle me with it."

"Hah." Cole was already dressed and ready to go. His three-piece suit made him look like he fit in more with the Wellington family than with the hotel staff. "The idea does have merit. Maybe I'll daydream about it later." In less than thirty seconds, Brant's tie was perfect and he was staring at himself in the mirror with wide eyes.

"What if she says no?" he whispered.

Cole slapped a hand on Brant's shoulder. "You don't let a woman like Nikki walk away from you. You walked away once, and I'll kick your ass if you let her do the same thing to you."

"Detailed and terrifying pep talk, Cole, thanks. You really suck as maid of honor."

Cole's eyes narrowed. "You know she wouldn't want it any other way. Besides, it's not like I'm wearing a dress."

Brock and Bentley walked into the hotel room followed by Grandfather, all of them in matching suits.

They were ready.

It was happening.

Really happening.

He had put a plan into action less than twelve hours ago. Never let it be said that money doesn't buy you just about anything. When Brant called his grandfather to let him know his plan, not only did his grandfather readily agree with it, but he cursed Brant to hell for making him losing a bet.

Another bet.

Seriously? Was that all his family did these days? Wager against him?

His grandfather refused to give him any details. All he knew was that Nadine bet that Brant, once he stopped being a jackass (her words, not his) would want to marry Nikki and do more than propose within the week.

His grandfather had bet that Brant would sleep with her and then run away with his tail between his legs.

Brant shook his head. Good to know that his own flesh and blood had that much confidence in him. Then again, Brant hadn't been doing much of anything in the past four years except fucking his way through life and drinking anything that would make him feel numb.

"It's time." Grandfather checked his watch.

Cole held up his cell. "Let me text Annie and see where the girls are with their appointments." He walked to the corner of the room.

Grandfather picked up a folder off the table and handed it over to Brant. "Here's the paperwork from the divorce."

"Shit." Brant was already starting to sweat.

He didn't want to take them.

He had no *choice* but to take them.

They were just papers, papers with black ink, papers with black ink that either decided his future or brought closure to his past.

"Son." Grandfather grabbed Brant's hand and closed his fingertips over the manila folder. "You're giving her the choice she never had. The best gift you can give isn't just your love—but the promise that regardless of what she chooses, you will never stop that love from overflowing from you and into her life, wherever she may choose to live it."

"And if it's not with me?" He hated asking it out loud, he hated the way he felt when those words left his lips, empty, hollow, meaningless.

The room fell silent.

"Then you have us." Brock took a step forward and put a hand on his shoulder, followed by Bentley, and then Cole—the bastard grinned up from his phone and shrugged, as if to say, *Yeah, you have me, too*.

It was the first time in Brant's life he felt like he actually belonged with his family, actually had a place. Nikki had been part of his identity, and when that was ripped away from him, he'd pushed his family away, too.

And yet they'd stood by him this entire time. Especially Bentley.

Brant rolled his eyes, then grinned down at the floor so they wouldn't see the emotion on his face. "All right. Let's go."

Grandfather stopped Brant. "Before you go...I have an idea."

* * *

Maybe a spa day wasn't so bad. Nikki's hands had both been massaged with the best-smelling lavender lotion, followed by her feet and calves. Her hair was brushed—which any woman knew could be so hypnotic that you wanted to fall asleep.

Makeup was last.

But even the makeup smelled good. Like brown sugar, as the brushes slid across her face.

And then, lipstick. It felt red. She had no idea how it felt red—it just did.

"All done." Carol's voice sounded different, more reserved, than it had when she first sat in the makeup chair.

Panicked, Nikki wished she could see herself, just once, just to know if she looked as pretty as she felt. Then again, maybe it was easier if she didn't know. It meant her confidence had to come from some other place, a place that wouldn't fade with age or get broken down by people's stares.

"Do I look okay?" she asked, careful not to touch her

face, not after her hands had been slapped away numerous times by Carol, and then again by Nadine when she'd checked in on their progress. It wasn't her fault she was used to feeling everything in order to imagine what things looked like!

"You look"—Carol sucked in a sharp breath—"like Snow White."

Nikki grinned wide. "She was always my favorite, you know, minus the whole living with a whole bunch of single, messy men."

Carol snorted. "Okay, let's get you to the Zen room."

"The Zen room?" She frowned. "Why would I be going to the Zen room after getting all of this work done?"

"Stop asking questions." Carol helped her stand and then walked with her arm in arm.

"Where is everyone?"

"What did I say about questions?" Carol reminded her.

"Geez, you and Nadine Titus could be related."

Carol chuckled and then said, "She's my great-aunt."

"I hate how that makes sense."

"Annie's a distant cousin, not blood related."

"What?"

"And Cole, well, Cole will have to tell you that story someday. But he's the closest to the Titus blood line, I'm sure he had his reasons from keeping you in the dark. He doesn't necessarily like telling people his connections with one of the richest families in the U.S."

"Is that what this is about? Cole leaving?"

"Like I would ever abandon you," Cole said. "You look like a princess."

"Snow White," Nikki offered for him. "Does that mean I'm really pale?"

"You're perfect." Cole leaned in and wrapped an arm around her. "Are you ready?"

"For what?"

He paused and then said, "Everything."

They walked in silence and then the familiar scents of the Zen room, the peppermint and the lemon, hit her senses, making her feel instantly at ease.

"Do me a favor, Nik," Cole whispered in her ear. "Be brave."

Nadine Titus's words rang out in her mind as Cole released her arm and took a step back.

"What's going on?"

"I thought it made sense, having your best friend of four years walk you toward me." Brant's gruff voice pounded in her ears, making her heart leap in her chest. "After all, he refuses to let me forget that the day I walked away, he stepped in, and for that I'll never forgive myself. And I'll always be forever in his debt."

Don't cry. Do. Not. Cry.

"The thing is." Brant was suddenly a blur of black and white in front of her. He smelled like heaven. He smelled like memories. He smelled like her best mistake—and greatest triumph. He smelled like the rest of her life—her future. "I love you." Her heart stopped and then slammed so hard she had to suck in air to remember to breathe. "But pressuring you into staying with me, seducing the hell out of you, tying you to my bed, while they all sound like the best ideas I've ever had—they aren't practical, and they don't involve one very important thing." He sighed, his fingertips grazing her chin as he tipped her face toward his body. "True love doesn't trap. It doesn't bribe. It offers a choice."

A folder of papers were set in her right hand, and her fingers curled around it. "Our marriage contract is in here, along with a check for the money that should have been yours the minute you signed the divorce papers four years ago. I was too lost in my own grief to double-check that things were taken care of. I ignored my lawyer's calls, and finally he stopped calling."

"We really are still married," she said in a stunned voice, suddenly needing to sit down. What did that mean? What did any of it mean?

"But we don't have to be," he said, quietly shattering her heart into a million pieces.

Tears welled. She couldn't speak.

"This is your choice, Nik. In that folder is our marriage contract and our divorce papers. Sign them, and the settlement of twenty million dollars is yours."

She gaped.

"Or—" Movement happened in front of her and then he took her left hand and lowered to one knee. "You could make me the happiest man alive, and marry me again, right here, right now, in front of all of our friends."

Her right hand felt heavy with the documents, with the past that was included in them.

Her left—light.

"I'm not perfect." She clung to his voice like a lifeline. "I think we both know that I don't deserve you, but I want to spend the rest of my life proving to you that you're worth it, that love is worth it. I want to prove—" His voice hitched. "I want our little boy when he looks down from heaven to see his mama in love. I want him to know that his dad tried the hardest to make her smile, so she forgets all the days—years—that he made her cry." Tears fell in rapid succession down her cheeks. "Nikki, will you marry me? Again?"

The contracts fell out of her hands, making a slapping noise on the floor, and then she was on her knees reaching for Brant, trying to find his face, but before she could find his mouth, it was already pressed against hers in a healing kiss.

A kiss of both closure and new beginnings.

"Yes," she whispered against his lips. "I'll marry you... again."

He slid a ring on her left hand, linking his fingers between hers, deepening the kiss, and then he grabbed her right hand and pressed it against his chest.

It felt just like her shirt.

She skimmed her fingertips down.

It was in Braille, too!

She knew it!

Still kissing him, she felt out the word and then gasped against his mouth, and tried like hell to keep herself from crying harder. "*Groom.* Your shirt says *groom.*"

"Care to guess what yours says?"

"Sexy?" she teased.

"Not enough space to put all the adjectives, Nik, but I kept one of the most important ones." He grabbed her hand and slid her fingertips across the word.

"*Bride.*" She sucked in a harsh breath. "Well, that could have been awkward had I signed those contracts, huh?"

Their laughter floated between them, and then they were kissing again, the contracts forgotten. And the people waiting outside the room completely forgotten.

Until a certain shrill voice yelled, “Well!? Did she say yes?”

“Nadine.” They said the word in unison, like a curse, but with humor in their voices.

“She’ll just fight her way past Cole if we don’t let her in.” Brant stood and helped her to her feet. “Besides, we have a wedding to get to.”

Nikki froze. “Today?”

“Yup.” His grip tightened. “I hope you like your dress.”

The minute the door to the Zen room was pushed open, she was hauled away from Brant amid cheers and bursts of color.

CHAPTER THIRTY-SIX

The minute Nikki was ushered into the hotel's bridal suite she felt like crying.

How often had she avoided this very room?

And now? Now it was hers to enjoy.

"Ladies!" Nadine let out a piercing whistle. "We have ten minutes."

"Ten minutes?" Nikki shrieked.

"I've thought of everything," Nadine said. "Though Brant picked out the dress."

A blur appeared in front of her. A red blur.

That man. She loved that man. "My dress is red."

"He said he wanted you to be able to see it," Nadine whispered as sniffles sounded around the room. "And apparently bright colors were all over the runway this spring, so I allowed it."

Well, that and she was a matchmaking psychopath. Brant could have asked to get married underwater and the woman would have been okay with it as long as she could plan everything.

Nikki reached out and touched the silky material. It was so smooth against her fingertips. It had to be expensive. There were thick straps that crisscrossed around the neck and down the back of the dress.

When she was done touching it, the dress was jerked from the hanger, and suddenly hands were everywhere as the shirt she was wearing was whisked away and the wedding dressed was smoothed over her body.

The dress fit perfectly.

"Jane!" Nadine called. "The shoes!"

"These," Jane's voice came from behind her, "are your something borrowed. They're the first shoes Brock bought me and kind of how our story started. I know they'll be perfect with this dress."

"Thank you," Nikki breathed as she stepped into the tall heels.

Margot was next. "And this dress is clearly your something new. When Brant said he wanted something red, well, I begged him to help pick it out. He was one of my best friends when we were in high school—I've never seen him look at a woman the way he looks at you, it was an honor."

"Thank you." Nikki sniffed. "All of you. I don't know what to say."

"Welcome to the family," Margot whispered.

"No!" everyone yelled all at once, as Nikki reached to touch her face.

"No." Nadine slapped her hands away. "Don't ruin your makeup. No more tears. All right, ladies, let's do this."

* * *

It felt like an eternity.

It had been twelve minutes.

Bentley elbowed Brant. "Stop sighing, it's depressing as hell. She said yes, which usually means she's going to be walking down the aisle pretty soon."

"Right." Brant swallowed the dryness in his throat. "But—"

"She'll be here," Brock said sternly.

Cole shrugged from his spot on Nikki's side of the aisle. "Or she could have used the getaway car I left for her." All three men glared at him. "Sorry, too soon?"

Brant rolled his eyes.

And then the wedding march sounded.

"Holy shit." Brant breathed out a pained exhale and waited.

"Maybe save the romancing for later." Cole nodded. "And the shits."

Bentley nodded to Cole. "Brant. We're adopting him later. Already got the paperwork."

Brock covered a laugh with a cough as the hotel staff stood and waited.

Grandfather held out his arm to Nikki and slid her hand through it. Then he kissed her on the cheek and whispered something in her ear that had tears filling her eyes.

Seeing those tears brought him back to what his grandfather had said earlier that day.

"Son." Tears filled Grandfather's eyes. "Had I not been too hard on you, this may have all been

avoided." He shook his head. "But I can't bring myself to say sorry."

A stunned Brant waited in silence for whatever his grandfather was going to confess next.

"Four years ago you were a boy trying to prove you were a man." His eyes locked onto Brant's. "Today, you're a man saying good-bye to the boy."

Those words. They were words Brant would never forget. And this vision in front of him, of Nikki walking with his grandfather, would be burned into his memory forever and always.

When they finally reached them, Brant's fingers itched to grab her hand, to hold it close, to promise to never let go.

Cole stepped down and grabbed Nikki's other hand. She gasped and then laughed through her tears.

The hotel chaplain smiled at them. "Who gives this woman?"

"Her grandfather and I," Cole said in a loud voice. "Her best friend."

Nikki tucked her head against Cole's chest and sighed as he kissed her temple.

Grandfather joined Cole on Nik's side of the room, still standing up front since she truly had no family that would accept her after she married Brant—and though Brant had invited them at the last minute, even offering to pay for everything, he'd still been given the cold shoulder.

It didn't matter. Because he and Nikki were a family again. A true family.

"I almost forgot." Brant reached into his pocket and

placed a charm bracelet in Nikki's hand. "Your something blue."

Her fingers ran along little hands praying, with the name Noah in Braille, across the single silver and blue charm.

She covered her mouth with her hands as a sob escaped.

"He's here." Brant was barely able to get the words out. "With us. He's here, and I'd like to think he's really excited that his mom and dad finally figured out what he figured out a long time ago."

"What's that?" she whispered.

Brant squeezed her hands. "Love never dies."

CHAPTER THIRTY-SEVEN

The wedding was perfect." Nikki shook her head at her husband. Her *husband*.

It had been a busy day, and while she wanted to celebrate with family, a part of her, a large part of her, really wanted to just be with Brant.

Instead she'd just sat through the longest meal of her life.

"Toasts!" Nadine yelled. "We have to do toasts."

"No, we don't, nope." Grandfather held out his hands. "Why don't you just calm yourself down and get another glass of wine?"

"This man," Nadine snorted. "Always trying to get me soused."

"She's quieter when she's drunk, if you can believe that," Grandfather said.

"Does she even know what that is? Quiet?" Brock wondered aloud as a glass of wine was placed in Nikki's hand.

"You have a funny look on your face," Brant whispered in Nikki's ear. "Thinking about something?"

"You mean other than leaving and having you all to myself?" She leaned into him and pressed a kiss against his neck.

He moaned and then gripped her thigh underneath the table. She let out a harsh breath and shook her head.

"Room," Cole's voice interrupted. "We have a few hundred, take your pick, just don't have sex on the table."

"Some of the best sex I've ever had has been on a table," Nadine piped up.

"More wine?" Brock asked in a cheerful voice. Had she already finished that last glass?

"So, Cole." Nadine's voice lit up with excitement. "That Annie is quite special, isn't she?"

"Nope," Cole snapped. "Dig your claws into me and I'll only bleed. Can't you see I'm heartbroken? My best friend just married a Wellington."

"Yes, but our families are finally playing nice again. You can tell your father to stop playing his games—besides, now that I've got Brant working for me things are even."

"Father?" Brant asked. "Cole's last name is Masters."

Nadine smirked. "His legal name is Cole Masters Titus, the third."

"What?" Shrieks were heard around the table.

Then Bentley burst out laughing. "Holy shit, we adopted the enemy."

"Trust me, I'm very distantly related, I haven't seen Nadine in years," Cole answered, and then sighed with longing. "They were such quiet years. Happy years filled with laughter and—ouch!"

"Yes, well, now you'll be lucky to get rid of me," Nadine said in that haughty voice of hers.

"Any more of that wine left?" Cole asked the table.

Nikki couldn't stop smiling. Oddly, it made sense he would be a Titus. He was an amazing manager, and he hadn't been worried about the buyout at all.

"Let's go somewhere," Brant whispered in her ear.

"Yes." She stood and let him lead her away.

"We're going to get some fresh air," he said to the table.

"Sure you are," Bentley called back. "Let us know how all that hundred-and-five-degree fresh air feels in that three-piece suit."

They left as the jokes kept piling on top of one another. She assumed they were going to his room, but instead he veered down the hall and into the spa.

"Brant?"

"Shh." He opened and then closed a door. "I've been wanting to do this for days."

His hands were all over her, unzipping her dress, caressing her breasts, licking her neck, kissing her lips.

"My massage room? Really?"

"Where it all began," he said in a husky voice. "Now, get on the table."

Anticipation exploded within her. "Are you serious?"

"I'm going to put my hands on you. Torture you. Bring you to the brink of ecstasy so fast that you fall apart, and then I'm going to walk out of here and show you the real meaning of torture, just like you did to me the first time I walked into this room."

Nikki tipped her head back and laughed as Brant lifted her and gently placed her onto the table. And then he was on top of her, pressing her body against the cool sheets as he rubbed his hands up and down her shoulders. Then he was weighing her breasts, tasting them, sucking, driving her crazy as his lips moved across her most sensitive parts only to retreat and meet her mouth again.

"Brant!" She forgot what she was going to say when he tugged her expensive lingerie from her body and then kissed her harder.

She reached for his pants. "No more kissing, I need you."

"But I was going to torture you."

"Four years" was all she said.

And then he was helping her unzip his pants as he released himself and then slid into her with one earth-shattering thrust.

"We can always make up for it later." She moved with him, his rhythm fast, strong, unwavering, as pleasure rolled and rocked between the two of them.

"I'll always love you." His hands dug into her hips as he lifted her body to his one final time.

"Forever," she whispered against his mouth as he swallowed her cry of pleasure.

Panting, both of them were silent for a few seconds before Brant finally spoke. "Again."

"But—"

"Fresh air takes a hell of a lot longer than five minutes. Sorry, there's just something about this table."

She reached out and massaged his shoulders.

"Fuck." He hung his head, touching hers. "Or maybe it's just your hands." He lifted her hand, pressed her palm to his mouth, and kissed it. "Or just everything." He took her other hand. "I spent four years trying to drink you away."

"How'd that work out?" she breathed against his mouth.

"I tried to forget—and only ended up remembering... I remember it all, the soft cries you make during sex, the way you sing in the shower, how you dance in the kitchen when nobody's looking—I remember it all and I'm a fucking fool for ever thinking I wanted to forget."

"I love you so much." She kissed him.

And kissed him again.

Jane isn't entirely sure that Cinderella got such a raw deal. Didn't she eventually land a prince and a happily-ever-after? But while Brock Wellington isn't exactly a prince and there's definitely no fairy-tale ending…no one says they can't indulge in a little bit of fantasy.

An excerpt from *The Bachelor Auction* follows.

CHAPTER ONE

He's senile. Last night he asked if I believed in unicorns."

Brock suppressed a groan at Bentley's insensitive statement. No doubt about it, or way around it. Their grandfather, the CEO of Wellington, Incorporated, was losing his damn mind.

But still, someone should come to the old man's defense, and ever since he was twelve years old, that someone had always been Brock. Always.

His younger brothers—twins—were a united front against anything and everything that happened, not only within the family, but especially with Brock. It had always been them against the world, leaving Brock the awkward job of defending them to his grandfather while simultaneously living with the ever increasing aggravation of their sex- and alcohol-filled lifestyles.

"His medication... causes..." Brock clenched and

unclenched his fists, mainly so he wouldn't do something stupid like punch one of them. Sleep. He needed more sleep, and a life outside of running a company he'd never wanted to run in the first place. "Visions," he finished. Bitterness took hold like it always did when he thought of the company, his grandfather, and the heavy weight of the world on his shoulders.

"You think visions of unicorns is bad?" Brant, the younger of the twins, gave Brock a disgusted look. "Just last week I found him skinny-dipping in the pool."

Brock frowned as the elevator doors opened to the main offices of Wellington, Inc. "Why is that strange?"

"Alone," Brant said. "Who skinny-dips *alone*?"

Bentley smirked, pushing past both of them. "Not you... clearly."

Brant's lips pressed into a smug grin. "Jealous?"

"Of the skank from last night?" Bentley snorted and sent off a text, most likely to the very same girl who had left Brant's bed the night before. Always a competition with them. "Hardly."

"Hello, boys." Mrs. Everly, their grandfather's secretary, was like family. She refused to acknowledge the brothers were well past the "boy" stage and had been for years.

"Hello," they all said in unison. Bentley reached for her hand and kissed the top of it.

"You get younger every day. Amazing, almost like you're aging backwards." He winked.

Brock's patience was already on edge. Running the company for his grandfather was one thing. Keeping the twins from making asses of themselves was another.

"Bentley." Brock gripped his brother's shoulders with

a jerk and shoved him toward the door. “Don’t keep Grandfather waiting.”

The twins exchanged an eye roll.

“So responsible,” Brant said under his breath. It wasn’t meant to be a compliment.

“So . . . old,” Bentley added, because that’s what he did. “Brock, when was the last time you even got laid? If you say anything past seven days I may need to disown you.”

It had been more than seven.

Way more than fourteen.

But with a company to run . . .

And two brothers to keep under control . . .

Not to mention the accident that had nearly taken his grandfather’s life this last year. Resentment washed over him.

When would he even have time?

For fun?

Sex?

Women?

Anything?

“You’re not getting any younger,” Bentley interrupted Brock’s depressing thoughts. “Aren’t you turning thirty-eight this year?”

“I saw a gray hair when he turned his head,” Brant added. “Depressing as hell.”

“It’s not gray,” Brock snapped, clenching his jaw so tight his teeth ached. “And if you haven’t noticed I’ve been busy.”

“Boys?” Brock flinched at the sound of their grandfather’s booming voice. “Boys, is that you out there?”

“He may be losing his mind but he sure hasn’t lost

his vocal chords," Bentley murmured as all three of them stepped casually into the office and shut the large wooden door behind them.

It closed with a resounding thud and Brock felt an ominous current of anxiety travel down his spine.

It was the same feeling he'd had when he was twelve and his grandfather had told him his parents had died in a plane crash.

The same feeling he'd had last year when he'd gone head to head with his grandfather over an acquisition—and won. The board had approved his decision. And less than twenty-four hours later, he'd almost lost his grandfather in a car accident.

As if reading the direction of his thoughts, his grandfather winced. The pain was still there, Brock knew, even if Grandfather refused to admit it.

Charles Williams Wellington the Third was seated behind his desk as if he sat on a throne, his mass of silver hair flowing into a deep curl that fell over his forehead. His wrinkled and tanned face didn't look older than seventy, though he was pushing eighty-two, only weeks away from celebrating his birthday.

"I have decided"—he paused and stood to his full height of six-four—"to have an auction."

"Oh?" Brock was the first to speak. Business he could deal with. Numbers he could process. Anything outside of that and he was going to need a drink.

Or ten.

"What would you like to auction?" He pulled out his iPhone and started a new note. "One of your houses? A few of your stallions? Titus Enterprises had a car auction last year that was extremely profitable."

Grandfather's face transformed into a wicked grin. "Maybe the other two should sit down."

"I think he means us," Bentley said under his breath, while Brant shot Brock a worried glance.

"I mean to auction..." Grandfather took a deep breath and raised his finger to point at them. "You."

Brant, the fastest of the bunch, jerked his chair to the right. "He's pointing at Bentley."

Bentley, never the more clever of the two, faked a coughing fit and fell forward in a vain attempt to kick Brock's chair closer to the middle.

Rolling his eyes, Brock said, "He's pointing at all of us."

"Actually..." Grandfather's voice deepened. "I was pointing at you, Brock."

Brock had always done everything his grandfather asked. When he graduated high school he'd been pressured into going to Harvard, because wouldn't it be so wonderful to go to the same school as his father? In honor of his memory?

Football, not basketball.

Chess, never checkers.

It was easier to keep the peace, to keep the smile on his grandfather's face. And because he'd do anything to keep the old man from more grief and sadness. He'd seen those emotions on his grandfather's tear-stained face when he'd told him his parents were dead. And ever since, Brock had said yes.

To Harvard.

To football.

To business school.

To taking over the company.

To the women his grandfather thought it best he be seen with.

But this? This was too far.

"Auction a person?" Brock tried to clarify. "Why?"

Immediately relieved they were no longer the focus of attention, both of his brothers had already directed their attention to their phones.

Not even paying attention.

Story of his life.

Grandfather limped around his massive desk. Guilt slammed into Brock's chest in perfect cadence with his increasingly erratic heartbeat.

With a curse, Grandfather grabbed his cane and wiped his brow with the back of his hand.

His eyes locked in on Brock. "Please."

Brock opened and closed his mouth.

"It's for a good cause." His grandfather didn't blink, just kept limping toward Brock until he had to crane his neck to stare up at the man he'd do anything for and had sacrificed everything for.

The final nail in the coffin was when the older man lowered his chin and humbled himself by uttering, "Do it for me."

Fuck.

CHAPTER TWO

Jane!" Esmeralda shouted. "Hurry up! You're taking way too long! We're going to be late to the party!"

"Maybe you should just go without me," Jane offered in what she hoped sounded like the perfect balance between depressed and content. She was exhausted from work—the last thing she needed was to babysit her sisters while they drank their body weight in vodka tonics.

Esmeralda's voice was loud and clear as day. "Jane! If you don't come who's going to fix my dress if something happens? Or watch over Essence; you know how she gets shy with guys! And you're the best wingman."

Jane clenched her teeth together. What girls actually had their own personal seamstress? Though Jane was really more of a jack-of-all-trades. And she was probably the worst wingman in history.

"You girls ready?" Essence asked.

"Jane! Hurry up! We don't want to arrive too late. It's rude, and he may not notice us."

Jane barely managed to hold in her gasp as Esmeralda and Essence tumbled down the stairs and presented their dresses.

Esmeralda's tight black dress had just enough fabric to cover her surgically enhanced boobs and barely covered her ass.

Essence's was nearly the same style, except it was white.

One wore purple lipstick, the other had on gray; they were always on top of the newest trends even if the trends were stupid—and ugly.

At Fashion Week, they could get away with it.

In Phoenix they just looked like Bratz dolls.

"Yeah, I think"—Jane coughed into her hand—"he'll notice."

"Aw!" Esmeralda clapped her hands and flicked her dark hair over her shoulder. "That's so nice of you to say."

"Yes." Essence twirled a few times to show off her dress to full effect. "How sweet of you, Jane." With her eyebrows drawn in perfect arches, it was amazing she could even move them. "Jane, why aren't you dressed?"

"I think I'm just going to stay in," Jane answered, tugging at her dress self-consciously. It was the best one she could find at the last minute. She hadn't even known about the party until an hour ago, and the best she'd been able to scrounge up was a dress she'd borrowed for prom four years ago from one of her sisters.

She'd tried her best to make the black cocktail dress appealing.

But you couldn't fix plain.

And that's what it was.

What Jane was.

Plain Jane.

Her sisters gave her the same empty-eyed stare. Arguing with them was completely useless. When it was two against one, she never won, not that it mattered in the long run. Her sisters typically got their way regardless of what Jane said. They were pushy—but they were family.

Swallowing back her insecurity, she nodded quickly. "I'll just grab my purse, then."

Her sisters whispered under their breaths, though Jane heard every mean word.

"Doesn't she have any other dresses? Poor Jane."

"Hey, I offered to help her shop and she said no."

Jane snorted quietly. She'd said no because Essence's shopping style was more like buy everything name brand and go into major credit card debt. At one point, Jane had had to use all of the money her parents had left them to pay off the bill.

"Poor Jane," Esmeralda said again.

She hated pity.

Especially theirs.

She would move out of the house if she thought her sisters wouldn't starve without her. Well, that and the fact that they were family and family stuck together. Even if family exhausted you, stressed you out, and made you want to scream at least ninety percent of the time.

"Let's go!" Esmeralda clapped her hands loudly and they were off...headed to a party that Jane didn't even care about.

ACKNOWLEDGMENTS

This part doesn't get repetitive, even after sixty-plus books. This is the part where I get to acknowledge all the people, but first I get to acknowledge and thank God for his incredible grace in my life. When I was little all I wanted to do was exist in the make-believe worlds in my head. I'd like to think that He knew that desire in my heart and was like, well, I can't make you a dinosaur slayer, but this is almost the same thing. Thank you, Jesus, for this amazing career; thank you for many blessings!

Nate, Thor—you dudes are my rocks. I'm so blessed to have you in my life and so thrilled that we get to do life together hand in hand. My greatest accomplishment is having a son with the love of my life. Thank you, babe, for always taking him when I need to hit a deadline and for being not just a husband but a partner and my best friend.

Jill and Nina—Wait, you're still here! It's been crazy busy this year, totally my fault for taking on so many projects, but you've been with me every step of the way, holding my hand, telling me not to panic, and even helping me brainstorm this book along with all the others. Jill, you're family—my sister, thank you for being a constant in my life; and Nina, thank you for not laughing at me when I told you all the things we had to accomplish. I feel like you and I met, fell in love, then hit the ground running and I'm so thankful for you!

Erica, awesome superhero of an agent, thanks for always being such a support system for me. I don't know what I would do without you—it actually makes me sick to my stomach to think about! You are the best of the best and I'm so grateful to have you as my agent and my friend.

Kristin, Liza, Heather, Michelle, Jessica—whoa, all of you guys (including Jill) did an awesome job beta-reading. Thank you for going through this process with me and for helping me make it the best! And Becca Manual, thank you for all your feedback and help with graphics and ordering all the things that make my life so much easier (ha-ha!). I have no idea what I would do without you!

Kay, as always, thank you for editing before I send it in—you always have the best suggestions for what I need to do to make every manuscript perfect.

And Amy—man, I feel like we went through a war and then came out on the other side complete winners... ha-ha. It took some time, but I'd like to think that by book three we found our stride and I'm so happy that we were able to work together for this series and put out such fun stories.

You challenged me in ways I've never been challenged before and I'm so grateful that you don't allow authors to get lazy; you push us to be more, and I know I'm better because of you.

Lauren Layne, Bae, Staci Hart, Jessica Prince, Audrey Carlan, Molly McAdams, Mia Sheridan, Jennifer Van Wyk—GAH, I knew I shouldn't have started this list because, well, now I know I'm forgetting about a billion people that I'm going to be upset I forgot about in this section. To my support system, to all the authors I talk with, you guys are incredible. Thank you for being you.

Rachel's new Rockin Readers—you guys are legit the best group on Facebook. Thank you for being more family than anything!

To all the bloggers who helped support this release, the editors, the people who made this book amazing, thank you so much. I know I'm forgetting people but know that I'm constantly in awe of this amazing community and the support given to romance!

HUGS,
RVD

SIGN UP FOR RACHEL'S NEWSLETTER HERE:
RACHELVANDYKENAUTHOR.COM

AND FOLLOW HER ON SOCIAL MEDIA TO KEEP UP-TO-THE-MINUTE ON HER NEXT RELEASE:
FACEBOOK.COM/RACHELVANDYKEN
TWITTER @RACHVD

ABOUT THE AUTHOR

Rachel Van Dyken is the *New York Times*, *Wall Street Journal*, and *USA Today* best-selling author of Regency and contemporary romances. When she's not writing, you can find her drinking coffee at Starbucks and plotting her next book while watching *The Bachelor*.

She keeps her home in Idaho with her husband, her adorable son, and two snoring boxers! She loves to hear from readers!

Want to be kept up-to-date on new releases? Text MAFIA to 66866!

Fall in Love with Forever Romance

NO OTHER DUKE WILL DO
By Grace Burrowes

From Grace Burrowes comes the next installment in the *New York Times* bestselling Windham Brides series! It's the house party of the decade, and everyone is looking for a spouse—especially Julian St. David, Duke of Haverford. The moment he meets Elizabeth Windham, their attraction is overwhelming, unexpected...and absolutely impossible. With meddling siblings, the threat of financial ruin, and gossips lurking behind every potted palm, will they find true love or true disaster?

Fall in Love with Forever Romance

ALWAYS YOU
By Denise Grover Swank

Matt Osborn had no idea coaching his five-year-old nephew's soccer team would get him so much attention from the mothers—attention he doesn't want now that he's given up on love and having a family of his own. Yep, Matt's the last of his bachelor buddies, and plans on staying that way. That is, until he finds himself face-to-face with the woman who broke his heart. The latest from *USA Today* bestselling author Denise Grover Swank is a winner!

Fall in Love with Forever Romance

THE BACHELOR CONTRACT
By Rachel Van Dyken

Brant Wellington could have spent the rest of his life living under the magical spell of alcohol, women, and forgetting his problems. That is, until a certain bachelor auction forces him back on the family payroll and off to assess one of the Wellington resorts. Only no one warned him that his past would be there waiting for him…Don't miss the newest book from #1 *New York Times* bestselling author Rachel Van Dyken!

WICKED INTENTIONS
By Elizabeth Hoyt

Don't miss *Wicked Intentions*, the *New York Times* bestseller that started Elizabeth Hoyt's classic Maiden Lane series!